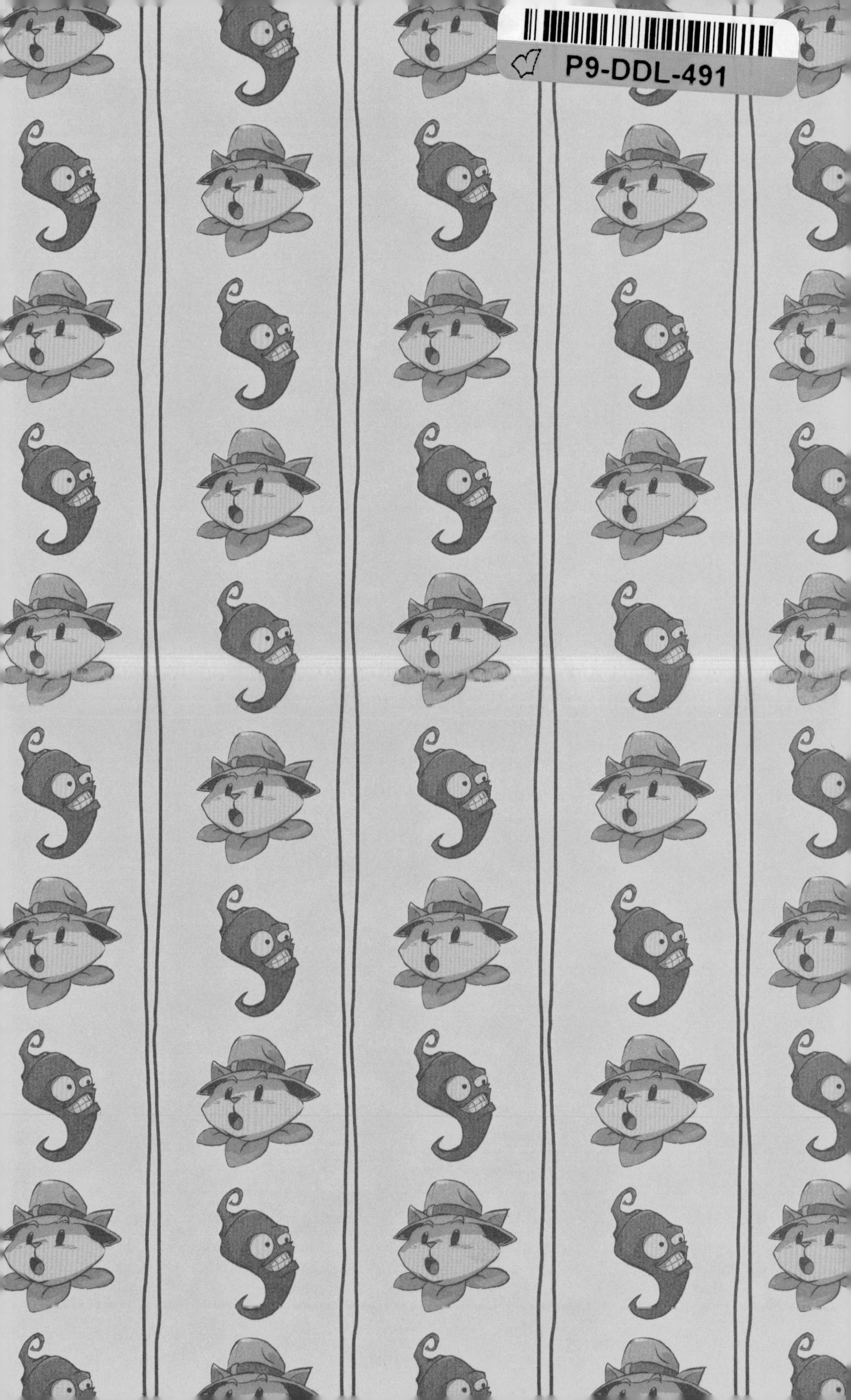

PLANTS VS. ZOMBIES™

GROWN SWEET HOME

Written by **PAUL TOBIN**
Art by **ANDIE TONG**
Colors by **MATTHEW J. RAINWATER**
Letters by **STEVE DUTRO**
Cover by **ANDIE TONG**

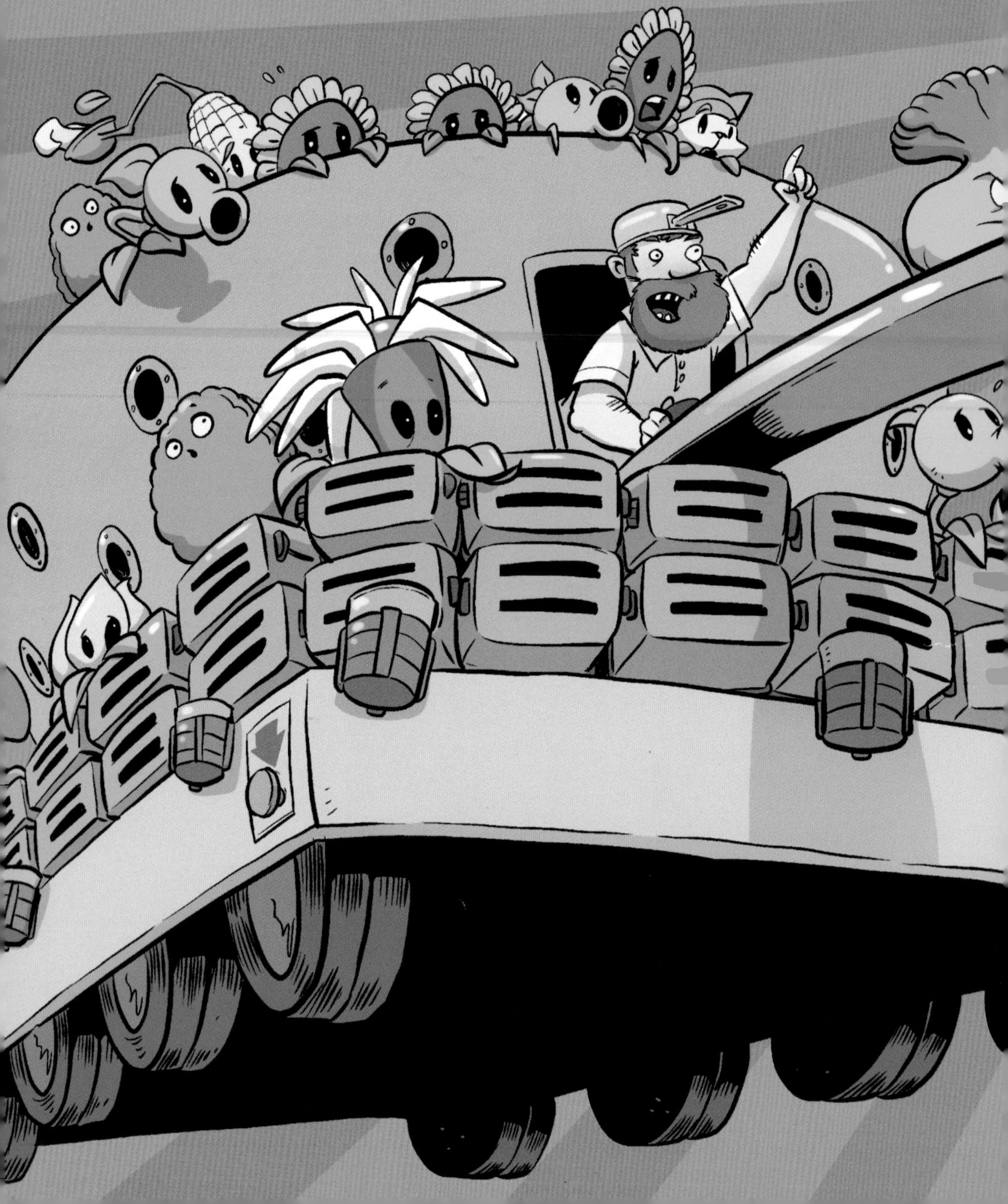

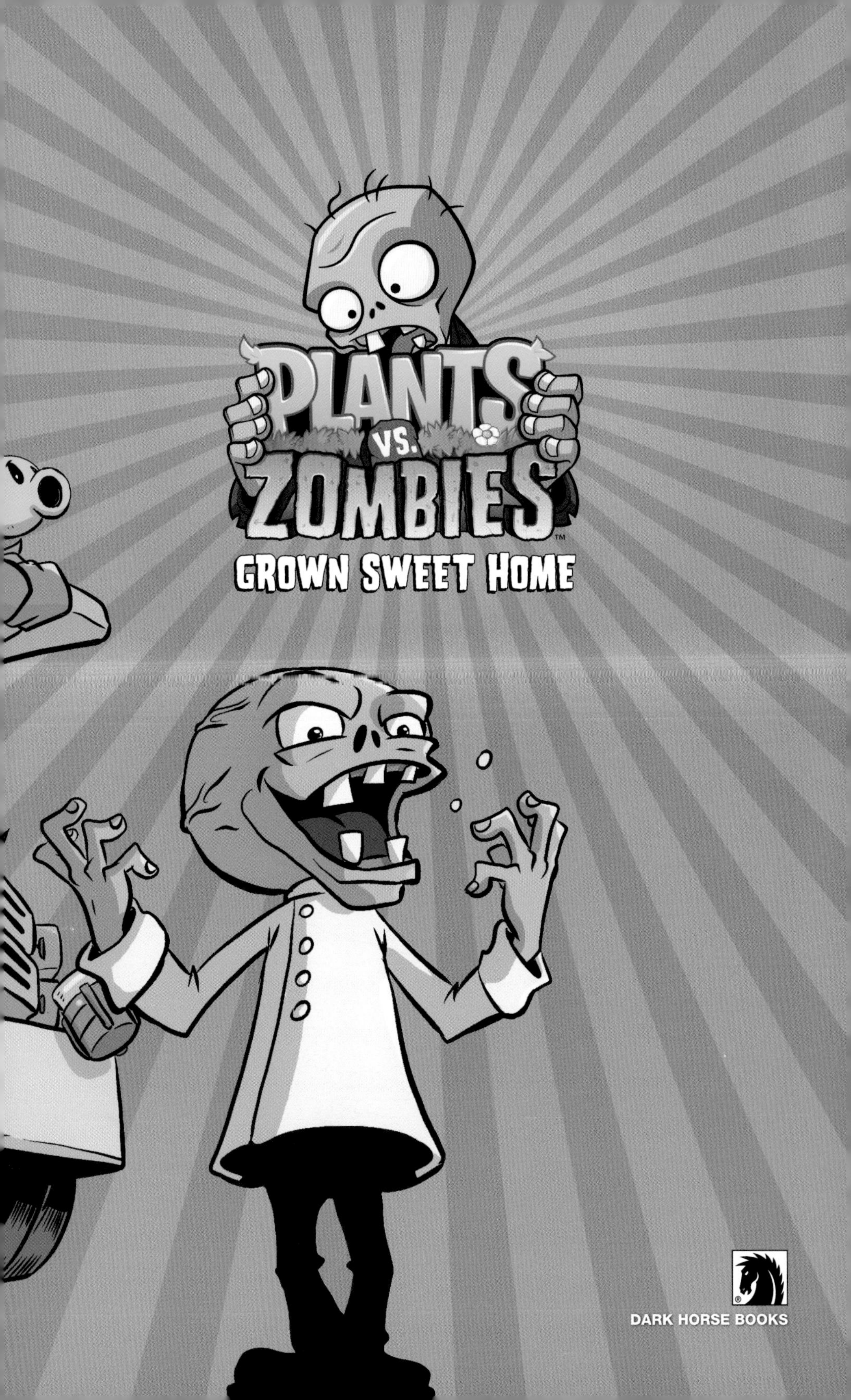
PLANTS VS. ZOMBIES™
GROWN SWEET HOME
DARK HORSE BOOKS

President and Publisher **MIKE RICHARDSON**
Senior Editor **PHILIP R. SIMON**
Associate Editor **HANNAH MEANS-SHANNON**
Assistant Editor **ROXY POLK**
Designer **CINDY CACEREZ-SPRAGUE**
Digital Art Technician **CHRISTINA McKENZIE**

Special thanks to LEIGH BEACH, GARY CLAY, SHANA
DOERR, A.J. RATHBUN, KRISTEN STAR, JEREMY
VANHOOZER, and everyone at PopCap Games.

First edition: June 2016
ISBN 978-1-61655-971-7

10 9 8 7 6 5 4 3 2
Printed in the United States of America

DarkHorse.com | PopCap.com

▷ No plants were harmed in the making of this comic. Numerous zombies
who could benefit from going to a finishing school to learn some
manners, however, definitely were.

NEIL HANKERSON Executive Vice President TOM WEDDLE Chief Financial Officer RANDY STRADLEY Vice President of Publishing
MICHAEL MARTENS Vice President of Book Trade Sales MATT PARKINSON Vice President of Marketing DAVID SCROGGY Vice
President of Product Development DALE LaFOUNTAIN Vice President of Information Technology CARA NIECE Vice President of
Production and Scheduling NICK McWHORTER Vice President of Media Licensing KEN LIZZI General Counsel DAVE MARSHALL
Editor in Chief DAVEY ESTRADA Editorial Director SCOTT ALLIE Executive Senior Editor CHRIS WARNER Senior Books Editor
CARY GRAZZINI Director of Print and Development LIA RIBACCHI Art Director MARK BERNARDI Director of Digital Publishing

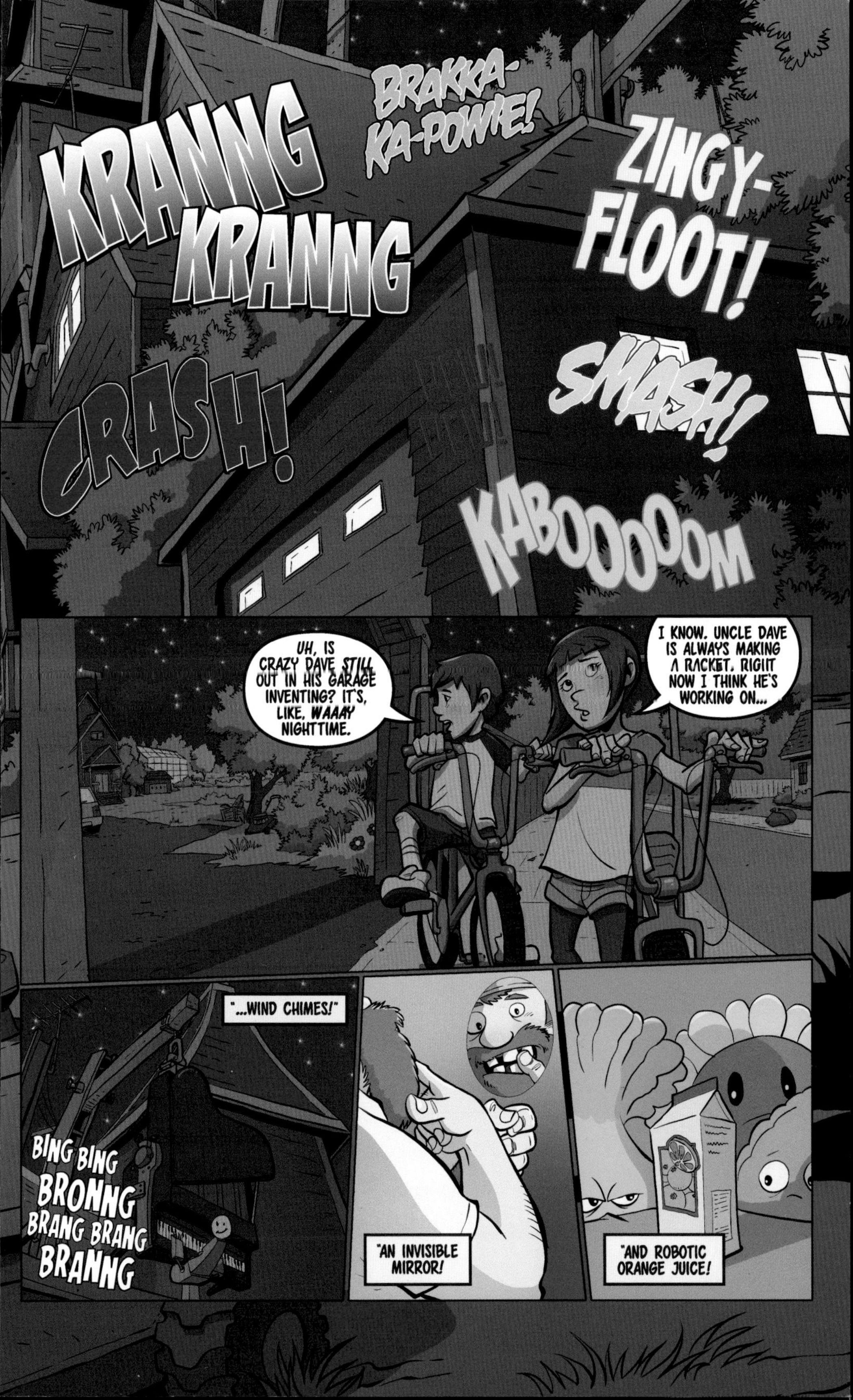
KRANNG KRANNG
BRAKKA-KA-POWIE!
ZINGY-FLOOT!
CRASH!
SMASH!
KABOOOOOM
UH, IS CRAZY DAVE STILL OUT IN HIS GARAGE INVENTING? IT'S, LIKE, WAAAY NIGHTTIME.
I KNOW. UNCLE DAVE IS ALWAYS MAKING A RACKET. RIGHT NOW I THINK HE'S WORKING ON...
"...WIND CHIMES!"
BING BING BRONNG BRANG BRANG BRANNG
"AN INVISIBLE MIRROR!
"AND ROBOTIC ORANGE JUICE!

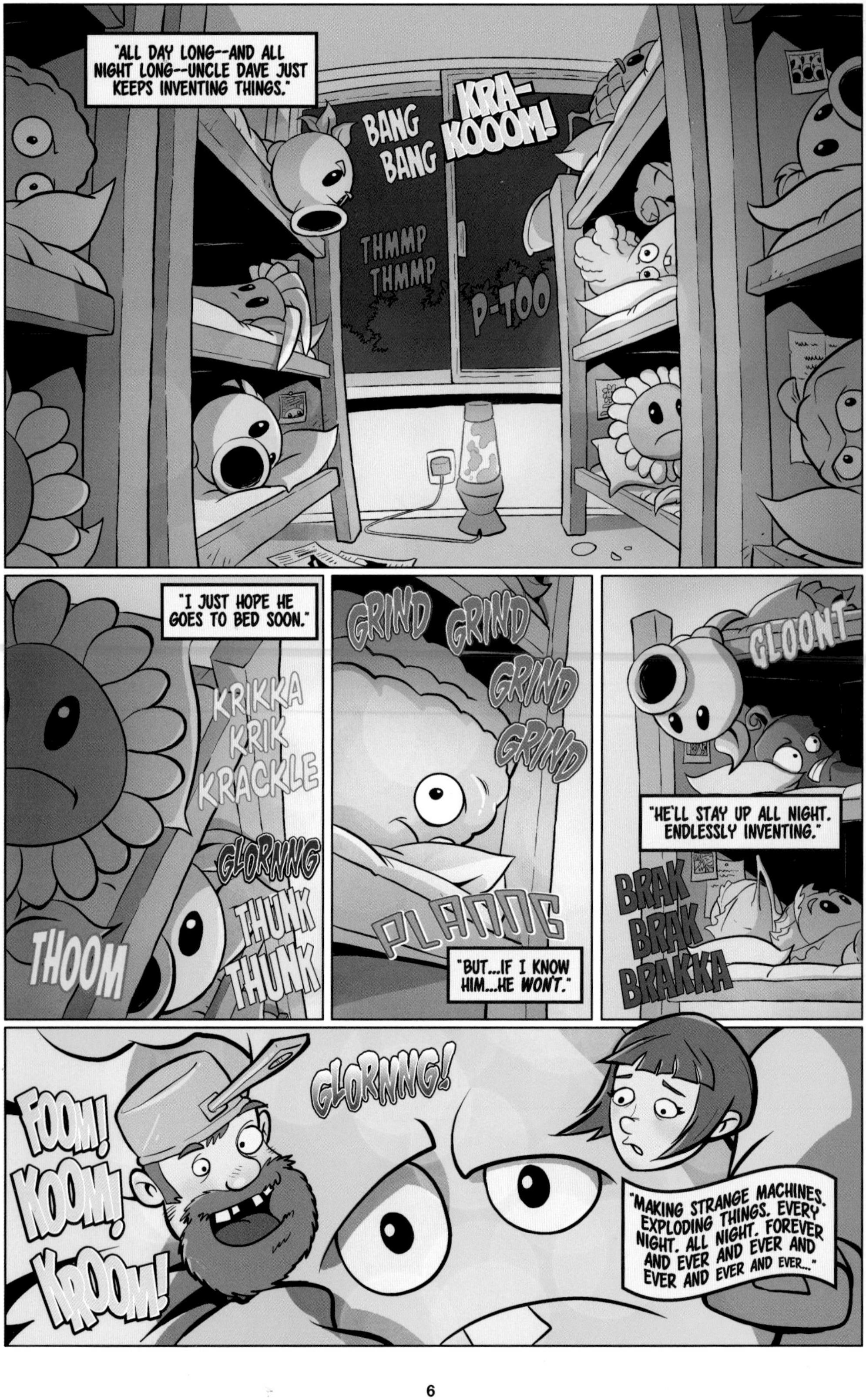
"ALL DAY LONG--AND ALL NIGHT LONG--UNCLE DAVE JUST KEEPS INVENTING THINGS."
BANG BANG
KRA-KOOOM!
THMMP THMMP
P-TOO
"I JUST HOPE HE GOES TO BED SOON."
KRIKKA KRIK KRACKLE
GLORNNG
THUNK THUNK
THOOM
GRIND GRIND GRIND GRIND
PLANNG
"BUT...IF I KNOW HIM...HE WON'T."
GLOONT
"HE'LL STAY UP ALL NIGHT. ENDLESSLY INVENTING."
BRAK BRAK BRAKKA
FOOM! KOOM! KROOM!
GLORNNG!
"MAKING STRANGE MACHINES. EXPLODING THINGS. EVERY NIGHT. ALL NIGHT. FOREVER AND EVER AND EVER AND EVER AND EVER AND EVER..."

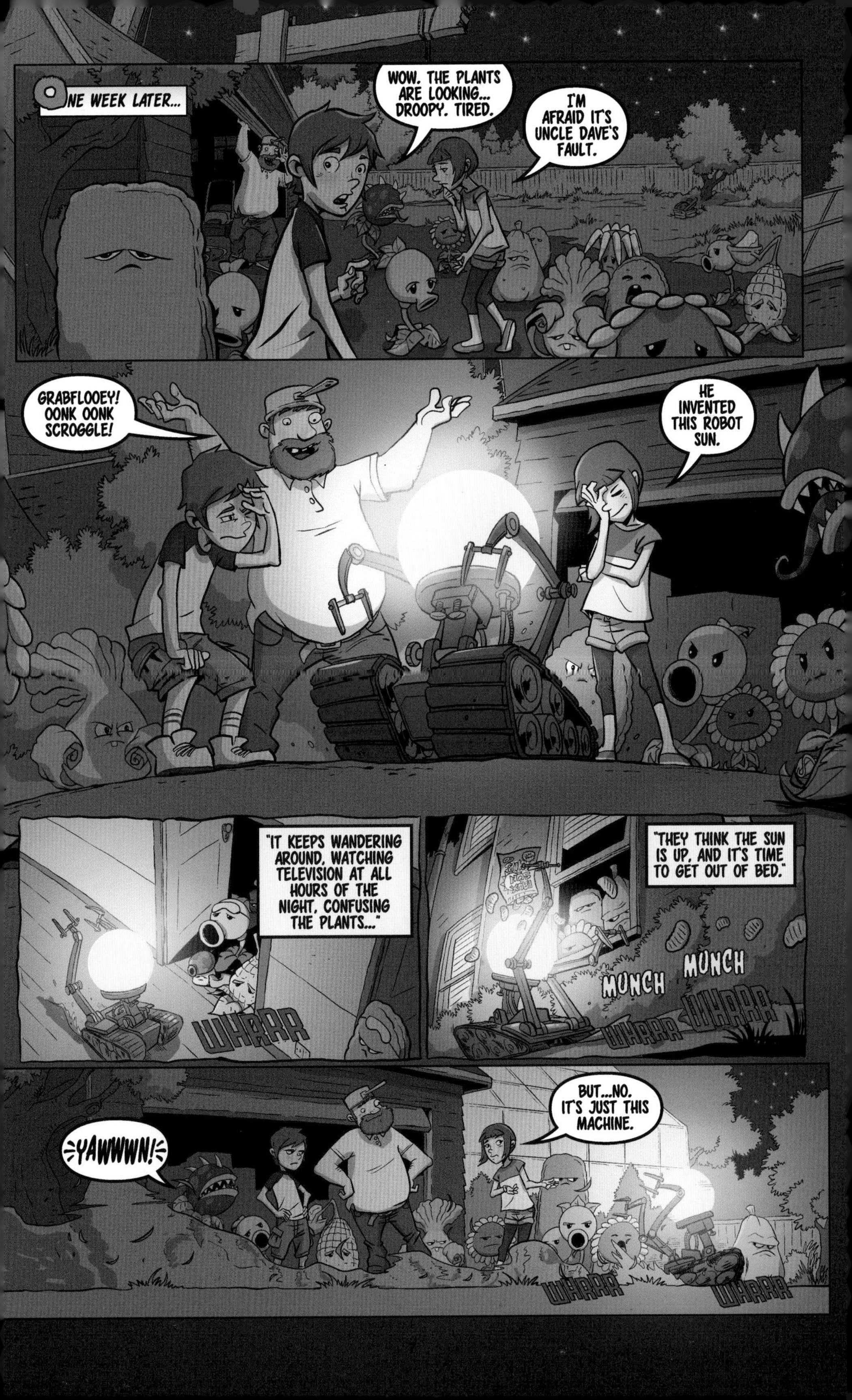
ONE WEEK LATER...
WOW. THE PLANTS ARE LOOKING... DROOPY. TIRED.
I'M AFRAID IT'S UNCLE DAVE'S FAULT.
GRABFLOOEY! OONK OONK SCROGGLE!
HE INVENTED THIS ROBOT SUN.
"IT KEEPS WANDERING AROUND, WATCHING TELEVISION AT ALL HOURS OF THE NIGHT, CONFUSING THE PLANTS..."
WHRRR
"THEY THINK THE SUN IS UP, AND IT'S TIME TO GET OUT OF BED."
MUNCH MUNCH
WHRRR WHRRR
YAWWWN!
BUT...NO. IT'S JUST THIS MACHINE.
WHRRR WHRRR

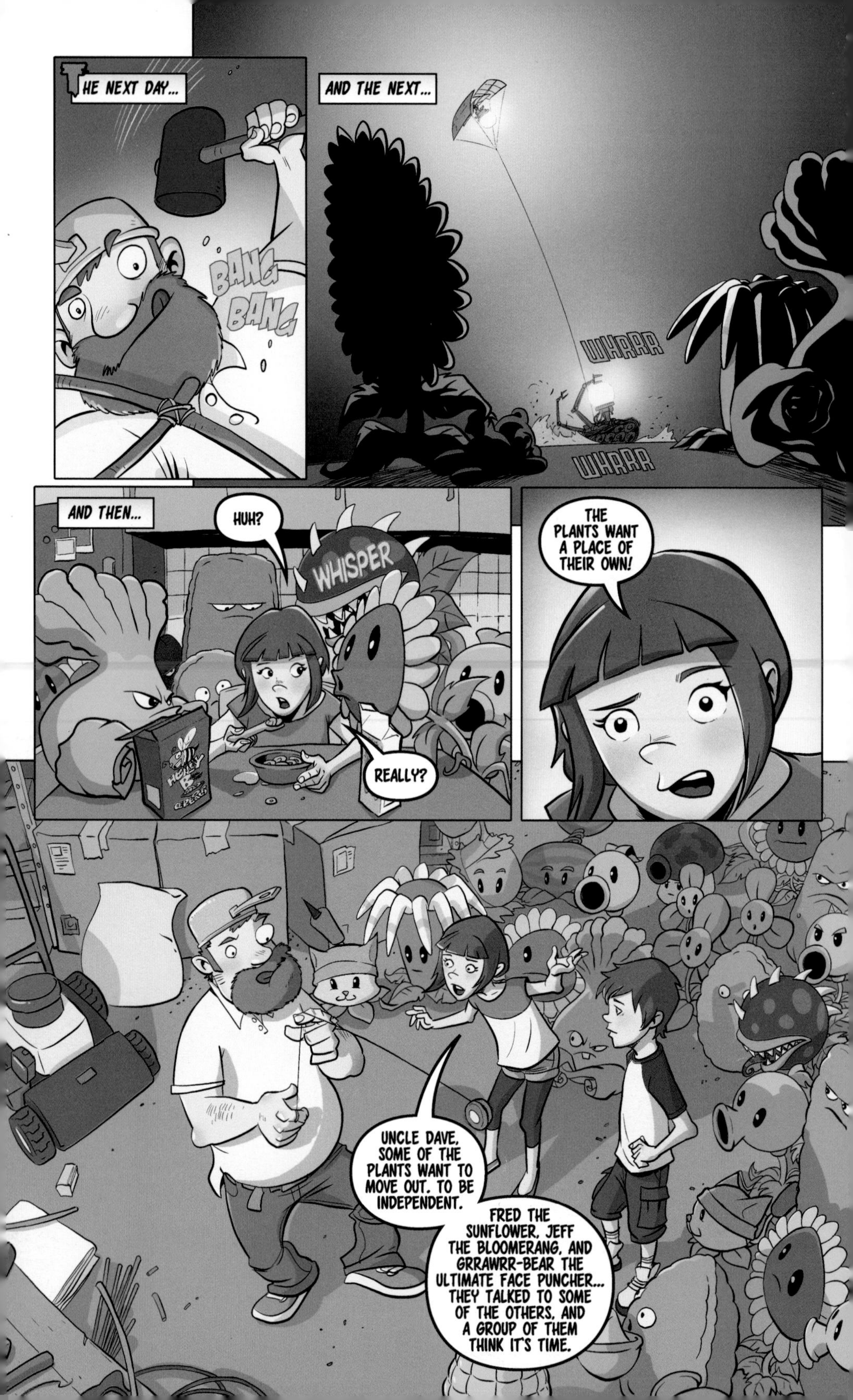
THE NEXT DAY...
BANG
BANG
AND THE NEXT...
WHRRR
WHRRR
AND THEN...
HUH?
WHISPER
REALLY?
THE PLANTS WANT A PLACE OF THEIR OWN!
UNCLE DAVE, SOME OF THE PLANTS WANT TO MOVE OUT. TO BE INDEPENDENT.
FRED THE SUNFLOWER, JEFF THE BLOOMERANG, AND GRRAWRR-BEAR THE ULTIMATE FACE PUNCHER... THEY TALKED TO SOME OF THE OTHERS, AND A GROUP OF THEM THINK IT'S TIME.

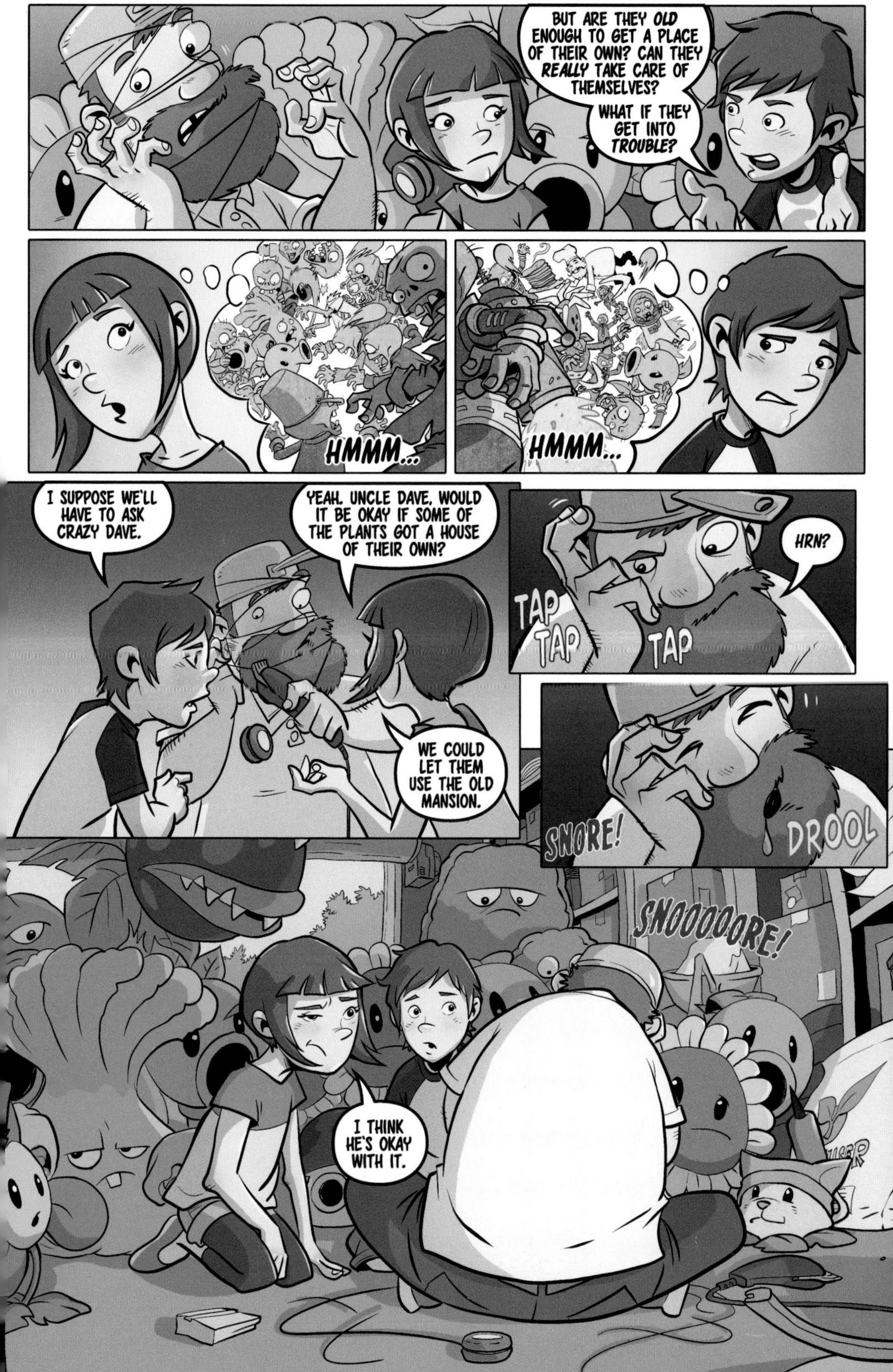
BUT ARE THEY OLD ENOUGH TO GET A PLACE OF THEIR OWN? CAN THEY REALLY TAKE CARE OF THEMSELVES?
WHAT IF THEY GET INTO TROUBLE?
HMMM...
HMMM...
I SUPPOSE WE'LL HAVE TO ASK CRAZY DAVE.
YEAH. UNCLE DAVE, WOULD IT BE OKAY IF SOME OF THE PLANTS GOT A HOUSE OF THEIR OWN?
WE COULD LET THEM USE THE OLD MANSION.
TAP
TAP
TAP
HRN?
SNORE!
DROOL
SNOOOOOORE!
I THINK HE'S OKAY WITH IT.

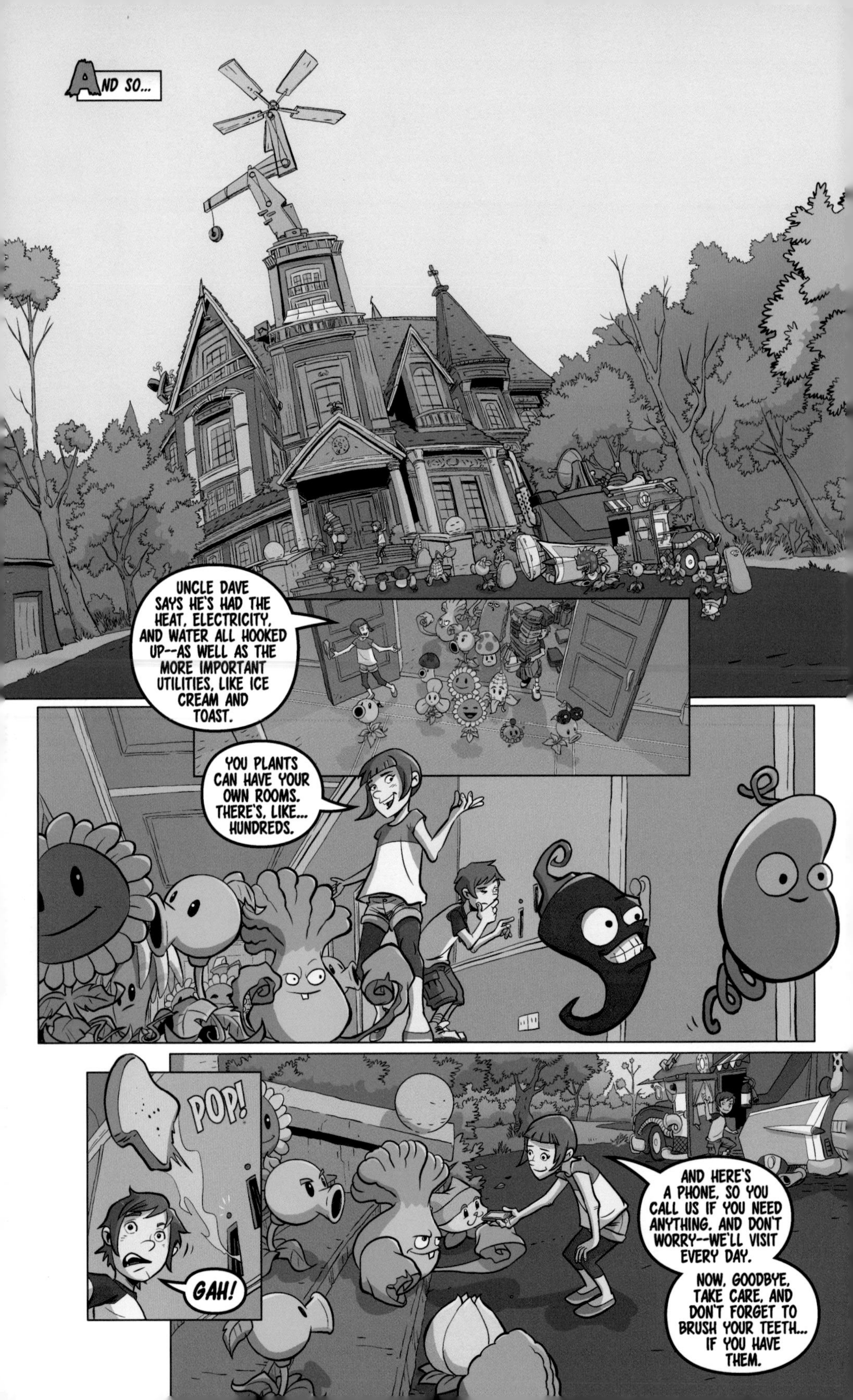
AND SO...
UNCLE DAVE SAYS HE'S HAD THE HEAT, ELECTRICITY, AND WATER ALL HOOKED UP--AS WELL AS THE MORE IMPORTANT UTILITIES, LIKE ICE CREAM AND TOAST.
YOU PLANTS CAN HAVE YOUR OWN ROOMS. THERE'S, LIKE... HUNDREDS.
POP!
GAH!
AND HERE'S A PHONE, SO YOU CALL US IF YOU NEED ANYTHING. AND DON'T WORRY--WE'LL VISIT EVERY DAY.
NOW, GOODBYE, TAKE CARE, AND DON'T FORGET TO BRUSH YOUR TEETH... IF YOU HAVE THEM.

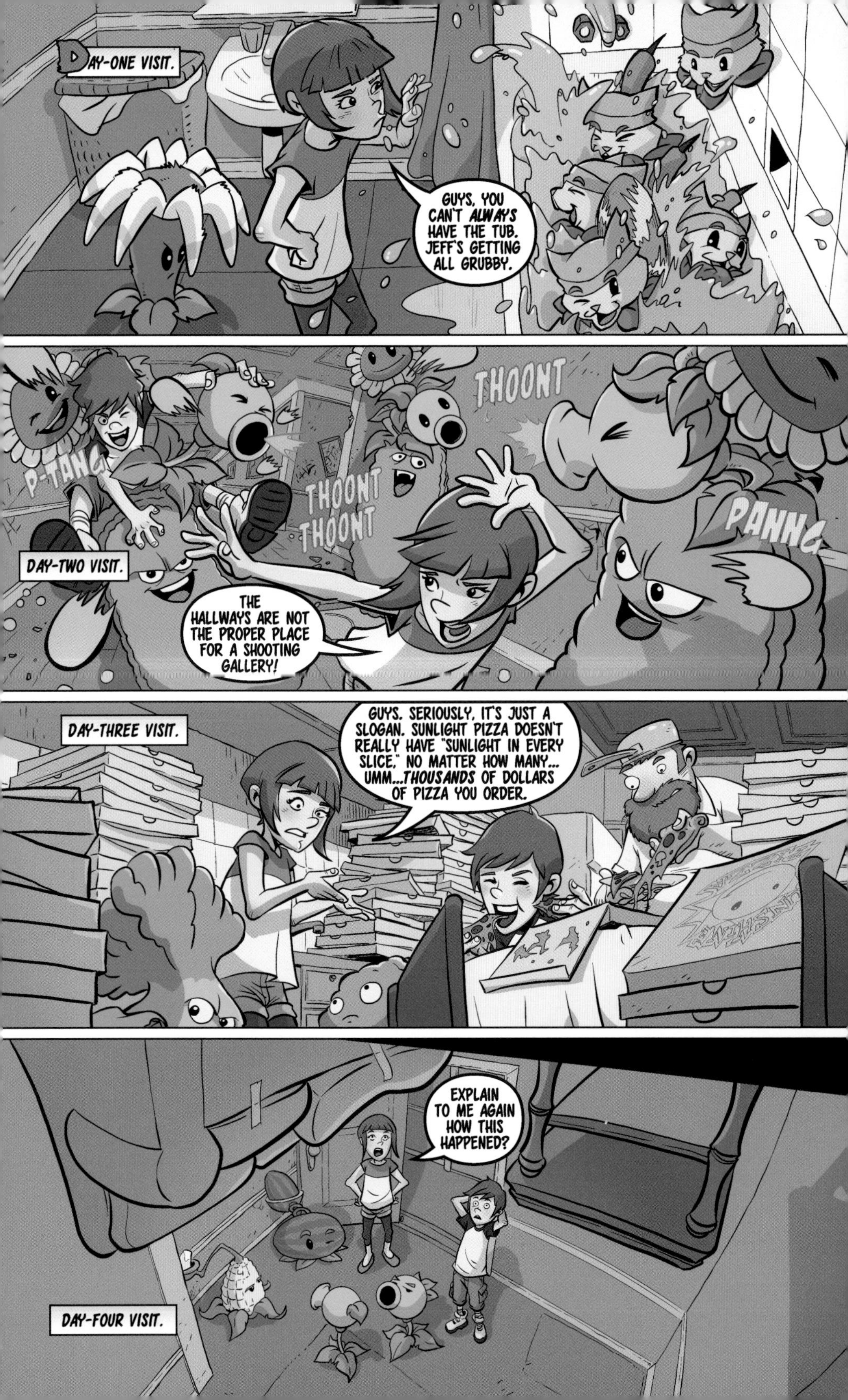
DAY-ONE VISIT.
GUYS, YOU CAN'T ALWAYS HAVE THE TUB. JEFF'S GETTING ALL GRUBBY.
THOONT
P-TANG
THOONT THOONT
PANNG
DAY-TWO VISIT.
THE HALLWAYS ARE NOT THE PROPER PLACE FOR A SHOOTING GALLERY!
DAY-THREE VISIT.
GUYS. SERIOUSLY, IT'S JUST A SLOGAN. SUNLIGHT PIZZA DOESN'T REALLY HAVE "SUNLIGHT IN EVERY SLICE," NO MATTER HOW MANY... UMM...THOUSANDS OF DOLLARS OF PIZZA YOU ORDER.
EXPLAIN TO ME AGAIN HOW THIS HAPPENED?
DAY-FOUR VISIT.

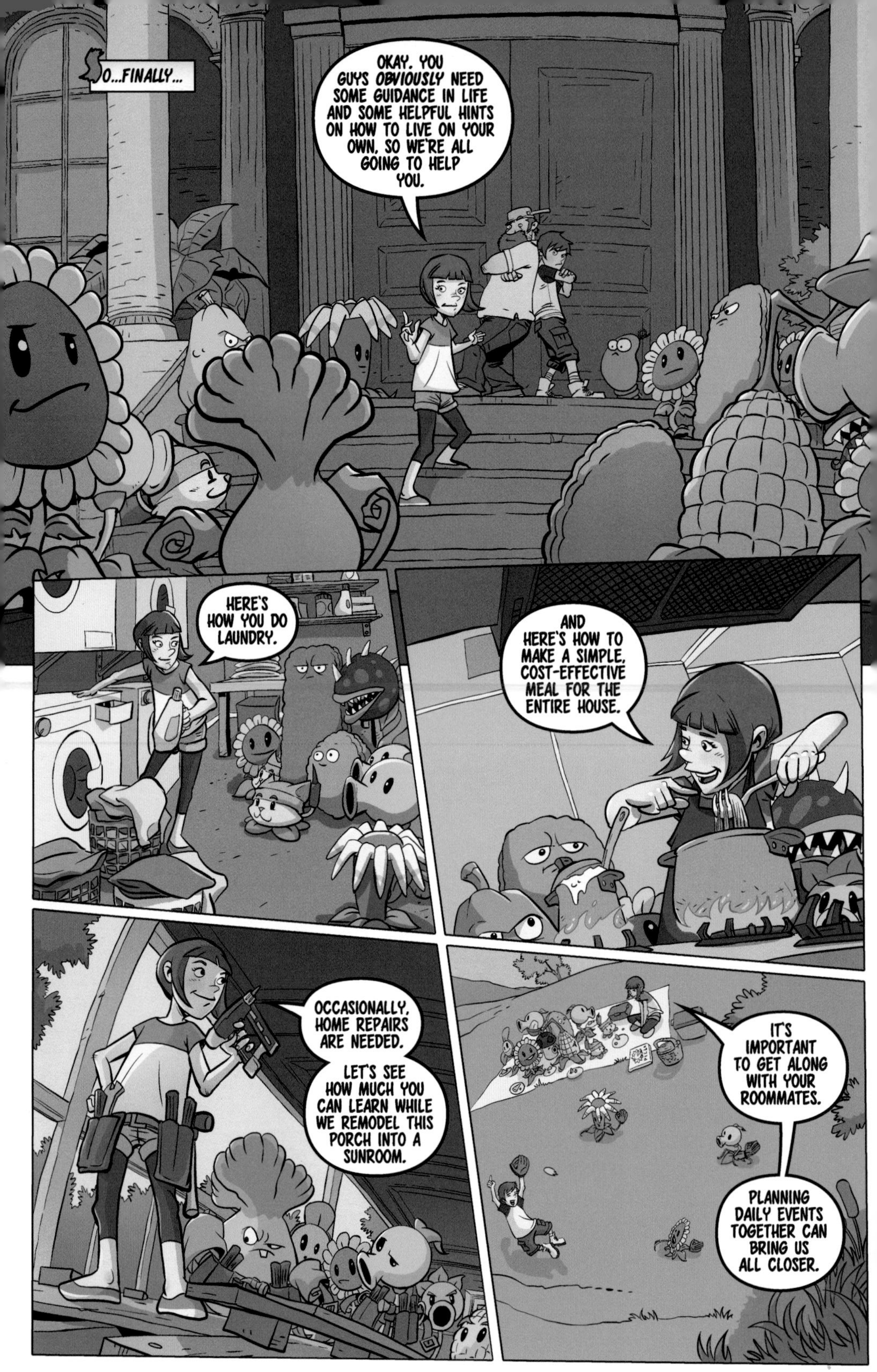
SO...FINALLY...
OKAY. YOU GUYS OBVIOUSLY NEED SOME GUIDANCE IN LIFE AND SOME HELPFUL HINTS ON HOW TO LIVE ON YOUR OWN, SO WE'RE ALL GOING TO HELP YOU.
HERE'S HOW YOU DO LAUNDRY.
AND HERE'S HOW TO MAKE A SIMPLE, COST-EFFECTIVE MEAL FOR THE ENTIRE HOUSE.
OCCASIONALLY, HOME REPAIRS ARE NEEDED.
LET'S SEE HOW MUCH YOU CAN LEARN WHILE WE REMODEL THIS PORCH INTO A SUNROOM.
IT'S IMPORTANT TO GET ALONG WITH YOUR ROOMMATES.
PLANNING DAILY EVENTS TOGETHER CAN BRING US ALL CLOSER.

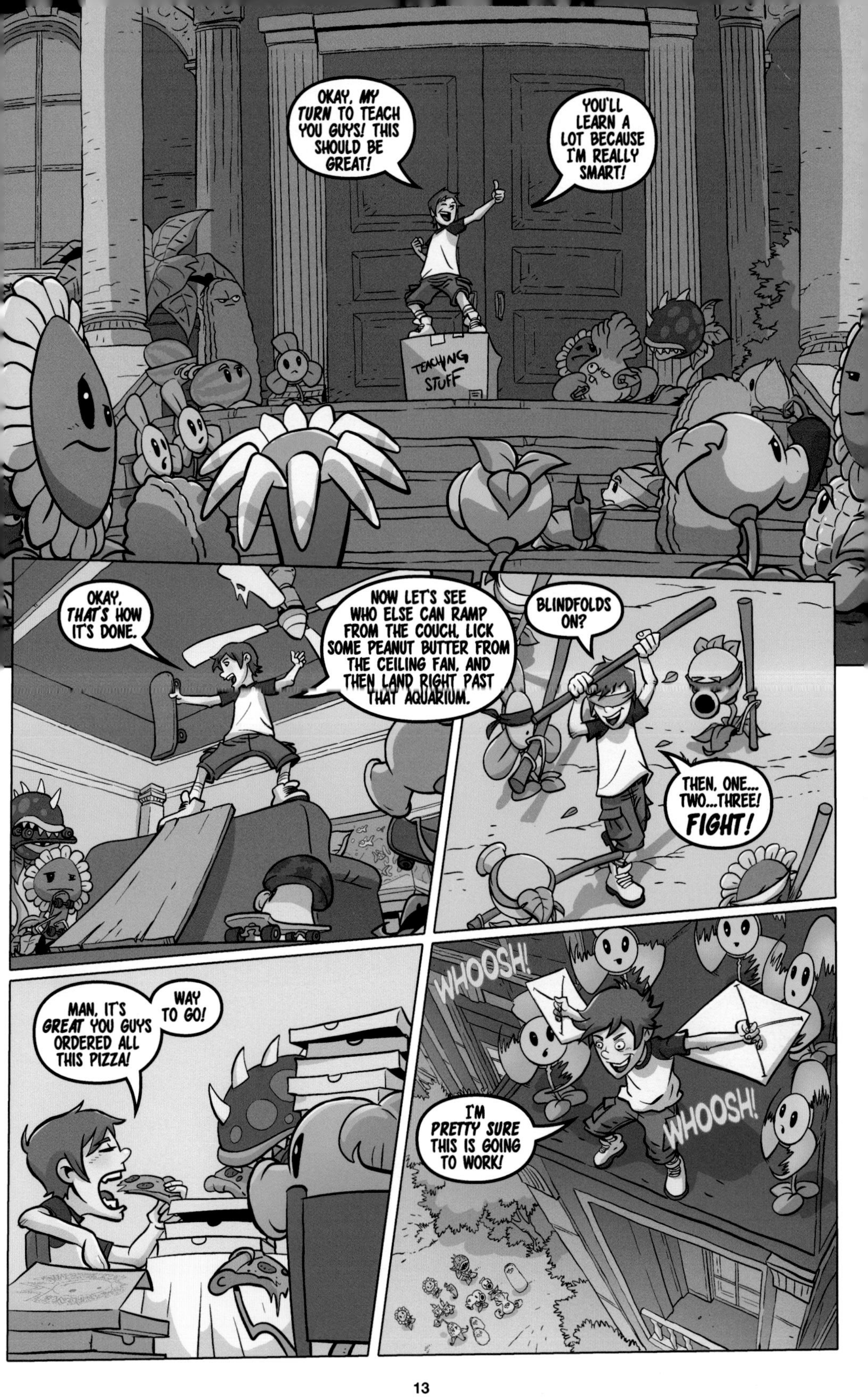
OKAY, MY TURN TO TEACH YOU GUYS! THIS SHOULD BE GREAT!
YOU'LL LEARN A LOT BECAUSE I'M REALLY SMART!
TEACHING STUFF
OKAY, THAT'S HOW IT'S DONE.
NOW LET'S SEE WHO ELSE CAN RAMP FROM THE COUCH, LICK SOME PEANUT BUTTER FROM THE CEILING FAN, AND THEN LAND RIGHT PAST THAT AQUARIUM.
BLINDFOLDS ON?
THEN, ONE... TWO...THREE! FIGHT!
MAN, IT'S GREAT YOU GUYS ORDERED ALL THIS PIZZA!
WAY TO GO!
WHOOSH!
I'M PRETTY SURE THIS IS GOING TO WORK!
WHOOSH!

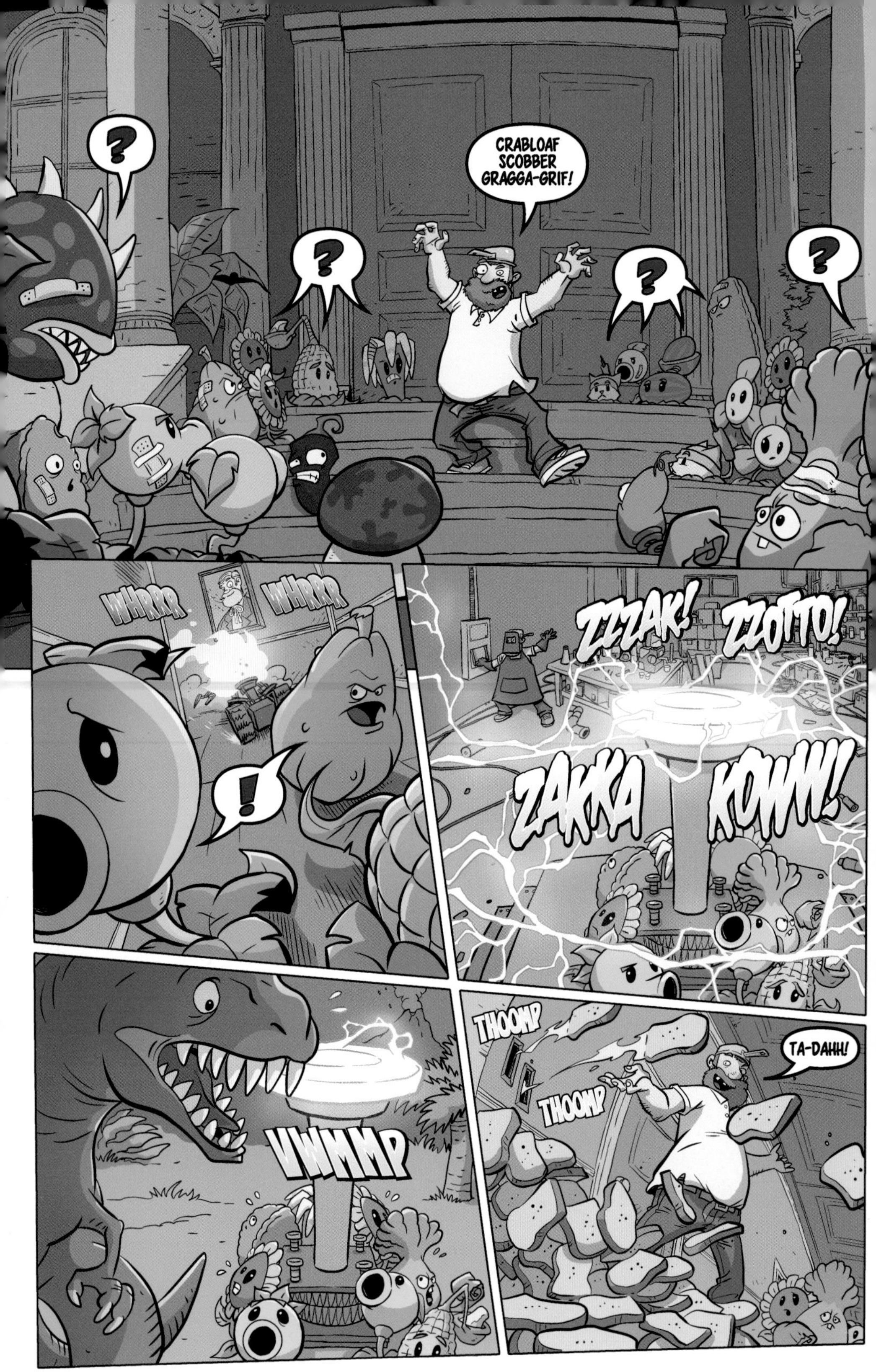
?
CRABLOAF SCOBBER GRAGGA-GRIF!
?
?
?
WHRRR
WHRRR
!
ZZZAK!
ZZOTTO!
ZAKKA
KOWW!
VWMMP
THOOMP
THOOMP
TA-DAHH!

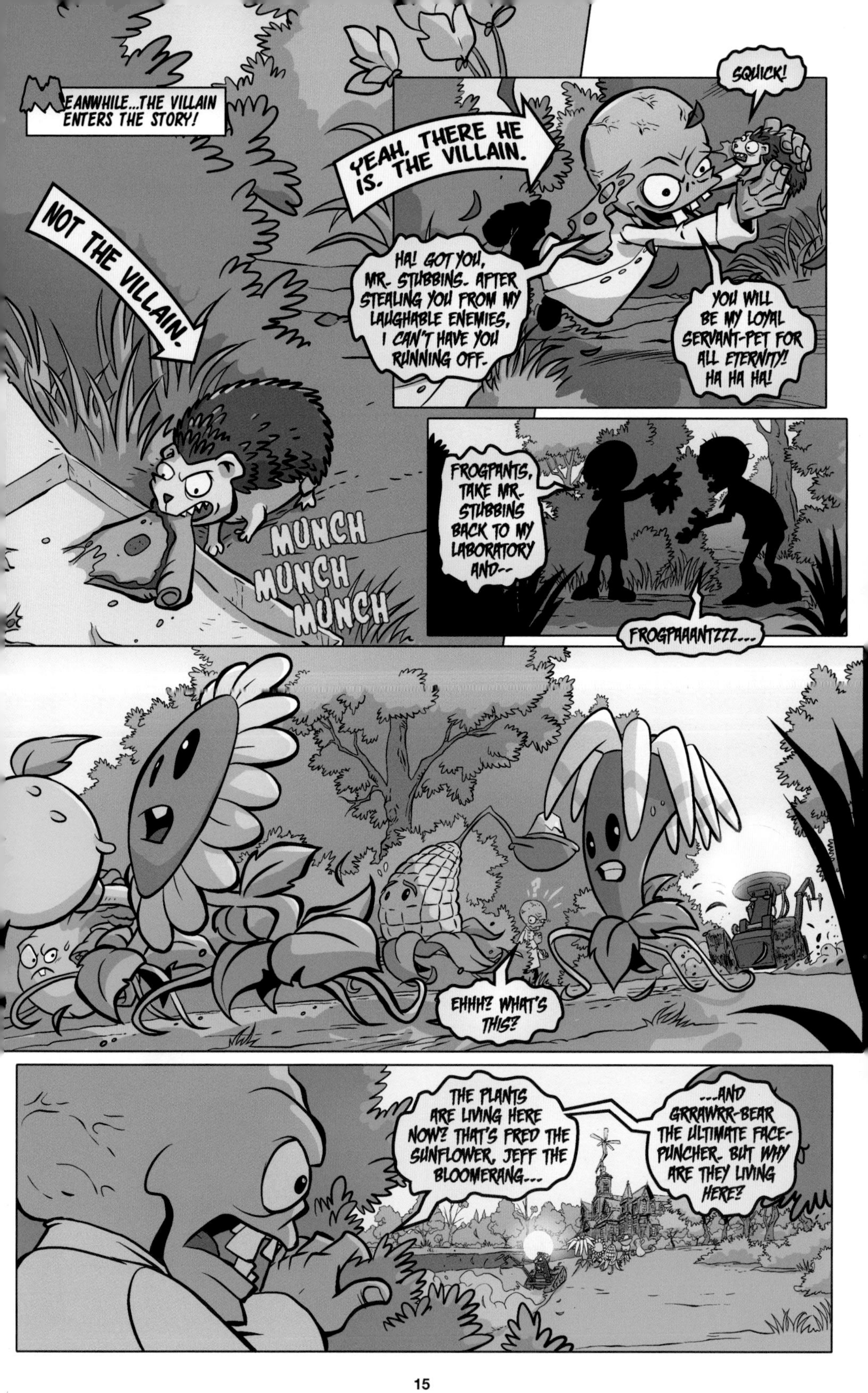
MEANWHILE...THE VILLAIN ENTERS THE STORY!
NOT THE VILLAIN.
YEAH, THERE HE IS. THE VILLAIN.
SQUICK!
HA! GOT YOU, MR. STUBBINS. AFTER STEALING YOU FROM MY LAUGHABLE ENEMIES, I CAN'T HAVE YOU RUNNING OFF.
YOU WILL BE MY LOYAL SERVANT-PET FOR ALL ETERNITY! HA HA HA!
MUNCH MUNCH MUNCH
FROGPANTS, TAKE MR. STUBBINS BACK TO MY LABORATORY AND--
FROGPAAANTZZZ...
EHHH? WHAT'S THIS?
THE PLANTS ARE LIVING HERE NOW? THAT'S FRED THE SUNFLOWER, JEFF THE BLOOMERANG...
...AND GRRAWRR-BEAR THE ULTIMATE FACE-PUNCHER. BUT WHY ARE THEY LIVING HERE?

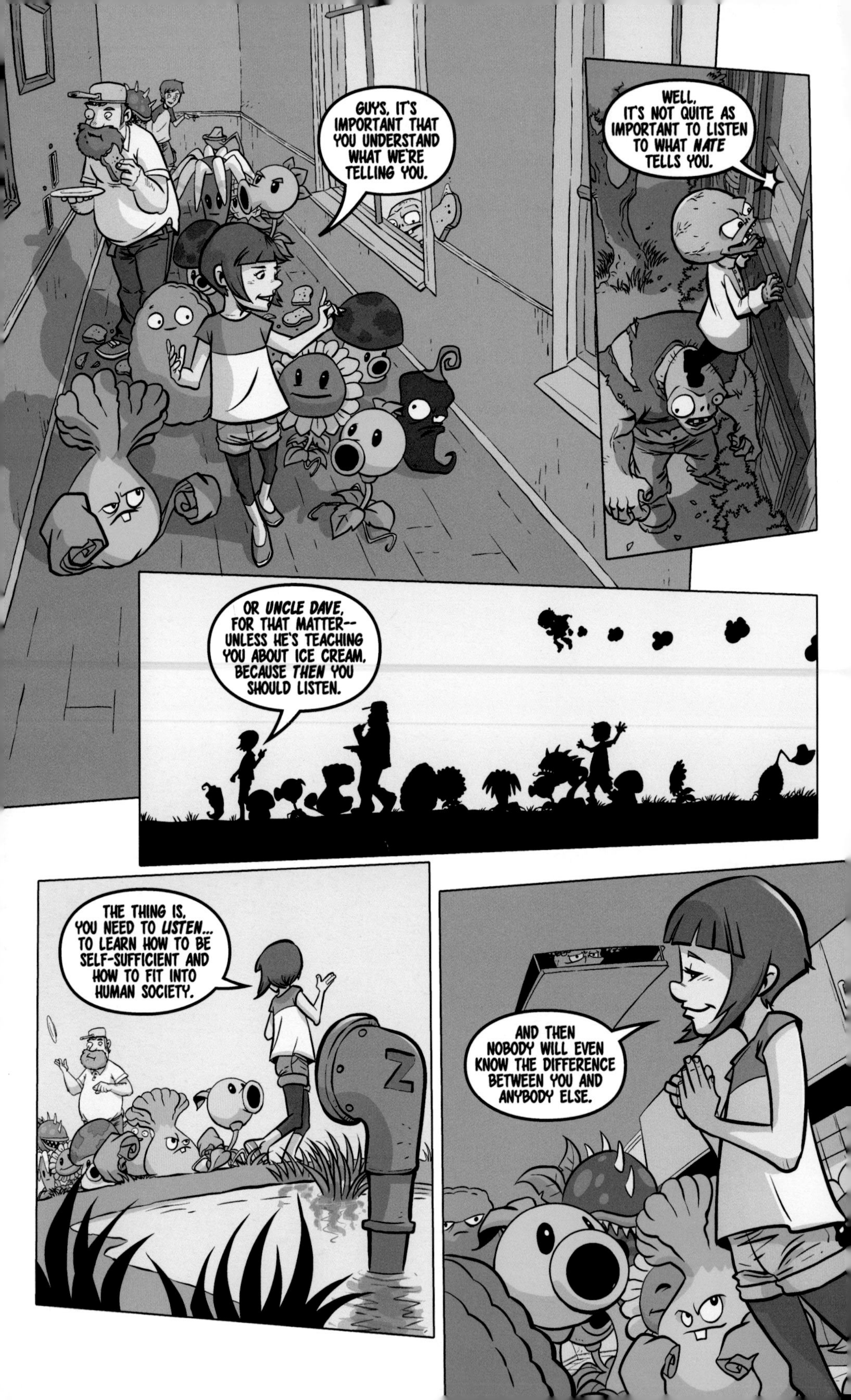
GUYS, IT'S IMPORTANT THAT YOU UNDERSTAND WHAT WE'RE TELLING YOU.
WELL, IT'S NOT QUITE AS IMPORTANT TO LISTEN TO WHAT *NATE* TELLS YOU.
OR *UNCLE DAVE*, FOR THAT MATTER-- UNLESS HE'S TEACHING YOU ABOUT ICE CREAM, BECAUSE *THEN* YOU SHOULD LISTEN.
THE THING IS, YOU NEED TO *LISTEN*... TO LEARN HOW TO BE SELF-SUFFICIENT AND HOW TO FIT INTO HUMAN SOCIETY.
Z
AND THEN NOBODY WILL EVEN KNOW THE DIFFERENCE BETWEEN YOU AND ANYBODY ELSE.

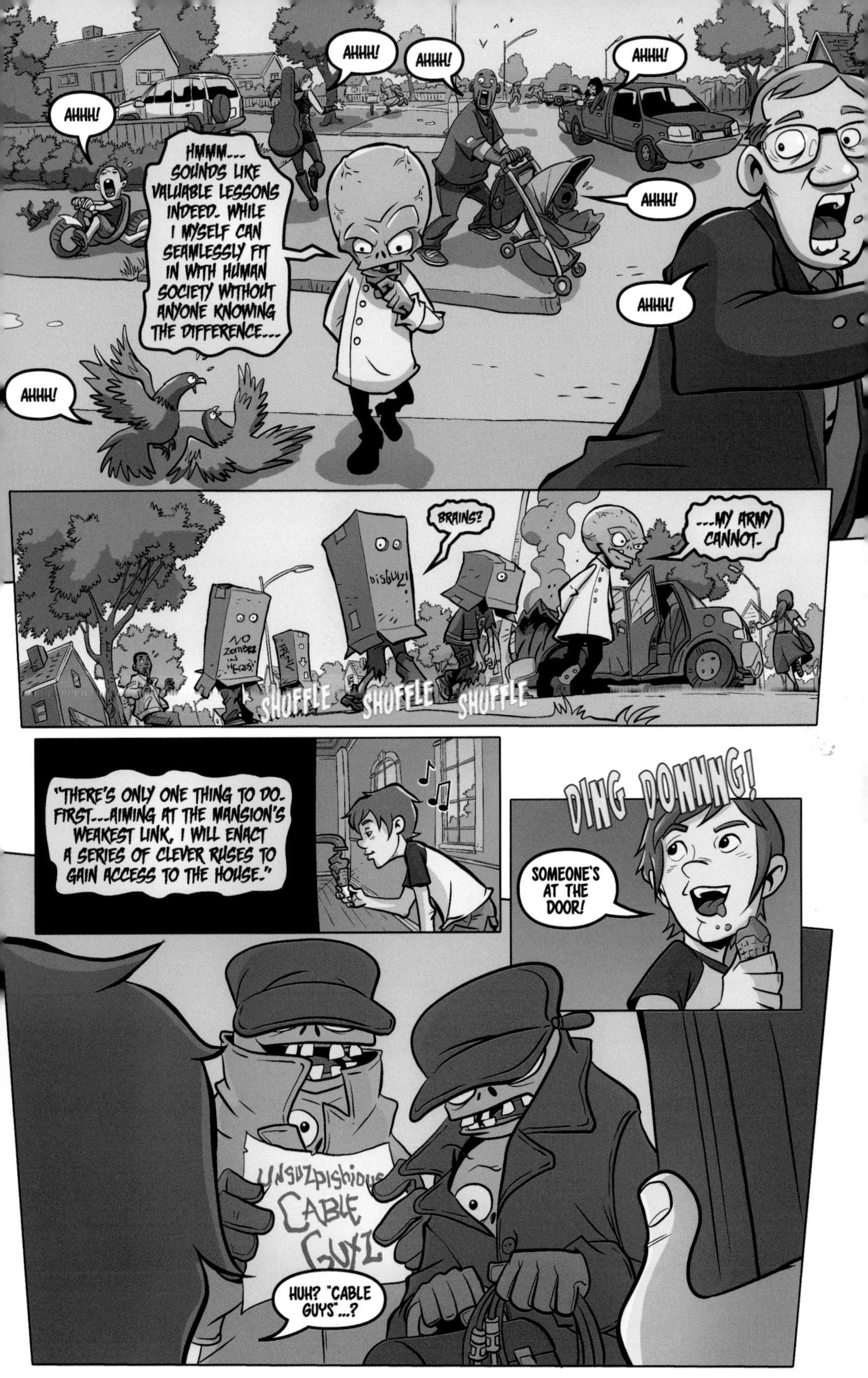
AHHH!
AHHH!
AHHH!
AHHH!
HMMM... SOUNDS LIKE VALUABLE LESSONS INDEED. WHILE I MYSELF CAN SEAMLESSLY FIT IN WITH HUMAN SOCIETY WITHOUT ANYONE KNOWING THE DIFFERENCE...
AHHH!
AHHH!
AHHH!
BRAINS?
...MY ARMY CANNOT.
SHUFFLE
SHUFFLE
SHUFFLE
"THERE'S ONLY ONE THING TO DO. FIRST...AIMING AT THE MANSION'S WEAKEST LINK, I WILL ENACT A SERIES OF CLEVER RUSES TO GAIN ACCESS TO THE HOUSE."
DING DONNNG!
SOMEONE'S AT THE DOOR!
UNSUZPISHIOUS CABLE GUYZ
HUH? "CABLE GUYS"...?

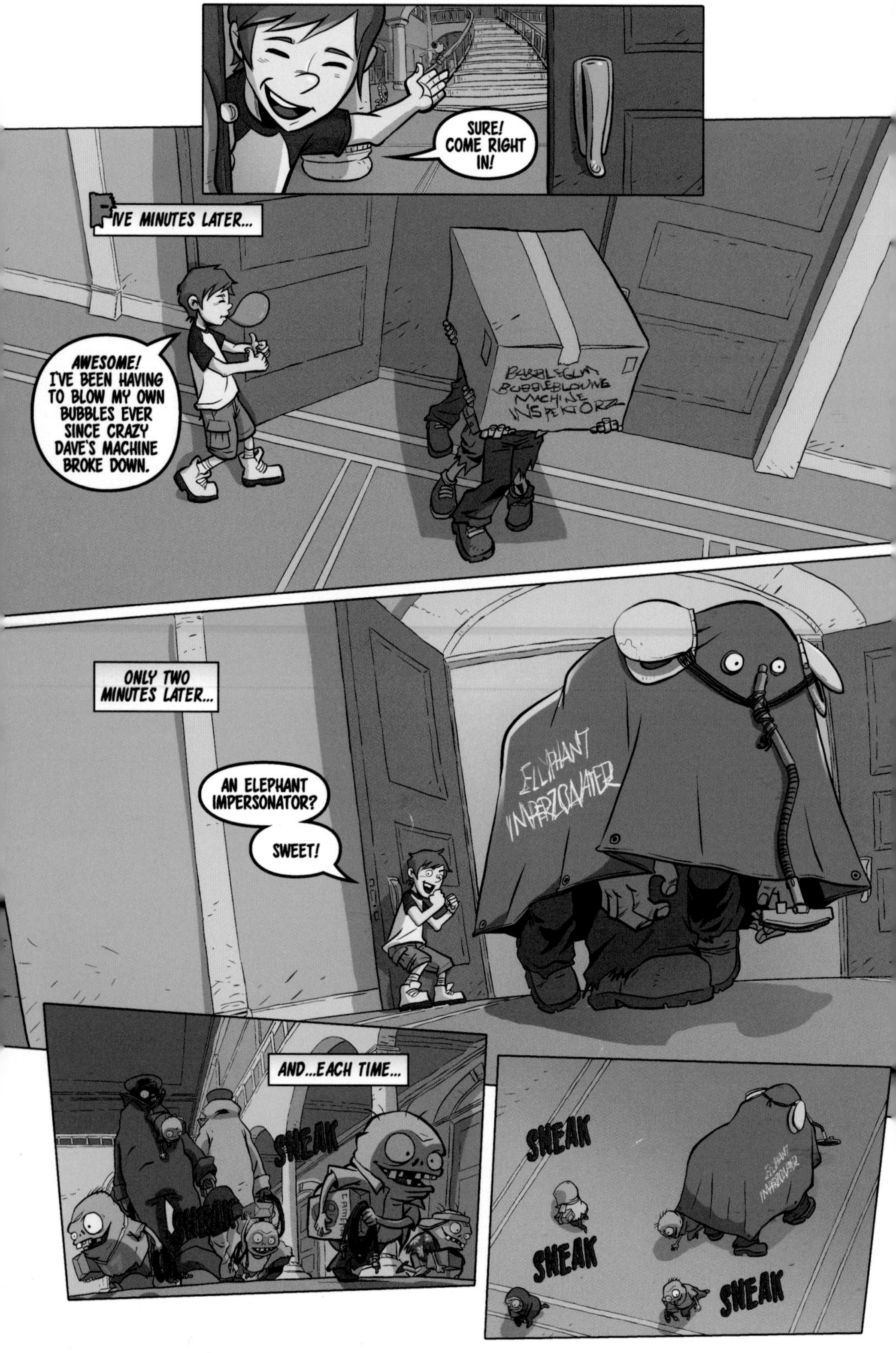
SURE! COME RIGHT IN!
FIVE MINUTES LATER...
AWESOME! I'VE BEEN HAVING TO BLOW MY OWN BUBBLES EVER SINCE CRAZY DAVE'S MACHINE BROKE DOWN.
ONLY TWO MINUTES LATER...
AN ELEPHANT IMPERSONATOR?
SWEET!
AND...EACH TIME...
SNEAK
SNEAK
SNEAK
SNEAK
SNEAK

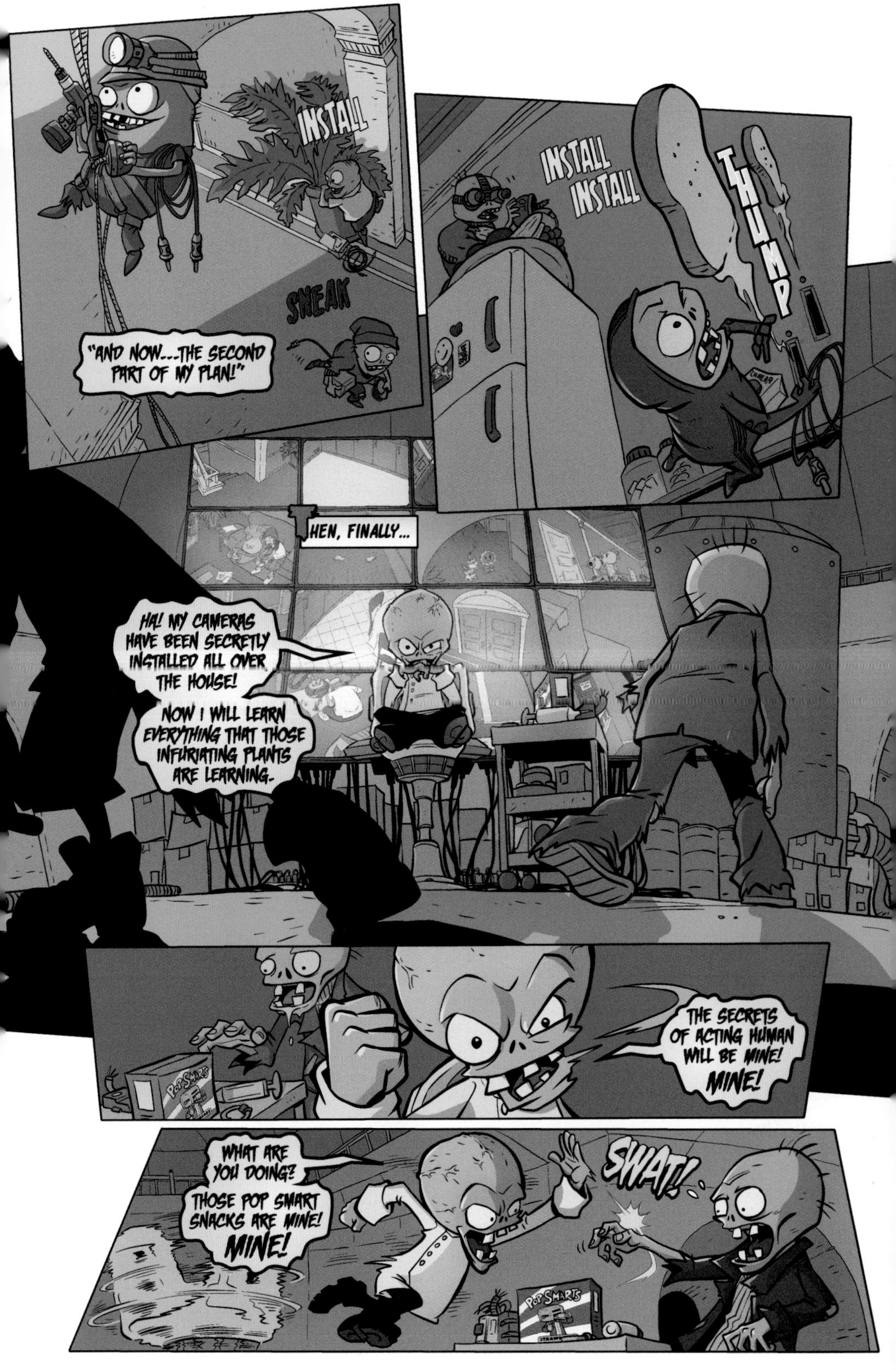
INSTALL
SNEAK
"AND NOW...THE SECOND PART OF MY PLAN!"
INSTALL INSTALL
THUMP
THEN, FINALLY...
HA! MY CAMERAS HAVE BEEN SECRETLY INSTALLED ALL OVER THE HOUSE!
NOW I WILL LEARN EVERYTHING THAT THOSE INFURIATING PLANTS ARE LEARNING.
THE SECRETS OF ACTING HUMAN WILL BE MINE! MINE!
WHAT ARE YOU DOING?
THOSE POP SMART SNACKS ARE MINE! MINE!
SWAT!

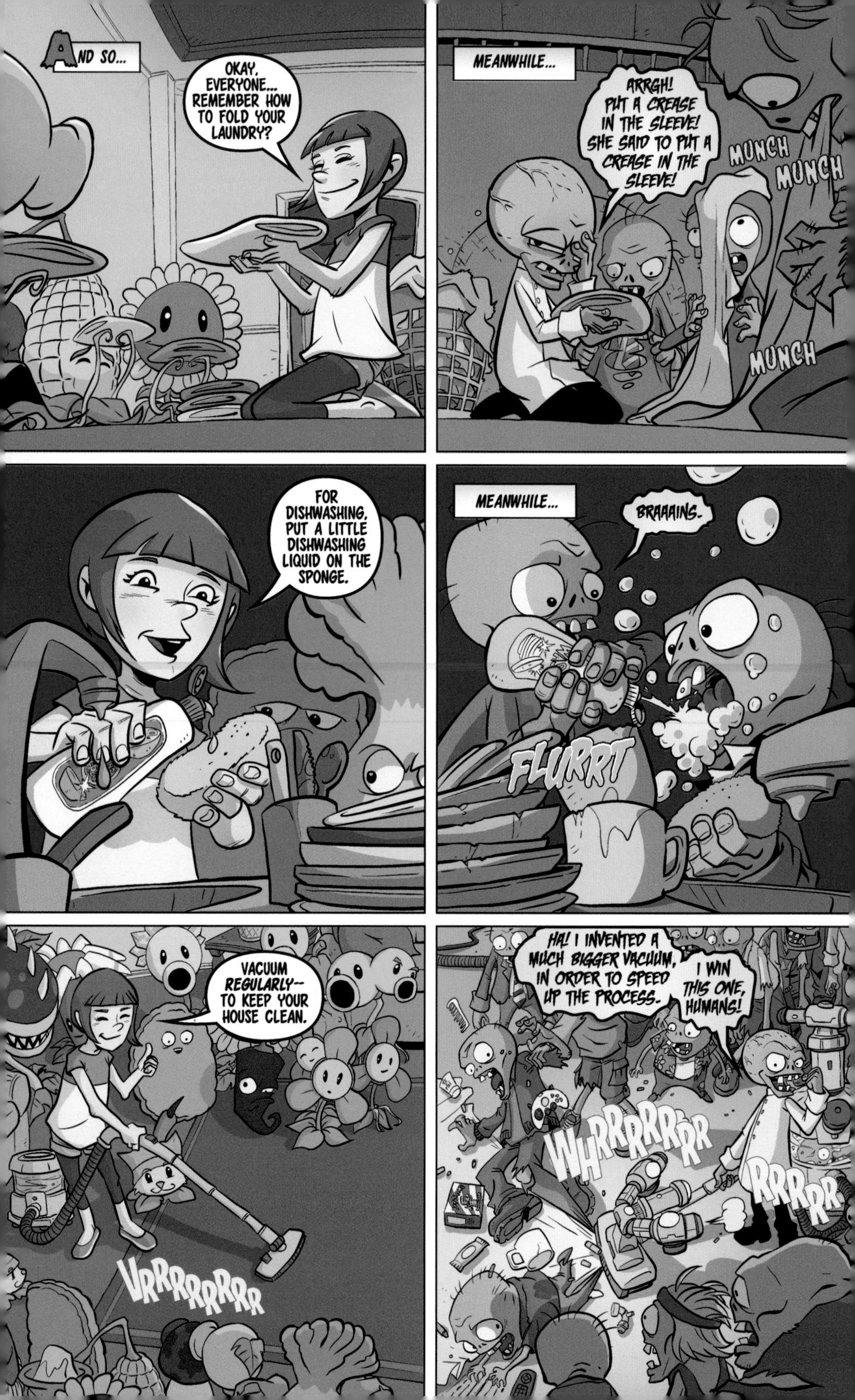
AND SO...
OKAY, EVERYONE... REMEMBER HOW TO FOLD YOUR LAUNDRY?
MEANWHILE...
ARRGH! PUT A CREASE IN THE SLEEVE! SHE SAID TO PUT A CREASE IN THE SLEEVE!
MUNCH
MUNCH
MUNCH
FOR DISHWASHING, PUT A LITTLE DISHWASHING LIQUID ON THE SPONGE.
MEANWHILE...
BRAAAINS.
FLURRT
VACUUM REGULARLY-- TO KEEP YOUR HOUSE CLEAN.
VRRRRRRRR
HA! I INVENTED A MUCH BIGGER VACUUM, IN ORDER TO SPEED UP THE PROCESS.
I WIN THIS ONE, HUMANS!
WHRRRRRRR
RRRRR

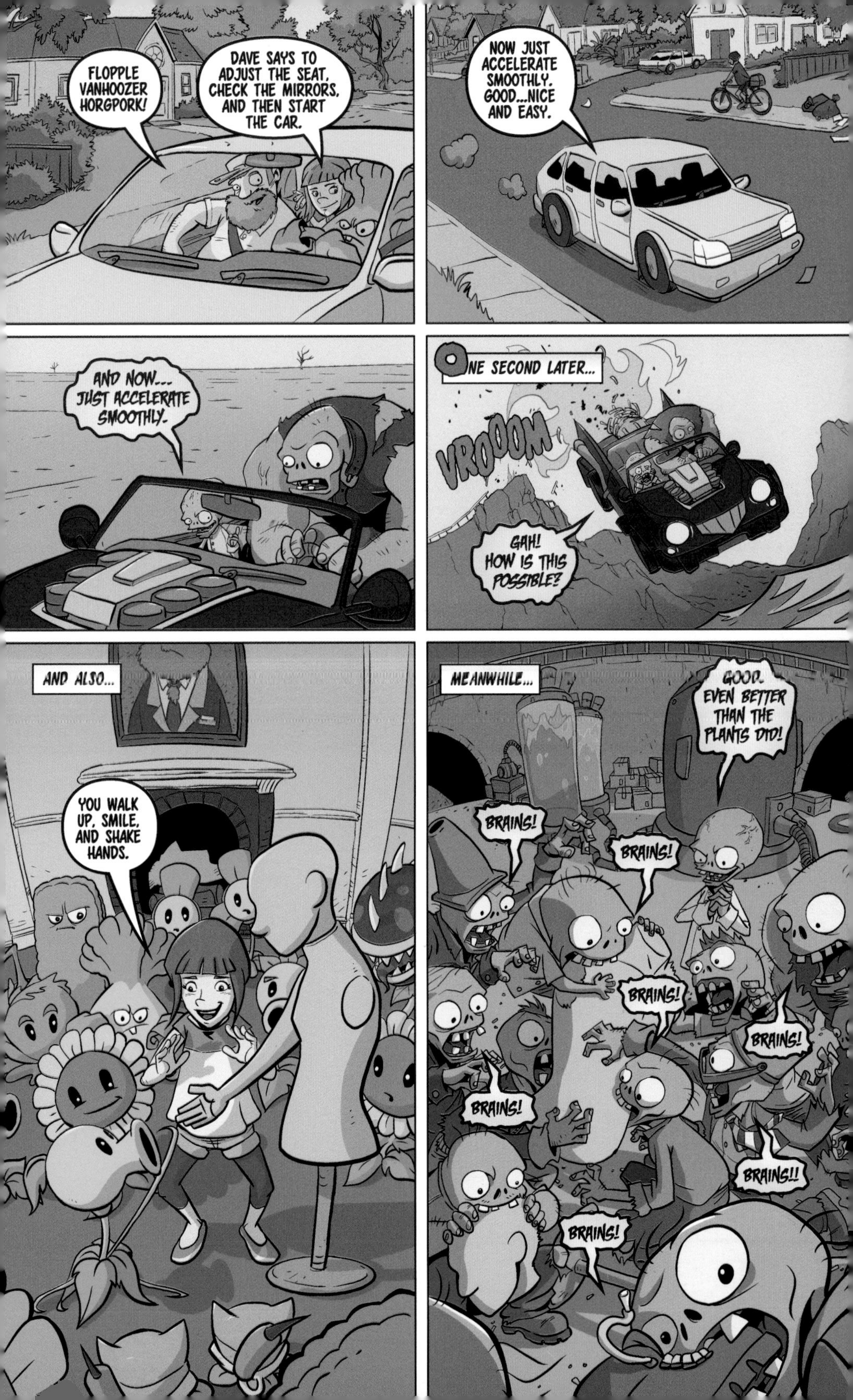
FLOPPLE VANHOOZER HORGPORK!
DAVE SAYS TO ADJUST THE SEAT, CHECK THE MIRRORS, AND THEN START THE CAR.
NOW JUST ACCELERATE SMOOTHLY. GOOD...NICE AND EASY.
AND NOW... JUST ACCELERATE SMOOTHLY.
ONE SECOND LATER...
VROOOM
GAH! HOW IS THIS POSSIBLE?
AND ALSO...
YOU WALK UP, SMILE, AND SHAKE HANDS.
MEANWHILE...
GOOD. EVEN BETTER THAN THE PLANTS DID!
BRAINS!
BRAINS!
BRAINS!
BRAINS!
BRAINS!
BRAINS!!
BRAINS!

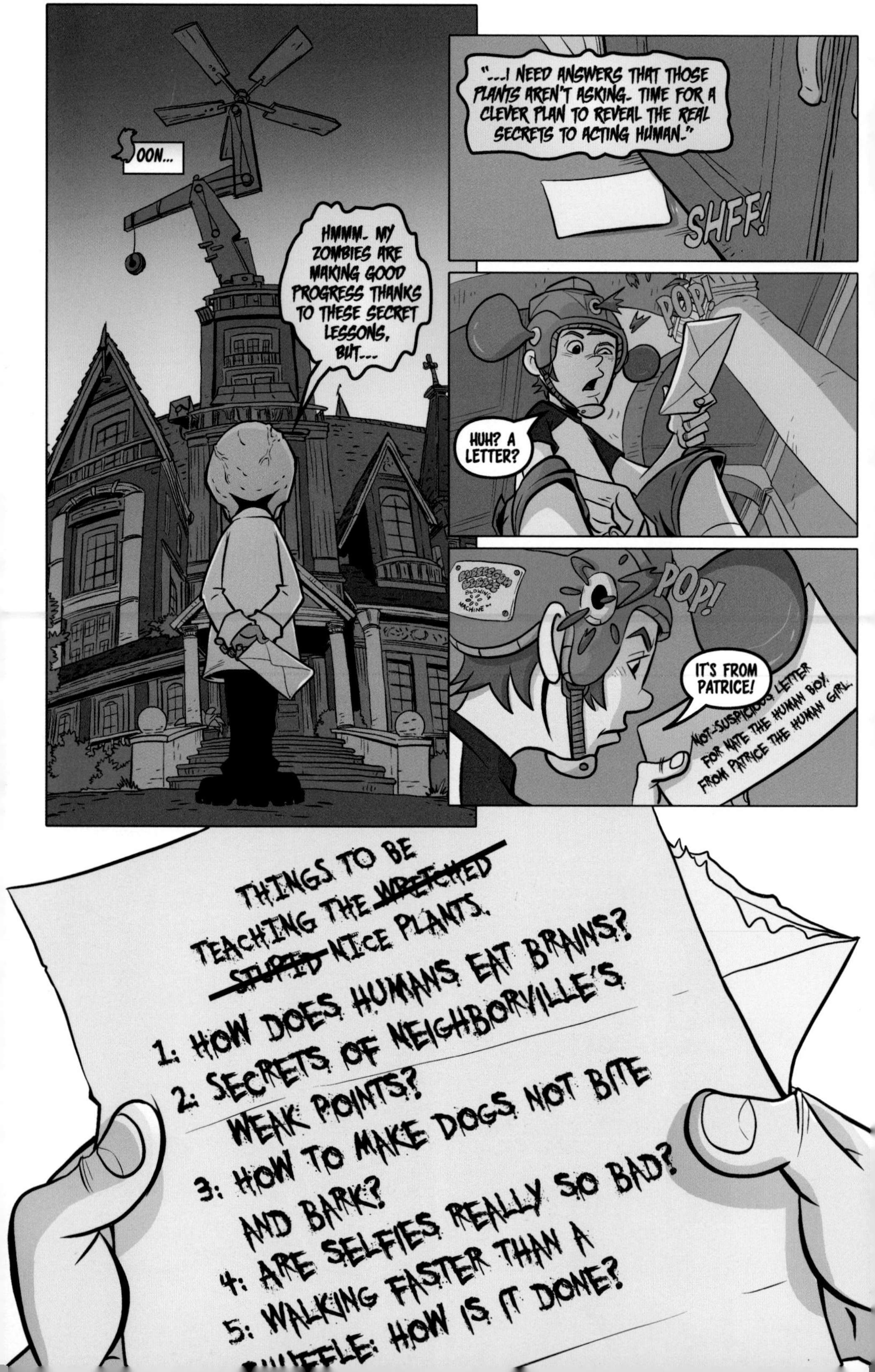
SOON...
HMMM. MY ZOMBIES ARE MAKING GOOD PROGRESS THANKS TO THESE SECRET LESSONS, BUT...
"...I NEED ANSWERS THAT THOSE PLANTS AREN'T ASKING. TIME FOR A CLEVER PLAN TO REVEAL THE REAL SECRETS TO ACTING HUMAN."
SHFF!
POP!
HUH? A LETTER?
POP!
BLOWING MACHINE
IT'S FROM PATRICE!
NOT-SUSPICIOUS LETTER
FOR NATE THE HUMAN BOY.
FROM PATRICE THE HUMAN GIRL.
THINGS TO BE
TEACHING THE ~~WRETCHED~~
~~STUPID~~ NICE PLANTS.
1: HOW DOES HUMANS EAT BRAINS?
2: SECRETS OF NEIGHBORVILLE'S
WEAK POINTS?
3: HOW TO MAKE DOGS NOT BITE
AND BARK?
4: ARE SELFIES REALLY SO BAD?
5: WALKING FASTER THAN A
UFFLE: HOW IS IT DONE?

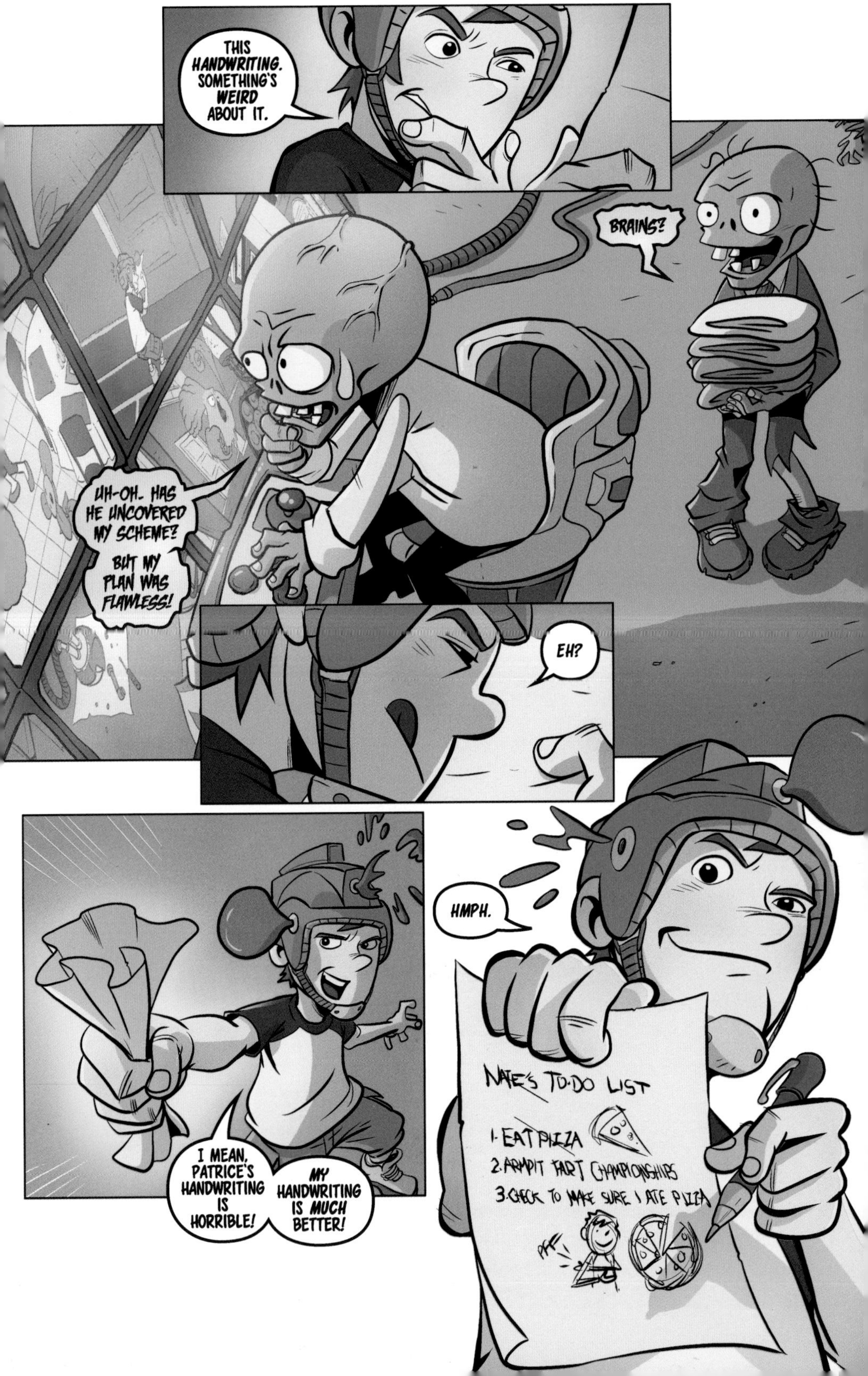
THIS HANDWRITING. SOMETHING'S WEIRD ABOUT IT.
BRAINS?
UH-OH. HAS HE UNCOVERED MY SCHEME?
BUT MY PLAN WAS FLAWLESS!
EH?
I MEAN, PATRICE'S HANDWRITING IS HORRIBLE!
MY HANDWRITING IS MUCH BETTER!
HMPH.
NATE'S TO-DO LIST
1. EAT PIZZA
2. ARMPIT FART CHAMPIONSHIPS
3. CHECK TO MAKE SURE I ATE PIZZA

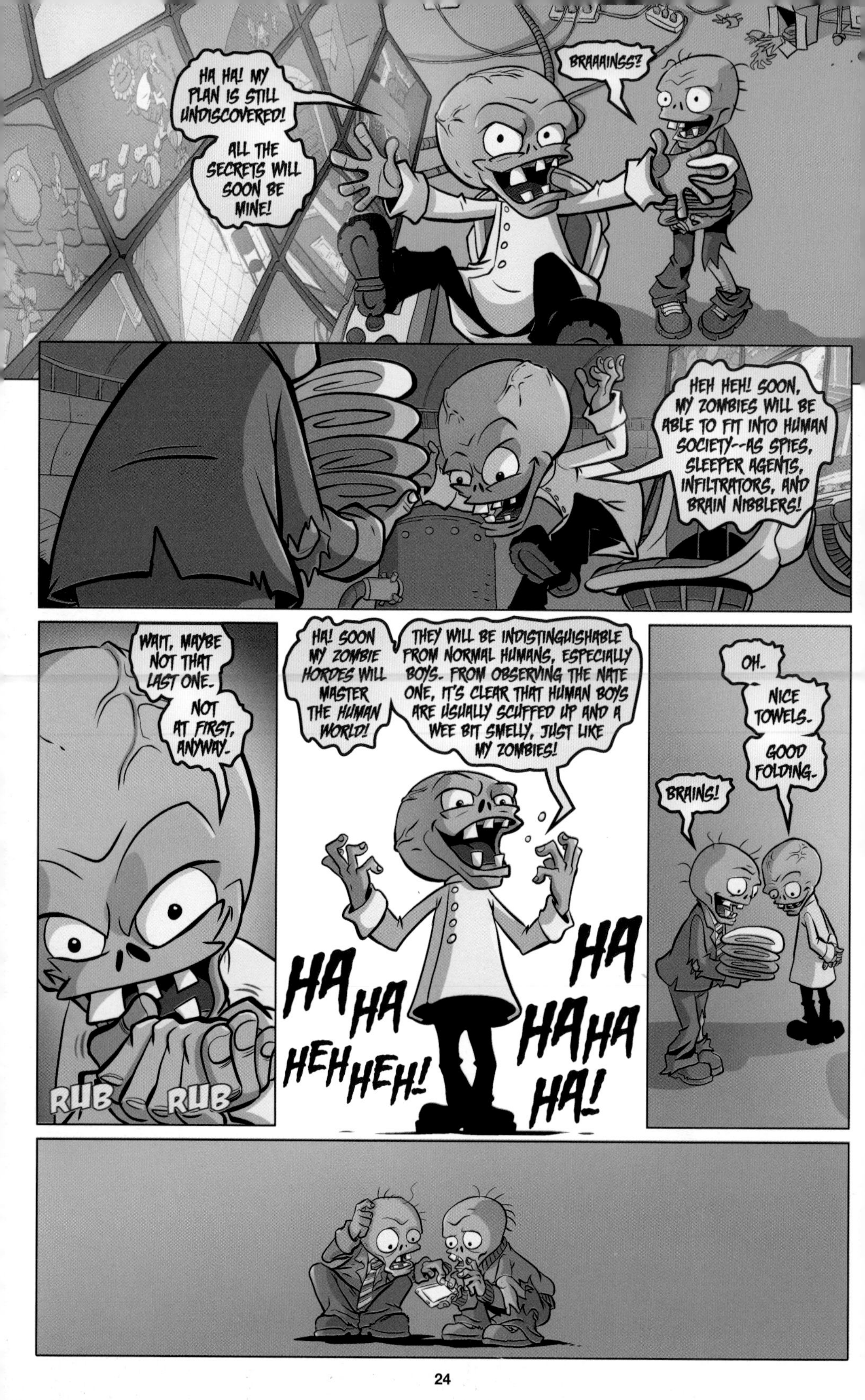
HA HA! MY PLAN IS STILL UNDISCOVERED!
ALL THE SECRETS WILL SOON BE MINE!
BRAAAINSS?
HEH HEH! SOON, MY ZOMBIES WILL BE ABLE TO FIT INTO HUMAN SOCIETY--AS SPIES, SLEEPER AGENTS, INFILTRATORS, AND BRAIN NIBBLERS!
WAIT, MAYBE NOT THAT LAST ONE.
NOT AT FIRST, ANYWAY.
RUB RUB
HA! SOON MY ZOMBIE HORDES WILL MASTER THE HUMAN WORLD!
THEY WILL BE INDISTINGUISHABLE FROM NORMAL HUMANS, ESPECIALLY BOYS. FROM OBSERVING THE NATE ONE, IT'S CLEAR THAT HUMAN BOYS ARE USUALLY SCUFFED UP AND A WEE BIT SMELLY, JUST LIKE MY ZOMBIES!
HA HA HEH HEH!
HA HA HA HA!
OH.
NICE TOWELS.
GOOD FOLDING.
BRAINS!

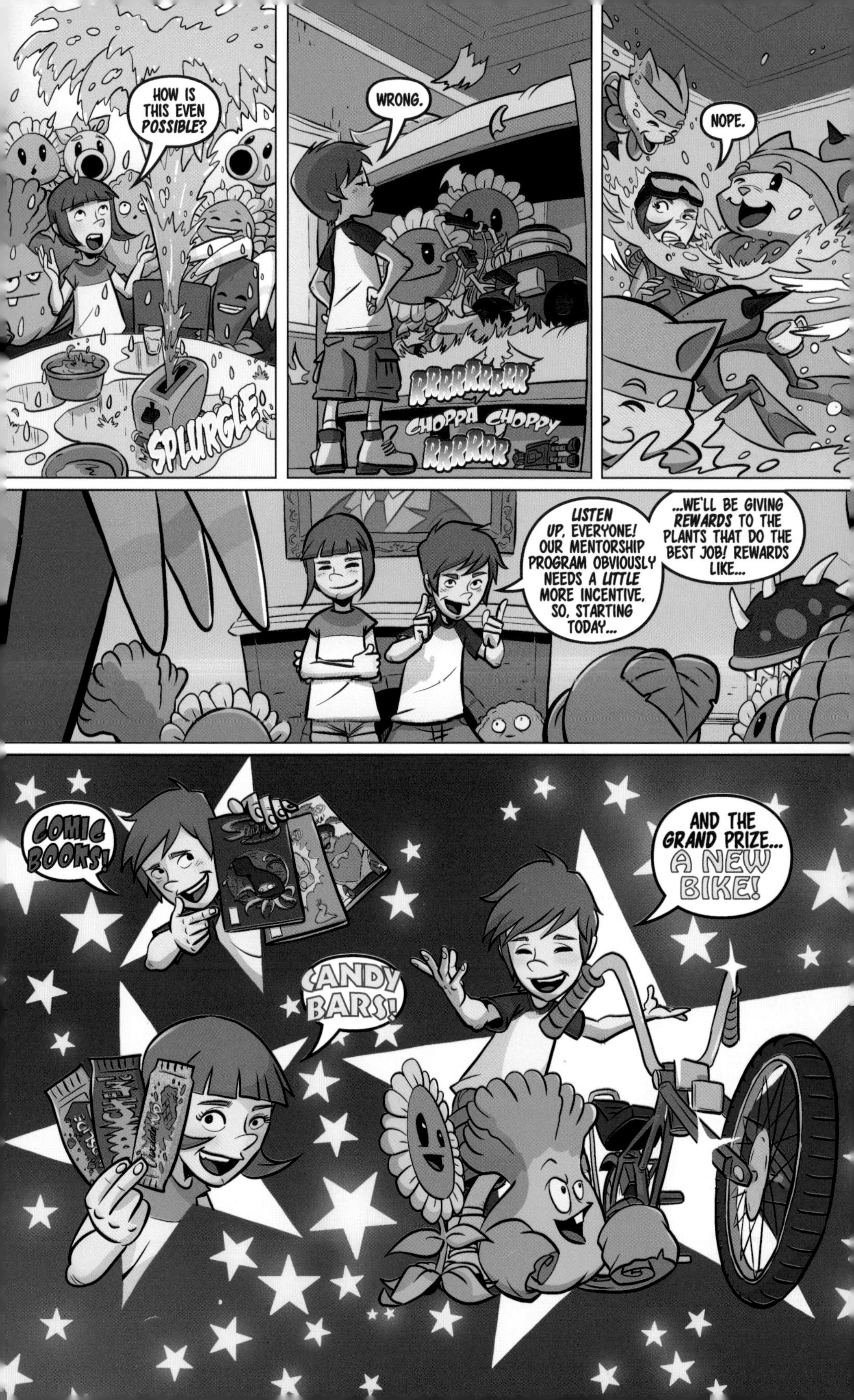
HOW IS THIS EVEN POSSIBLE?
SPLURGLE
WRONG.
RRRRRRRRR
CHOPPA CHOPPY
RRRRRR
NOPE.
LISTEN UP, EVERYONE! OUR MENTORSHIP PROGRAM OBVIOUSLY NEEDS A LITTLE MORE INCENTIVE, SO, STARTING TODAY...
...WE'LL BE GIVING REWARDS TO THE PLANTS THAT DO THE BEST JOB! REWARDS LIKE...
COMIC BOOKS!
CANDY BARS!
AND THE GRAND PRIZE... A NEW BIKE!

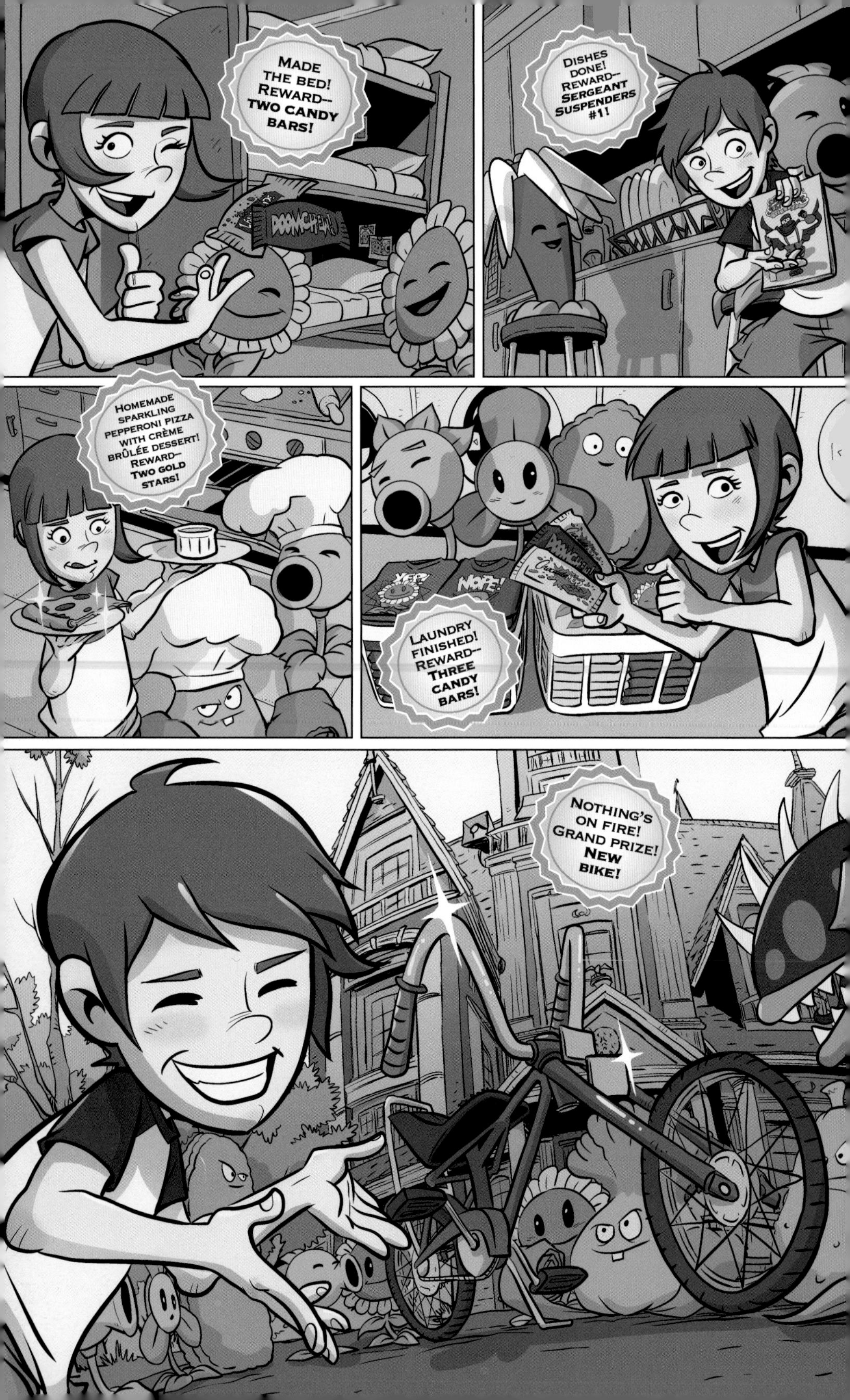

MADE THE BED! REWARD-- TWO CANDY BARS!
DOOMCHEW!
DISHES DONE! REWARD-- SERGEANT SUSPENDERS #1!
HOMEMADE SPARKLING PEPPERONI PIZZA WITH CRÈME BRÛLÉE DESSERT! REWARD-- TWO GOLD STARS!
YEP!
NOPE!
LAUNDRY FINISHED! REWARD-- THREE CANDY BARS!
NOTHING'S ON FIRE! GRAND PRIZE! NEW BIKE!

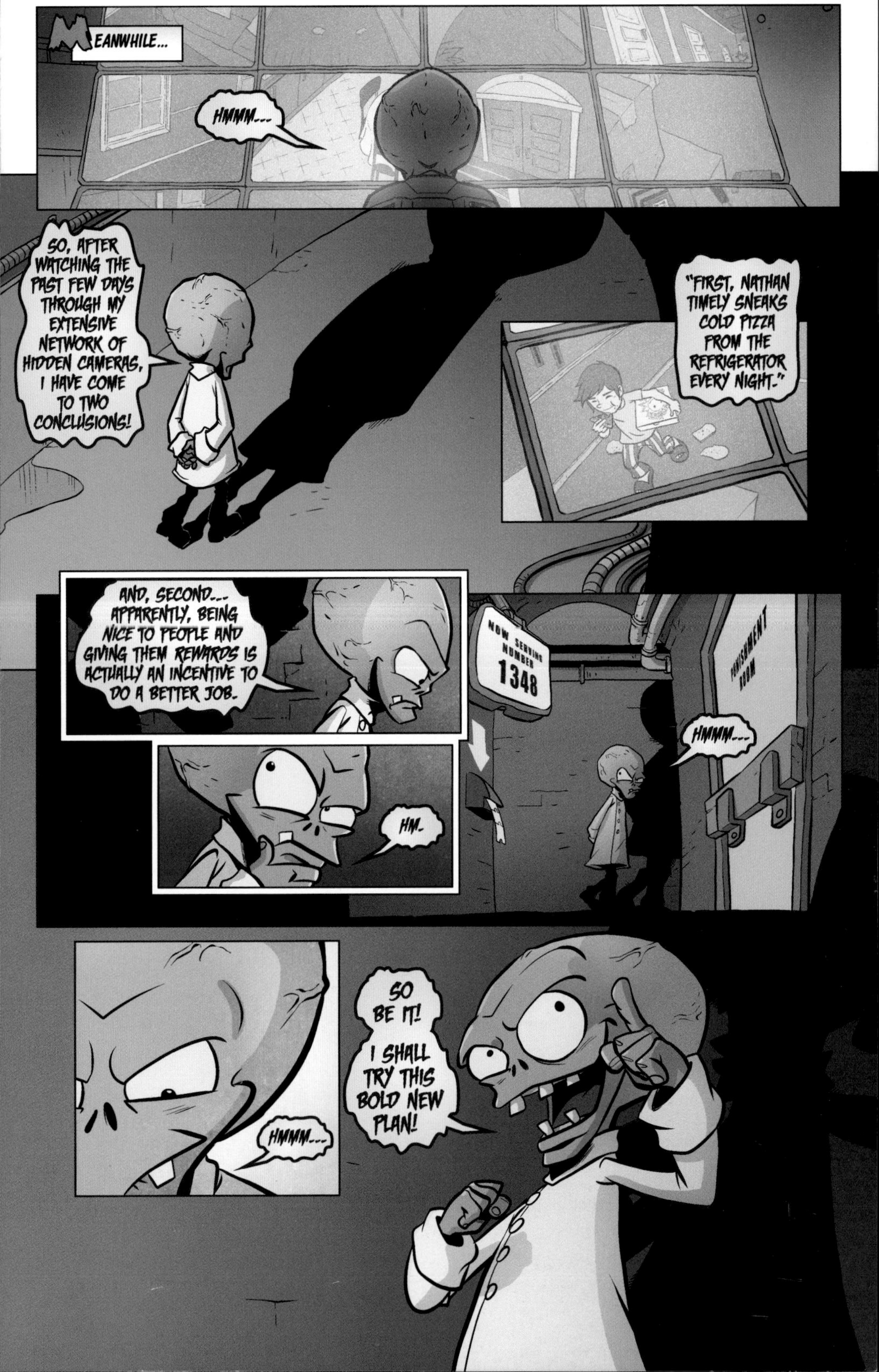
MEANWHILE...
HMMM...
SO, AFTER WATCHING THE PAST FEW DAYS THROUGH MY EXTENSIVE NETWORK OF HIDDEN CAMERAS, I HAVE COME TO TWO CONCLUSIONS!
"FIRST, NATHAN TIMELY SNEAKS COLD PIZZA FROM THE REFRIGERATOR EVERY NIGHT."
AND, SECOND... APPARENTLY, BEING NICE TO PEOPLE AND GIVING THEM REWARDS IS ACTUALLY AN INCENTIVE TO DO A BETTER JOB.
NOW SERVING NUMBER 1348
PUNISHMENT ROOM
HMMM...
HM.
HMMM...
SO BE IT!
I SHALL TRY THIS BOLD NEW PLAN!

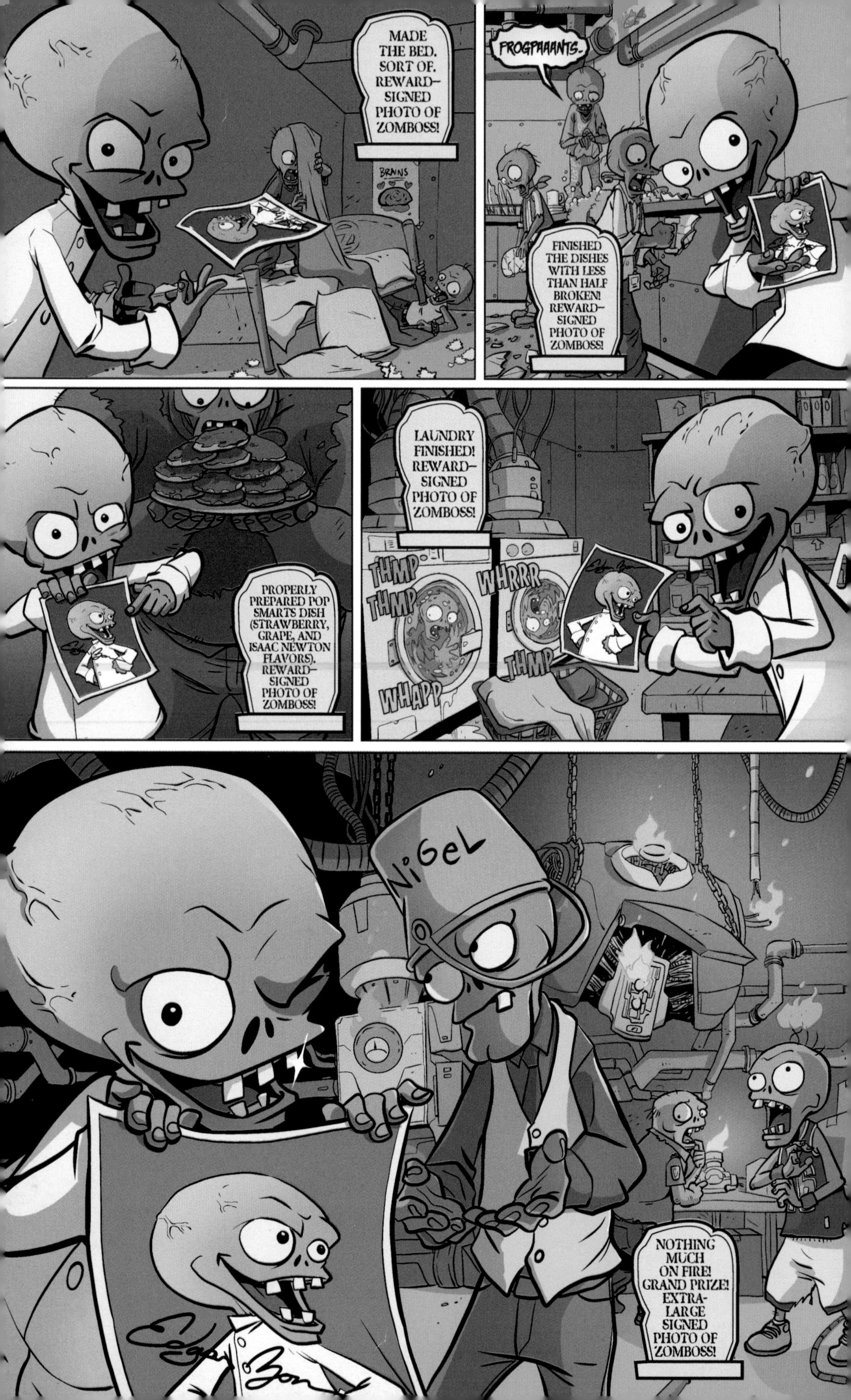
MADE THE BED. SORT OF. REWARD– SIGNED PHOTO OF ZOMBOSS!
BRAINS
FROGPAAANTS...
FINISHED THE DISHES WITH LESS THAN HALF BROKEN! REWARD– SIGNED PHOTO OF ZOMBOSS!
PROPERLY PREPARED POP SMARTS DISH (STRAWBERRY, GRAPE, AND ISAAC NEWTON FLAVORS). REWARD– SIGNED PHOTO OF ZOMBOSS!
LAUNDRY FINISHED! REWARD– SIGNED PHOTO OF ZOMBOSS!
THMP
THMP
WHRRR
THMP
WHAPP
NiGeL
NOTHING MUCH ON FIRE! GRAND PRIZE! EXTRA-LARGE SIGNED PHOTO OF ZOMBOSS!

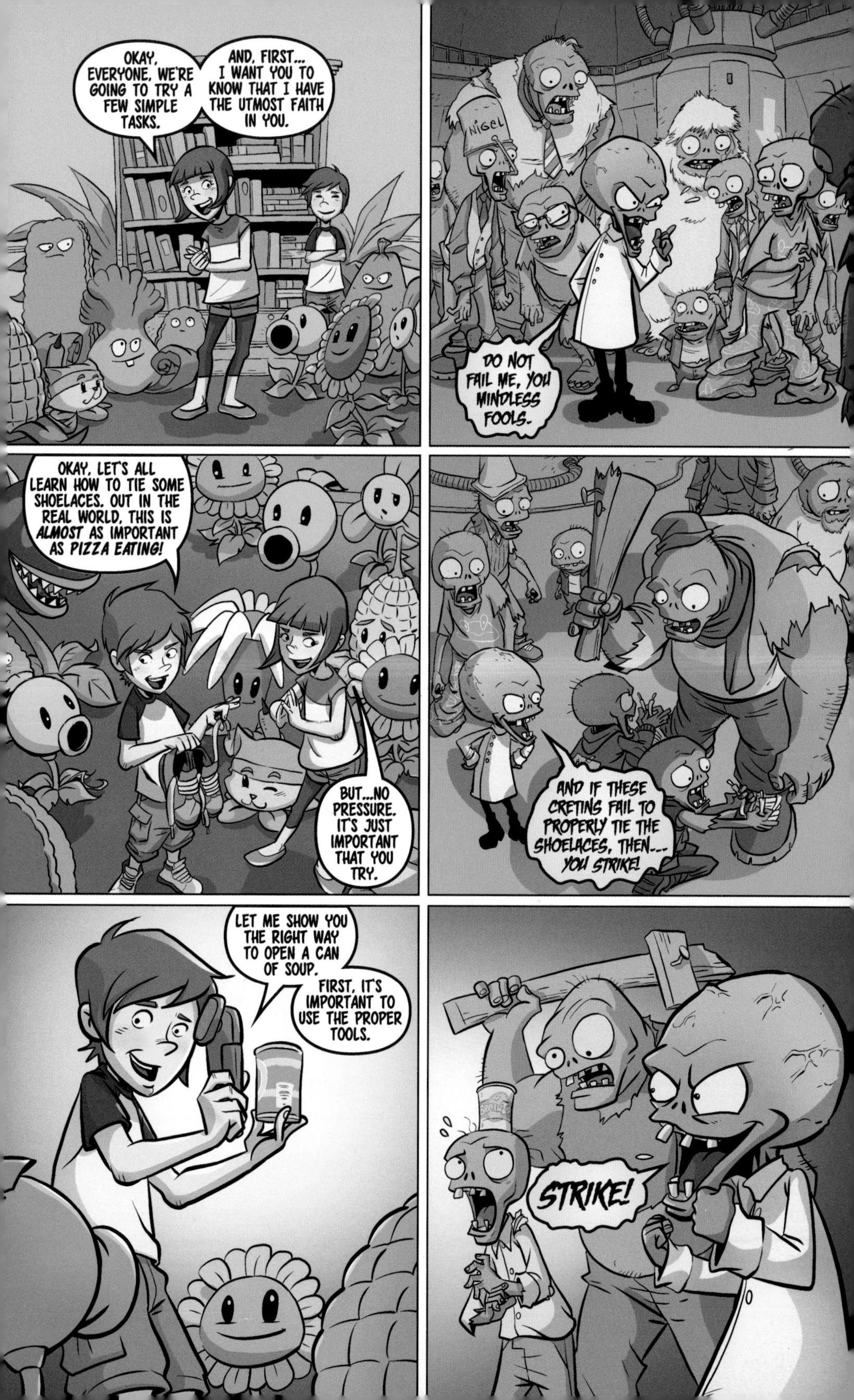
OKAY, EVERYONE, WE'RE GOING TO TRY A FEW SIMPLE TASKS.
AND, FIRST... I WANT YOU TO KNOW THAT I HAVE THE UTMOST FAITH IN YOU.
NIGEL
DO NOT FAIL ME, YOU MINDLESS FOOLS.
OKAY, LET'S ALL LEARN HOW TO TIE SOME SHOELACES. OUT IN THE REAL WORLD, THIS IS ALMOST AS IMPORTANT AS PIZZA EATING!
BUT...NO PRESSURE. IT'S JUST IMPORTANT THAT YOU TRY.
AND IF THESE CRETINS FAIL TO PROPERLY TIE THE SHOELACES, THEN... YOU STRIKE!
LET ME SHOW YOU THE RIGHT WAY TO OPEN A CAN OF SOUP.
FIRST, IT'S IMPORTANT TO USE THE PROPER TOOLS.
STRIKE!

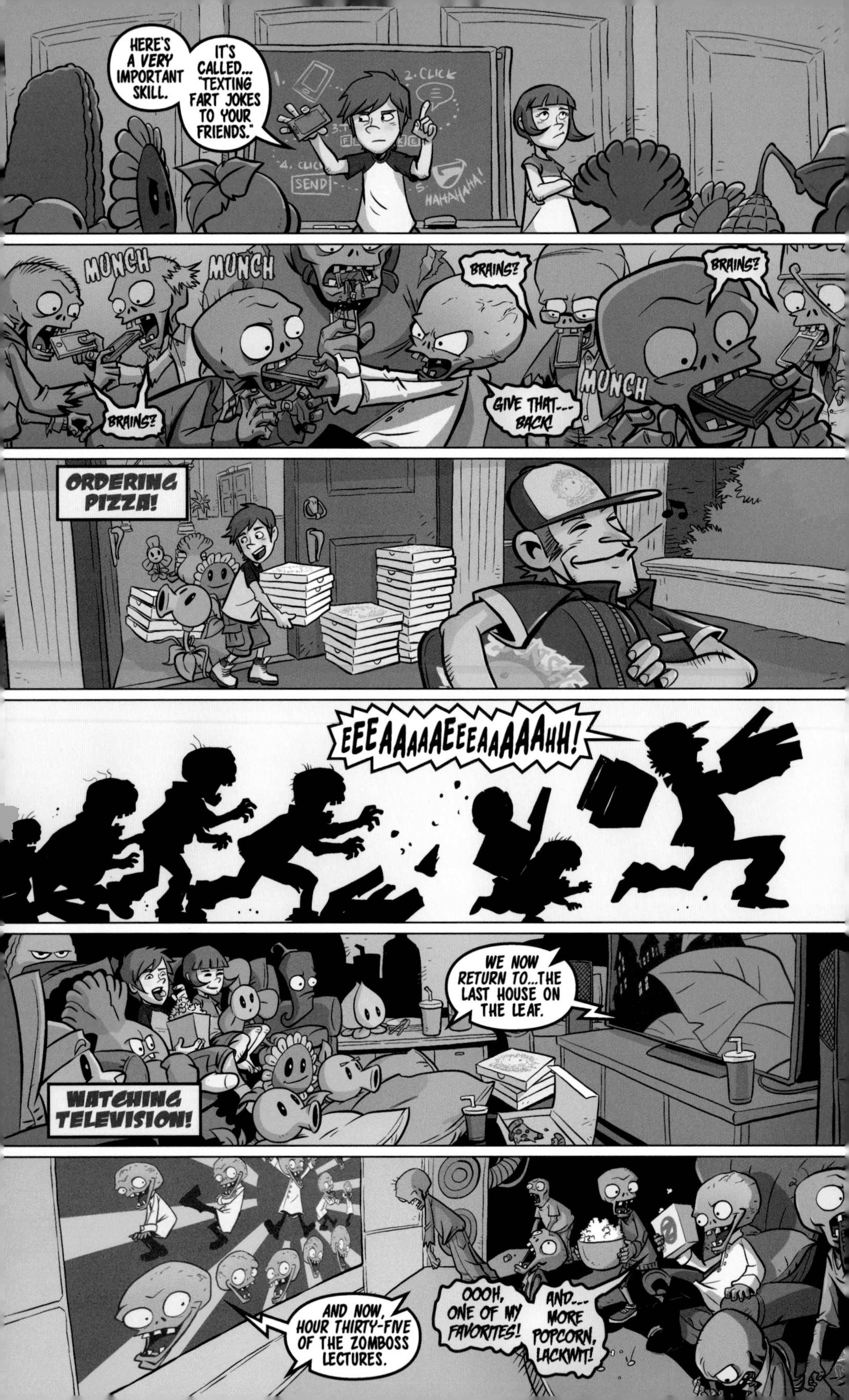
HERE'S A VERY IMPORTANT SKILL.
IT'S CALLED... "TEXTING FART JOKES TO YOUR FRIENDS."
2. CLICK
4. CLICK
SEND
5.
HAHAHAHA!
MUNCH
MUNCH
BRAINS?
BRAINS?
BRAINS?
GIVE THAT--- BACK!
MUNCH
ORDERING PIZZA!
EEEAAAAAEEEAAAAAHH!
WE NOW RETURN TO...THE LAST HOUSE ON THE LEAF.
WATCHING TELEVISION!
AND NOW, HOUR THIRTY-FIVE OF THE ZOMBOSS LECTURES.
OOOH, ONE OF MY FAVORITES!
AND--- MORE POPCORN, LACKWIT!

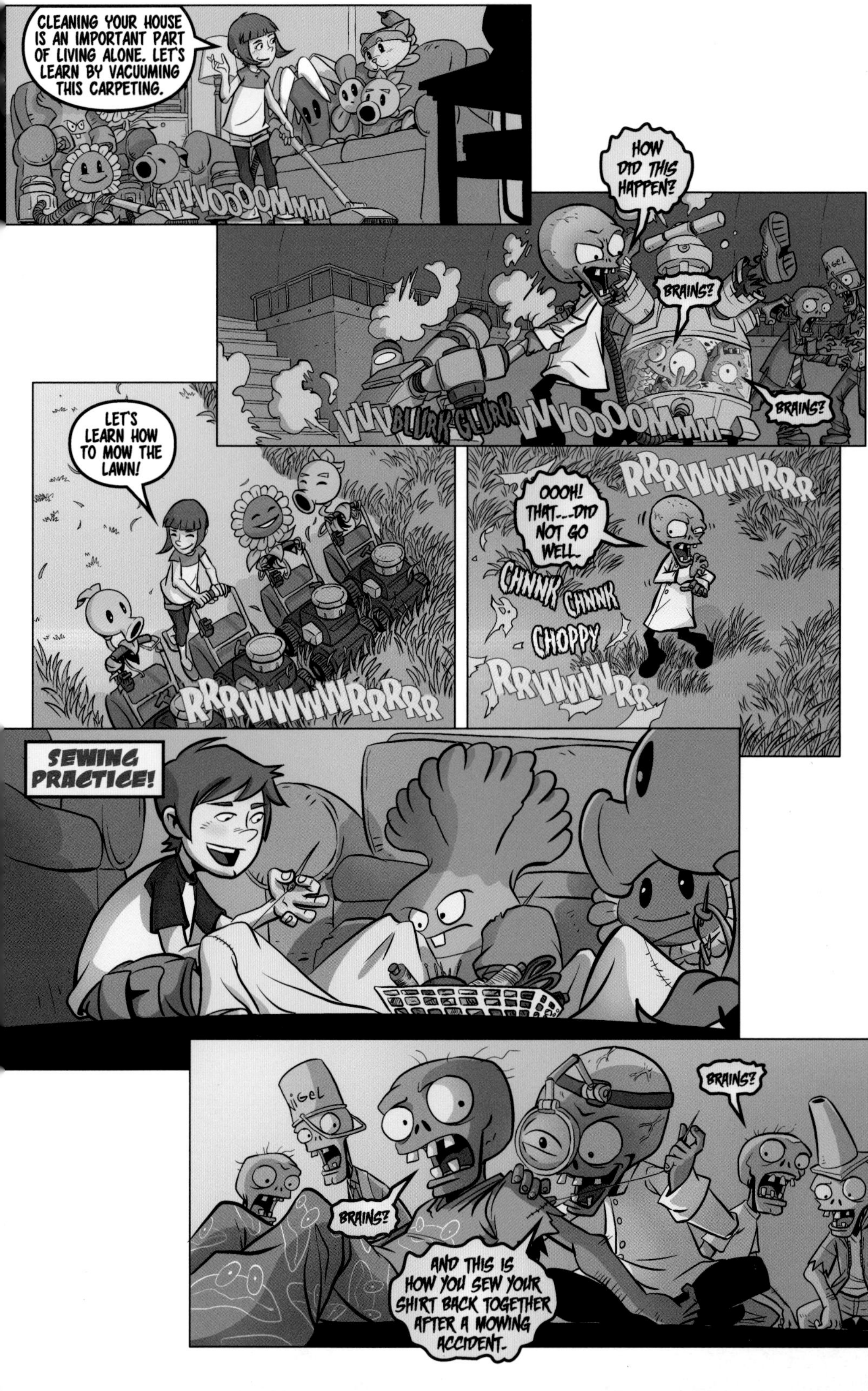
CLEANING YOUR HOUSE IS AN IMPORTANT PART OF LIVING ALONE. LET'S LEARN BY VACUUMING THIS CARPETING.
VVVOOOOMMM
HOW DID THIS HAPPEN?
BRAINS?
VVV BLURK GLURK VVVOOOOMMMM
BRAINS?
LET'S LEARN HOW TO MOW THE LAWN!
RRRWWWWWRRRRRR
RRRWWWWRRR
OOOH! THAT...DID NOT GO WELL.
CHNNK CHNNK
CHOPPY
RRWWWRR
SEWING PRACTICE!
BRAINS?
BRAINS?
AND THIS IS HOW YOU SEW YOUR SHIRT BACK TOGETHER AFTER A MOWING ACCIDENT.

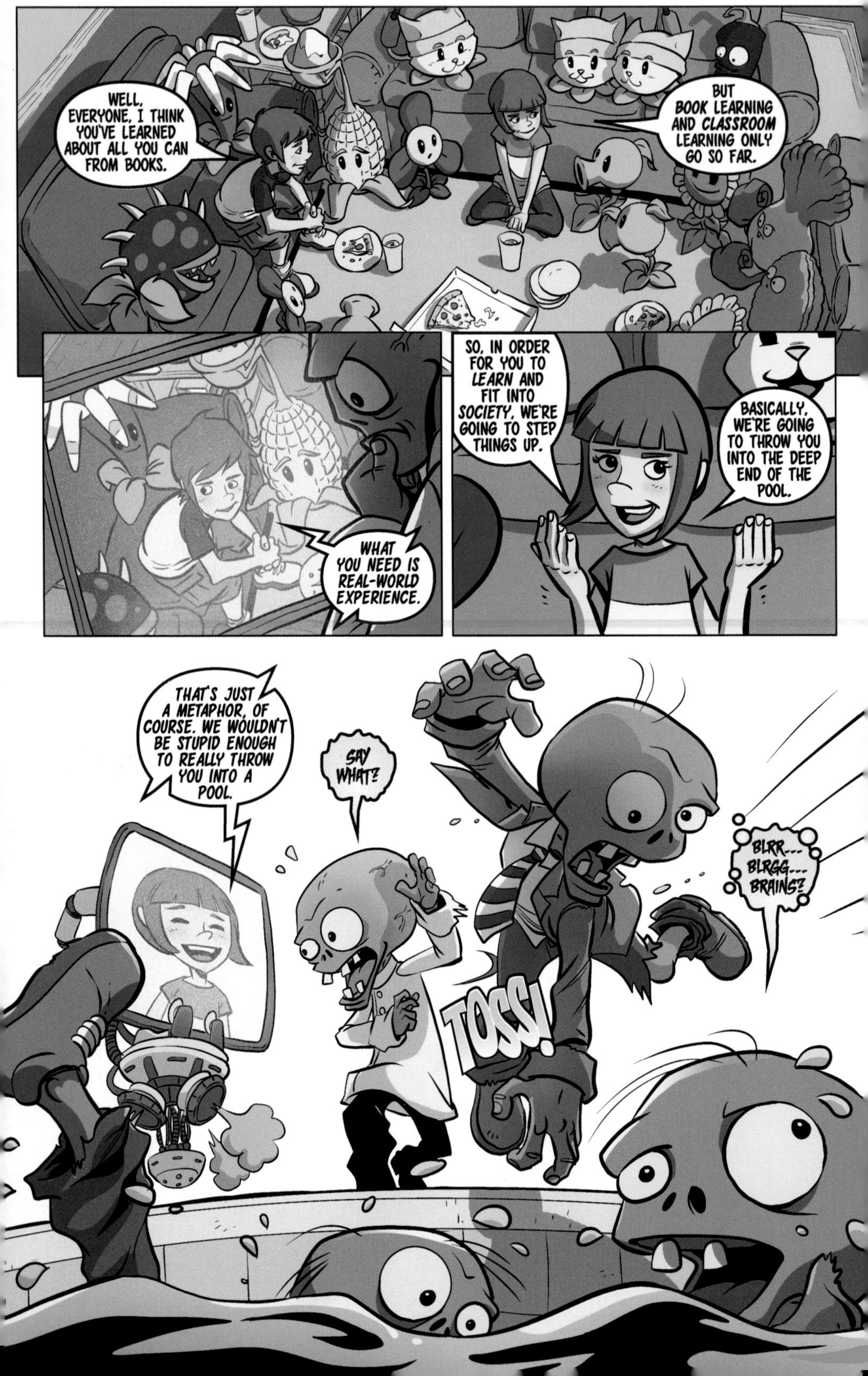
WELL, EVERYONE, I THINK YOU'VE LEARNED ABOUT ALL YOU CAN FROM BOOKS.
BUT BOOK LEARNING AND *CLASSROOM* LEARNING ONLY GO SO FAR.
WHAT YOU NEED IS REAL-WORLD EXPERIENCE.
SO, IN ORDER FOR YOU TO *LEARN* AND FIT INTO *SOCIETY*, WE'RE GOING TO STEP THINGS UP.
BASICALLY, WE'RE GOING TO THROW YOU INTO THE DEEP END OF THE POOL.
THAT'S JUST A METAPHOR, OF COURSE. WE WOULDN'T BE STUPID ENOUGH TO REALLY THROW YOU INTO A POOL.
SAY WHAT?
TOSS!
BLRR... BLRGG... BRAINS?

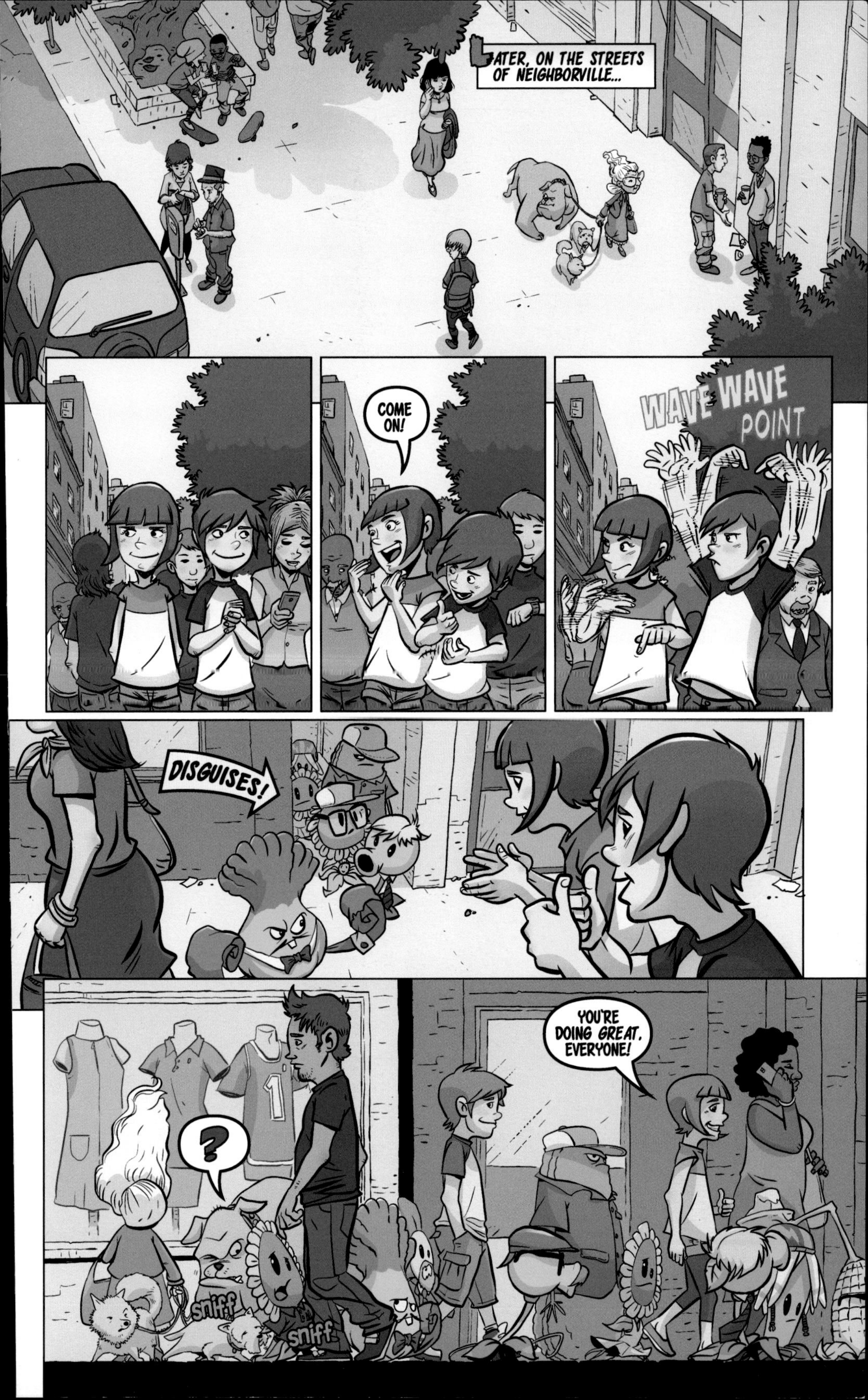
LATER, ON THE STREETS OF NEIGHBORVILLE...
COME ON!
WAVE WAVE POINT
DISGUISES!
?
YOU'RE DOING GREAT, EVERYONE!
sniff
sniff

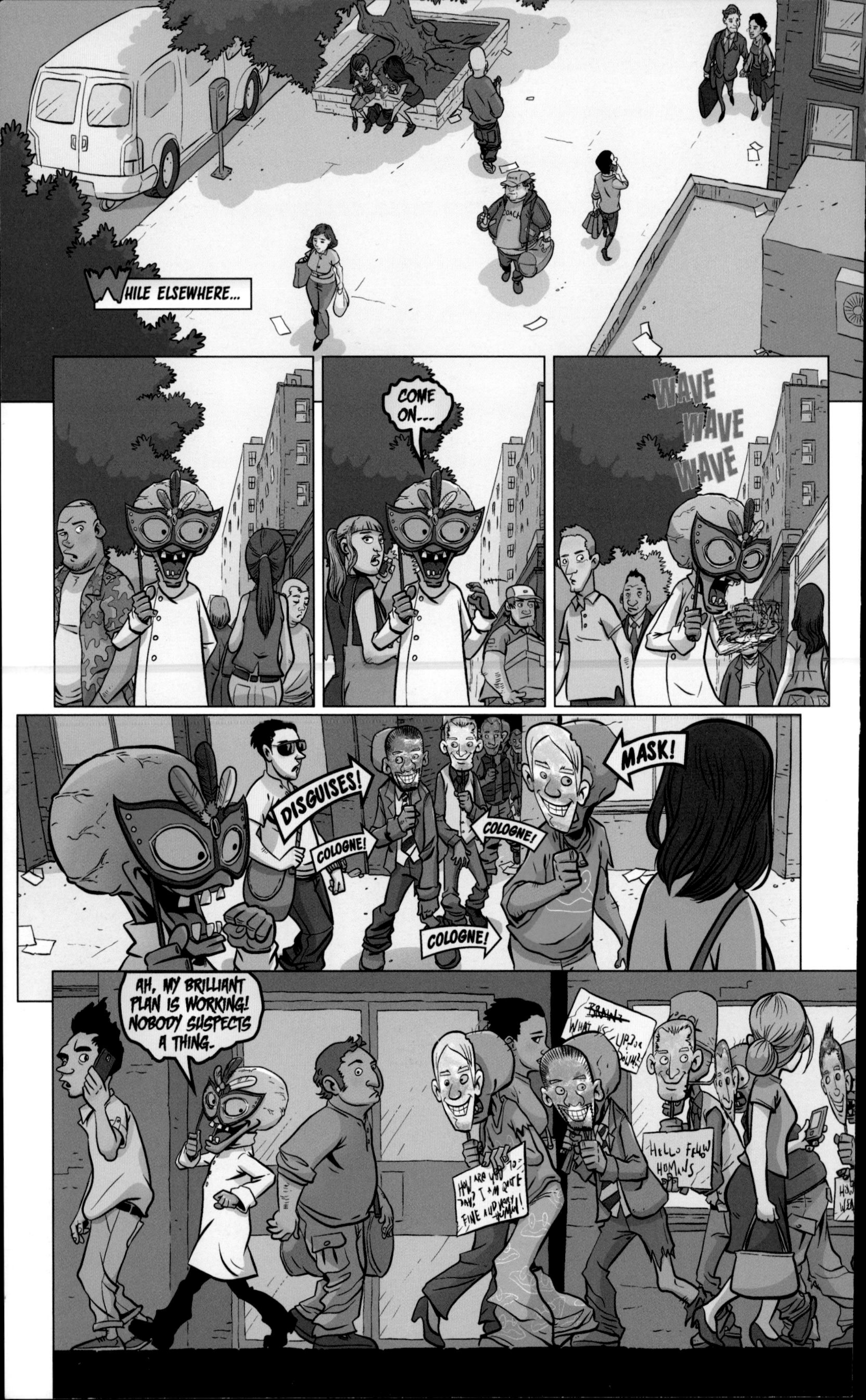
WHILE ELSEWHERE...
COME ON...
WAVE
WAVE
WAVE
DISGUISES!
COLOGNE!
COLOGNE!
COLOGNE!
MASK!
AH, MY BRILLIANT PLAN IS WORKING! NOBODY SUSPECTS A THING.
BRAINZ
WHAT IS UP? OR DOWN?
HOW ARE YOU TO-DAY? I AM QUITE FINE AND VERY HUMAN!
HELLO FELLOW HUMANS

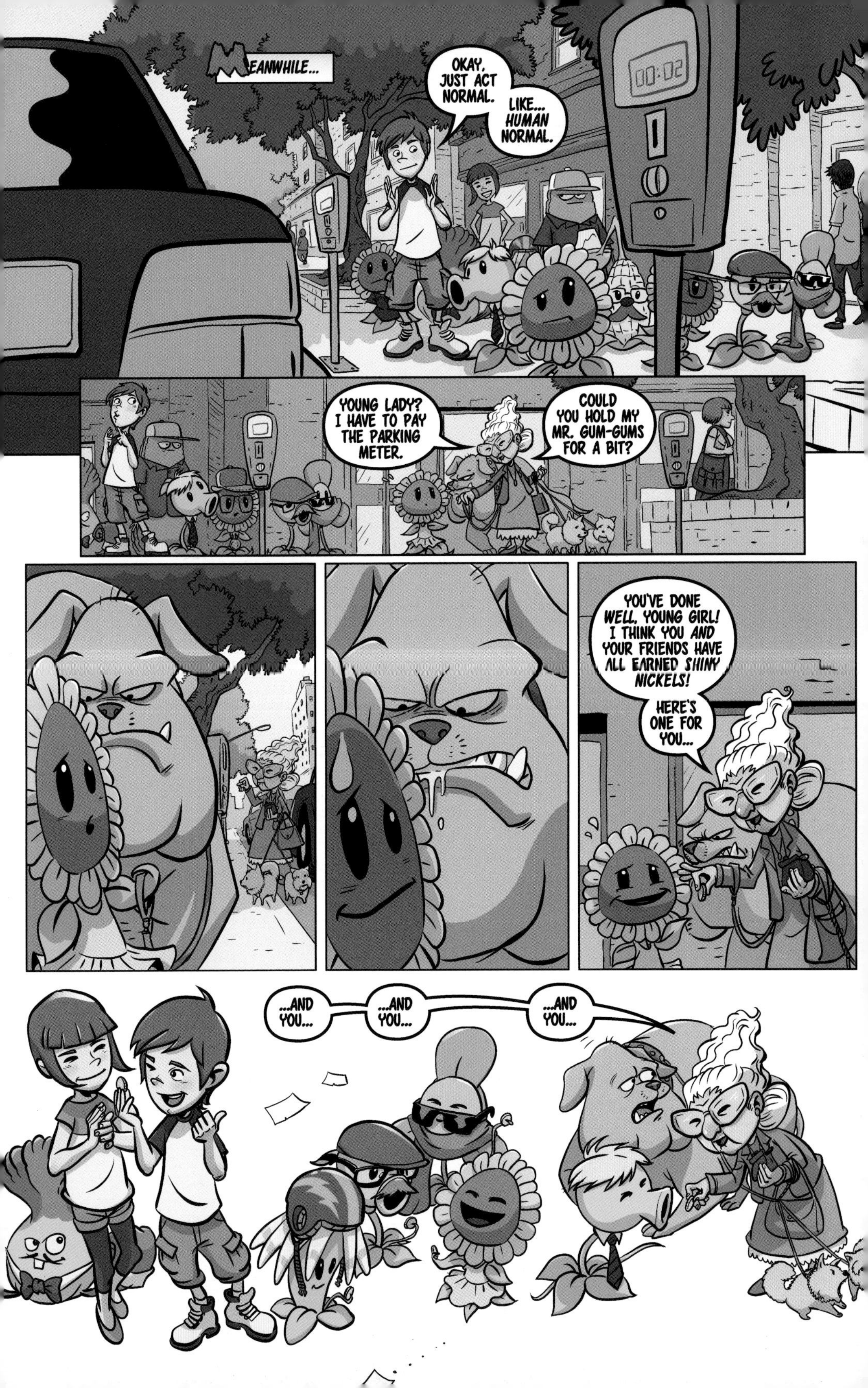
MEANWHILE...
OKAY, JUST ACT NORMAL.
LIKE... HUMAN NORMAL.
00:02
YOUNG LADY? I HAVE TO PAY THE PARKING METER.
COULD YOU HOLD MY MR. GUM-GUMS FOR A BIT?
YOU'VE DONE WELL, YOUNG GIRL! I THINK YOU AND YOUR FRIENDS HAVE ALL EARNED SHINY NICKELS!
HERE'S ONE FOR YOU...
...AND YOU...
...AND YOU...
...AND YOU...

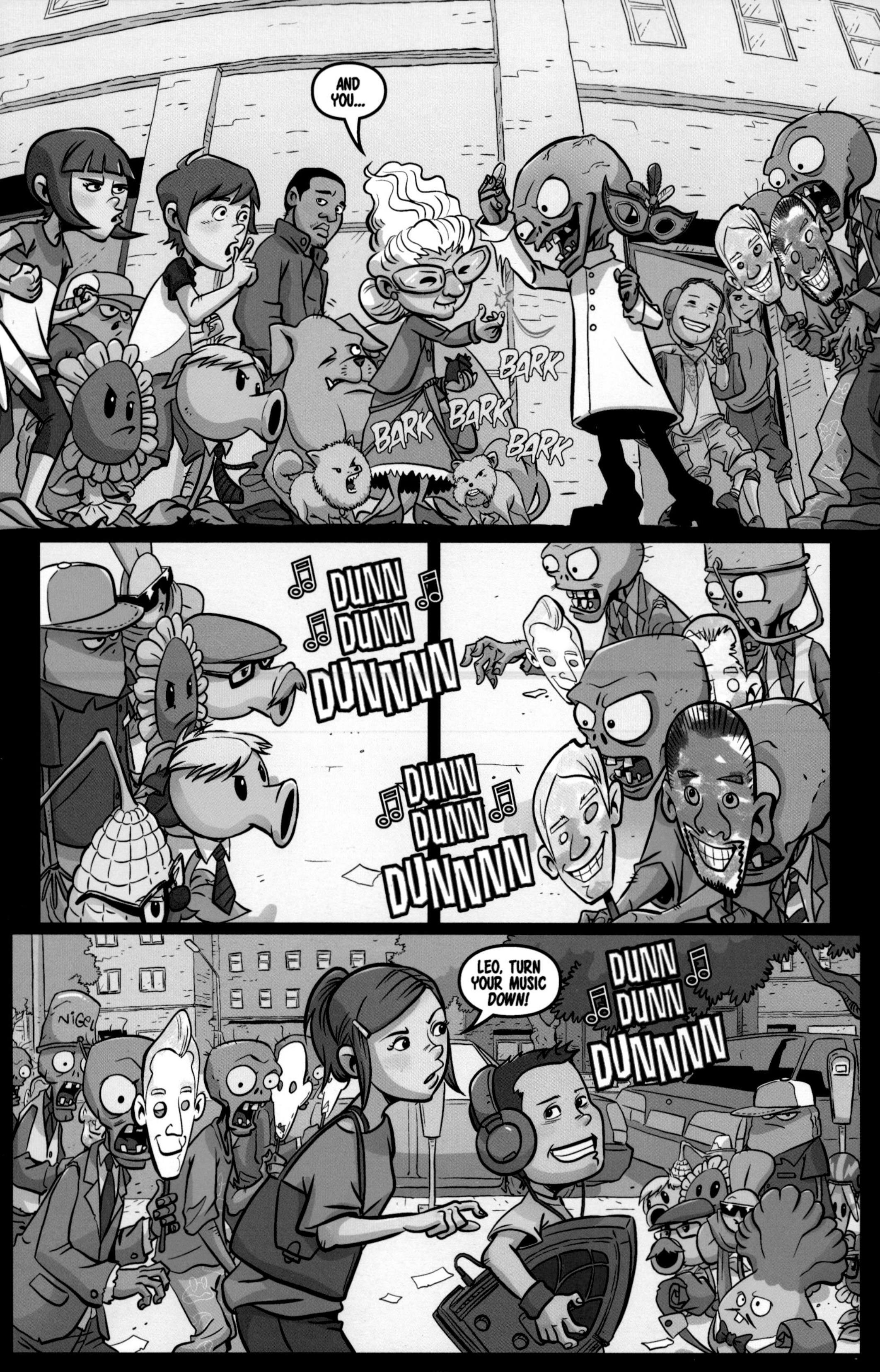
AND YOU...
BARK
BARK
BARK
BARK
DUNN DUNN DUNNNN
DUNN DUNN DUNNNN
NIGEL
LEO, TURN YOUR MUSIC DOWN!
DUNN DUNN DUNNNN

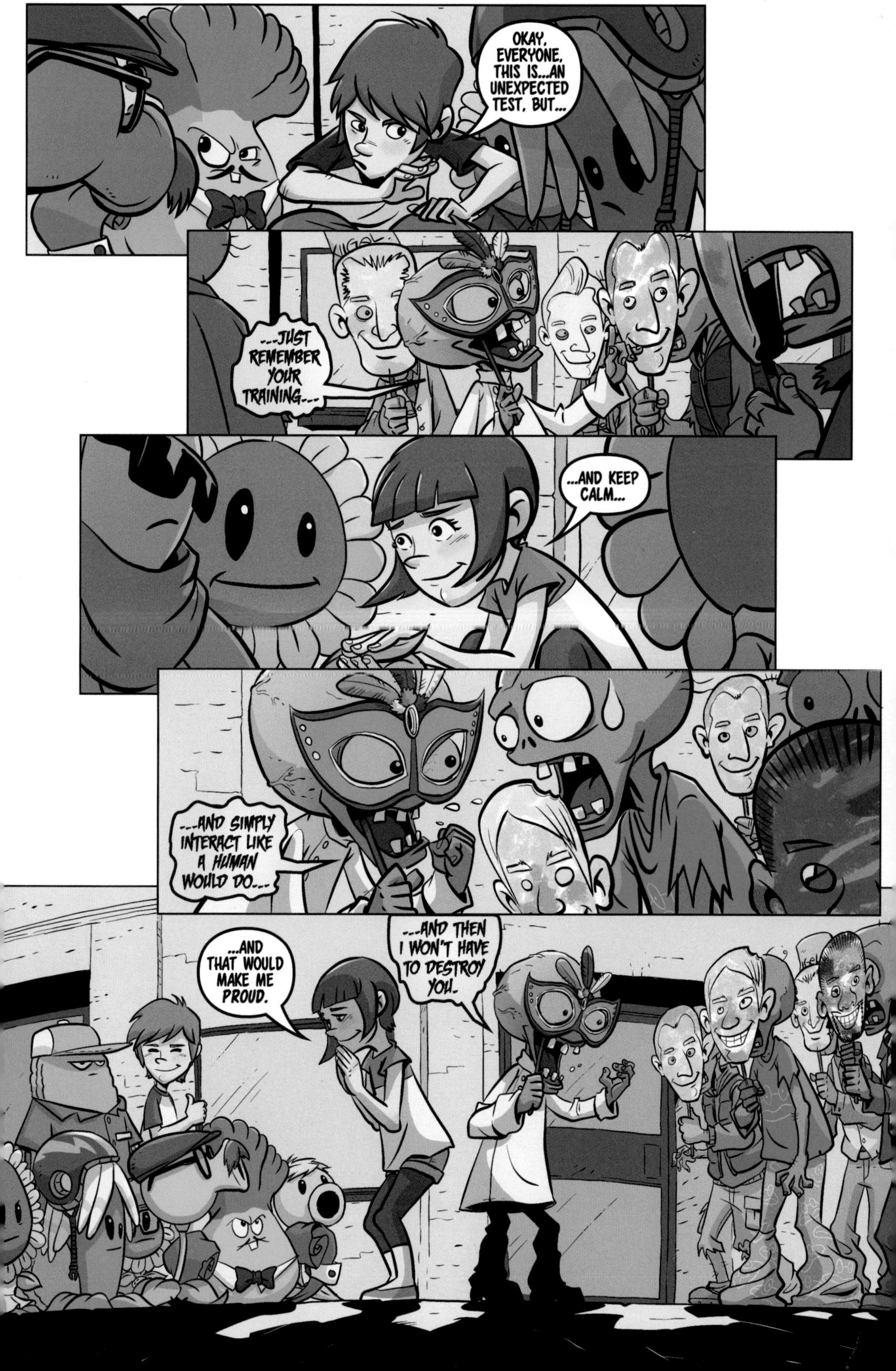
OKAY, EVERYONE, THIS IS...AN UNEXPECTED TEST, BUT...
---JUST REMEMBER YOUR TRAINING---
...AND KEEP CALM...
---AND SIMPLY INTERACT LIKE A HUMAN WOULD DO---
...AND THAT WOULD MAKE ME PROUD.
---AND THEN I WON'T HAVE TO DESTROY YOU.

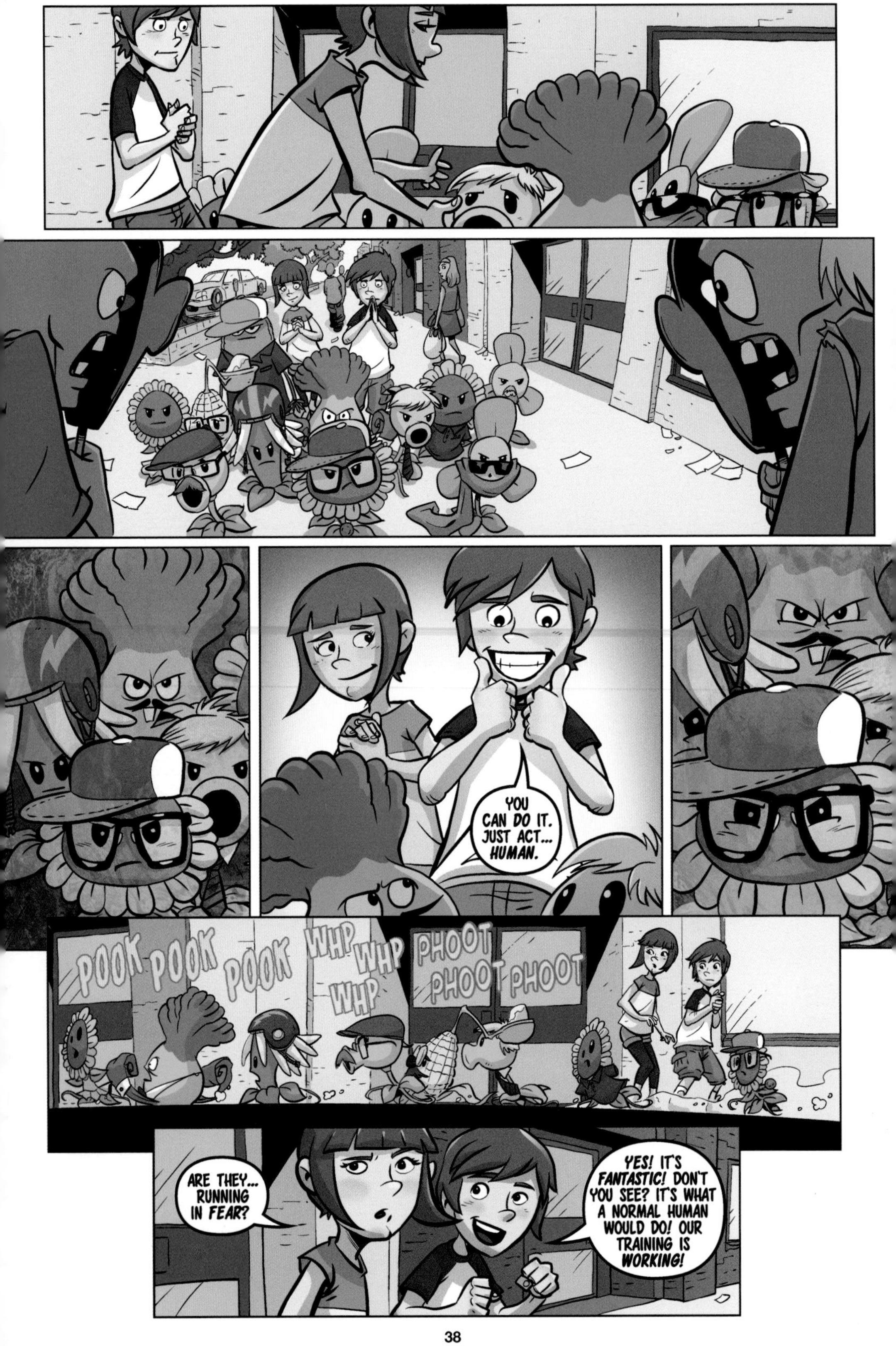
YOU CAN DO IT. JUST ACT... HUMAN.
POOK POOK POOK
WHP WHP WHP
PHOOT PHOOT PHOOT
ARE THEY... RUNNING IN FEAR?
YES! IT'S FANTASTIC! DON'T YOU SEE? IT'S WHAT A NORMAL HUMAN WOULD DO! OUR TRAINING IS WORKING!

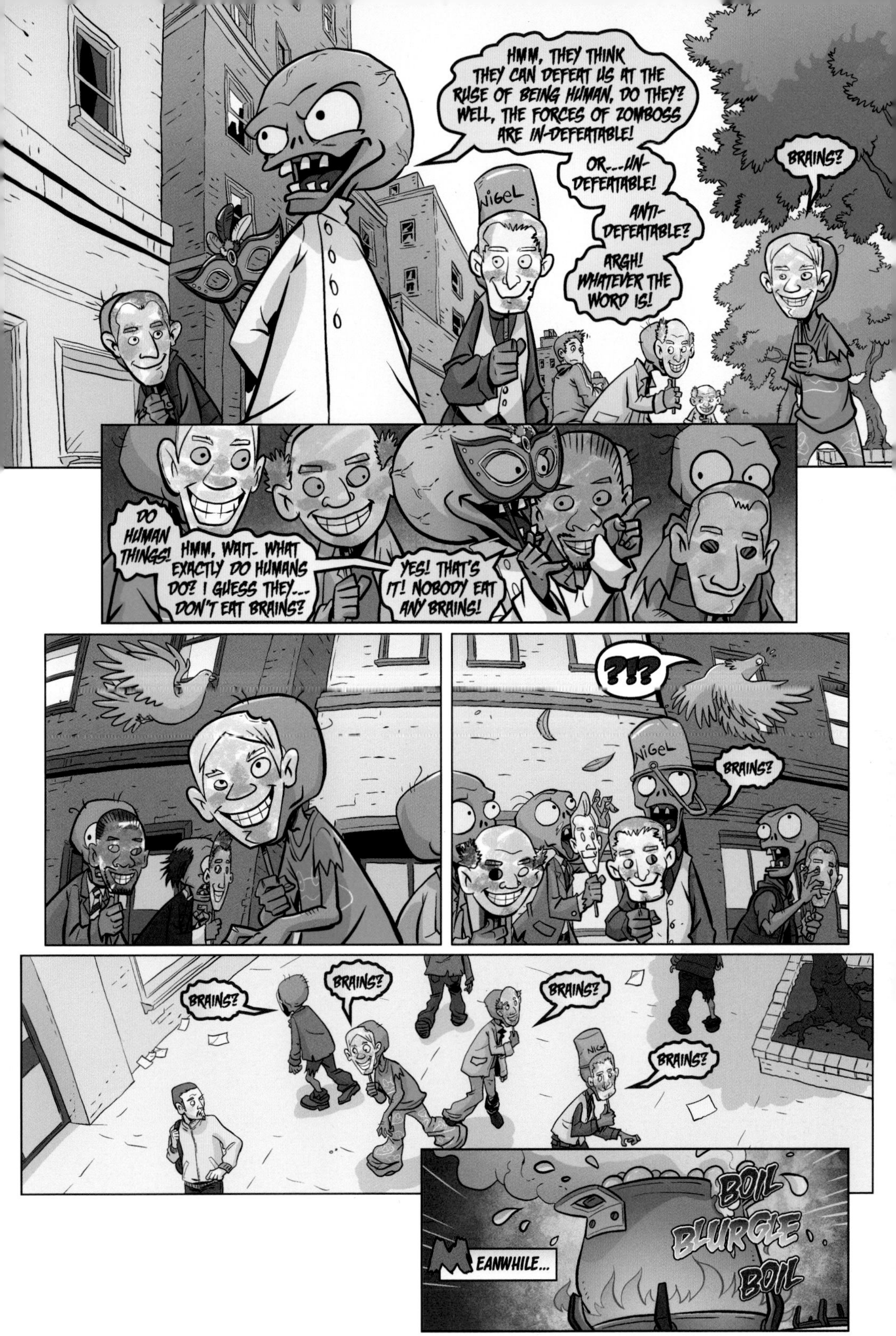
HMM, THEY THINK THEY CAN DEFEAT US AT THE RUSE OF BEING HUMAN, DO THEY? WELL, THE FORCES OF ZOMBOSS ARE IN-DEFEATABLE!
OR...UN-DEFEATABLE!
ANTI-DEFEATABLE?
ARGH! WHATEVER THE WORD IS!
BRAINS?
DO HUMAN THINGS!
HMM, WAIT. WHAT EXACTLY DO HUMANS DO? I GUESS THEY... DON'T EAT BRAINS?
YES! THAT'S IT! NOBODY EAT ANY BRAINS!
?!?
BRAINS?
BRAINS?
BRAINS?
BRAINS?
BRAINS?
MEANWHILE...
BOIL
BLURGLE
BOIL

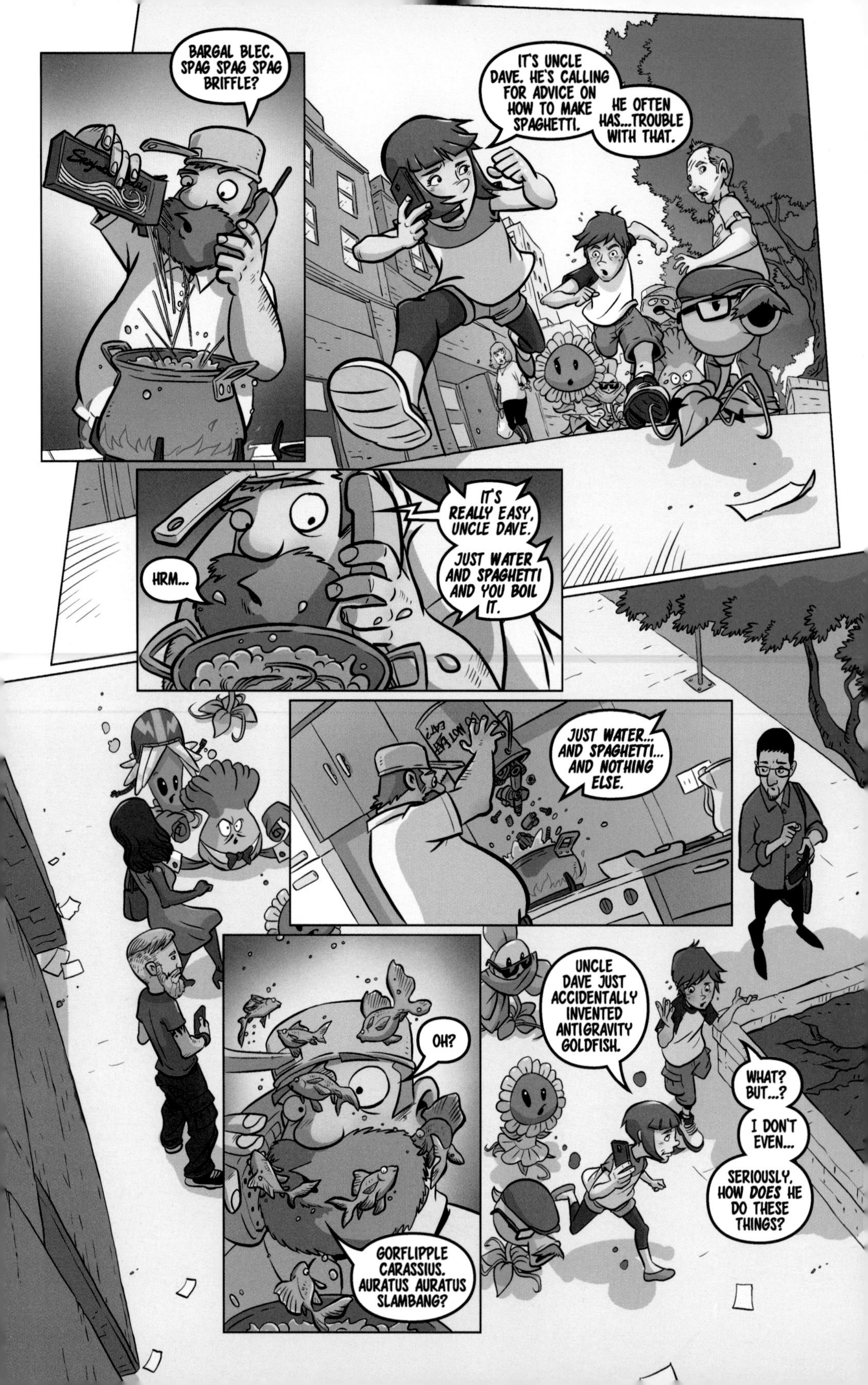
BARGAL BLEC. SPAG SPAG SPAG BRIFFLE?
IT'S UNCLE DAVE. HE'S CALLING FOR ADVICE ON HOW TO MAKE SPAGHETTI.
HE OFTEN HAS...TROUBLE WITH THAT.
IT'S REALLY EASY, UNCLE DAVE.
JUST WATER AND SPAGHETTI AND YOU BOIL IT.
HRM...
JUST WATER... AND SPAGHETTI... AND NOTHING ELSE.
DO NOT EAT
OH?
GORFLIPPLE CARASSIUS. AURATUS AURATUS SLAMBANG?
UNCLE DAVE JUST ACCIDENTALLY INVENTED ANTIGRAVITY GOLDFISH.
WHAT? BUT...?
I DON'T EVEN...
SERIOUSLY, HOW DOES HE DO THESE THINGS?

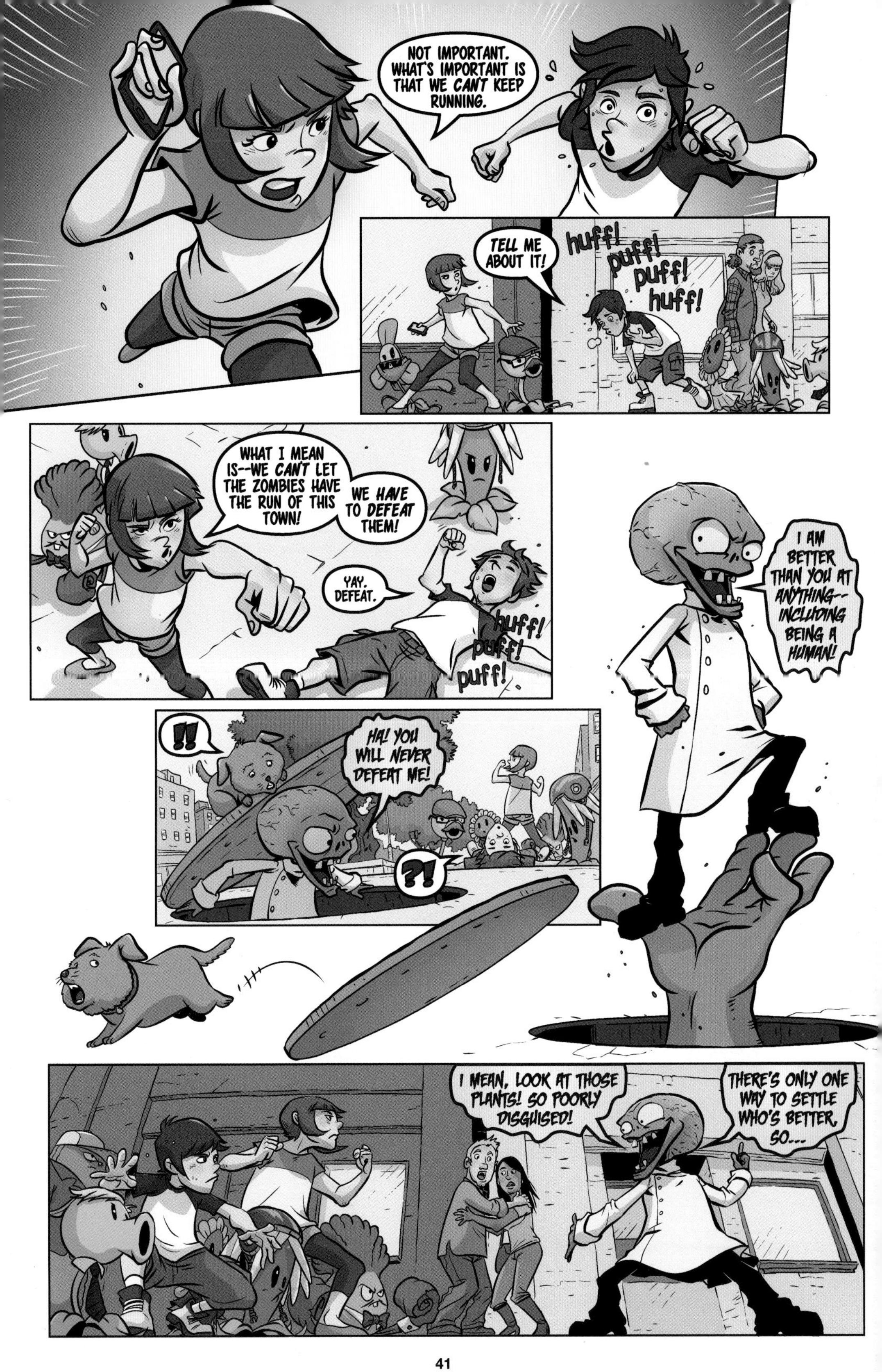
NOT IMPORTANT. WHAT'S IMPORTANT IS THAT WE CAN'T KEEP RUNNING.
TELL ME ABOUT IT!
huff! puff! puff! huff!
WHAT I MEAN IS--WE CAN'T LET THE ZOMBIES HAVE THE RUN OF THIS TOWN!
WE HAVE TO DEFEAT THEM!
YAY. DEFEAT.
huff! puff! puff!
!!
HA! YOU WILL NEVER DEFEAT ME!
?!
I AM BETTER THAN YOU AT ANYTHING--INCLUDING BEING A HUMAN!
I MEAN, LOOK AT THOSE PLANTS! SO POORLY DISGUISED!
THERE'S ONLY ONE WAY TO SETTLE WHO'S BETTER, SO...

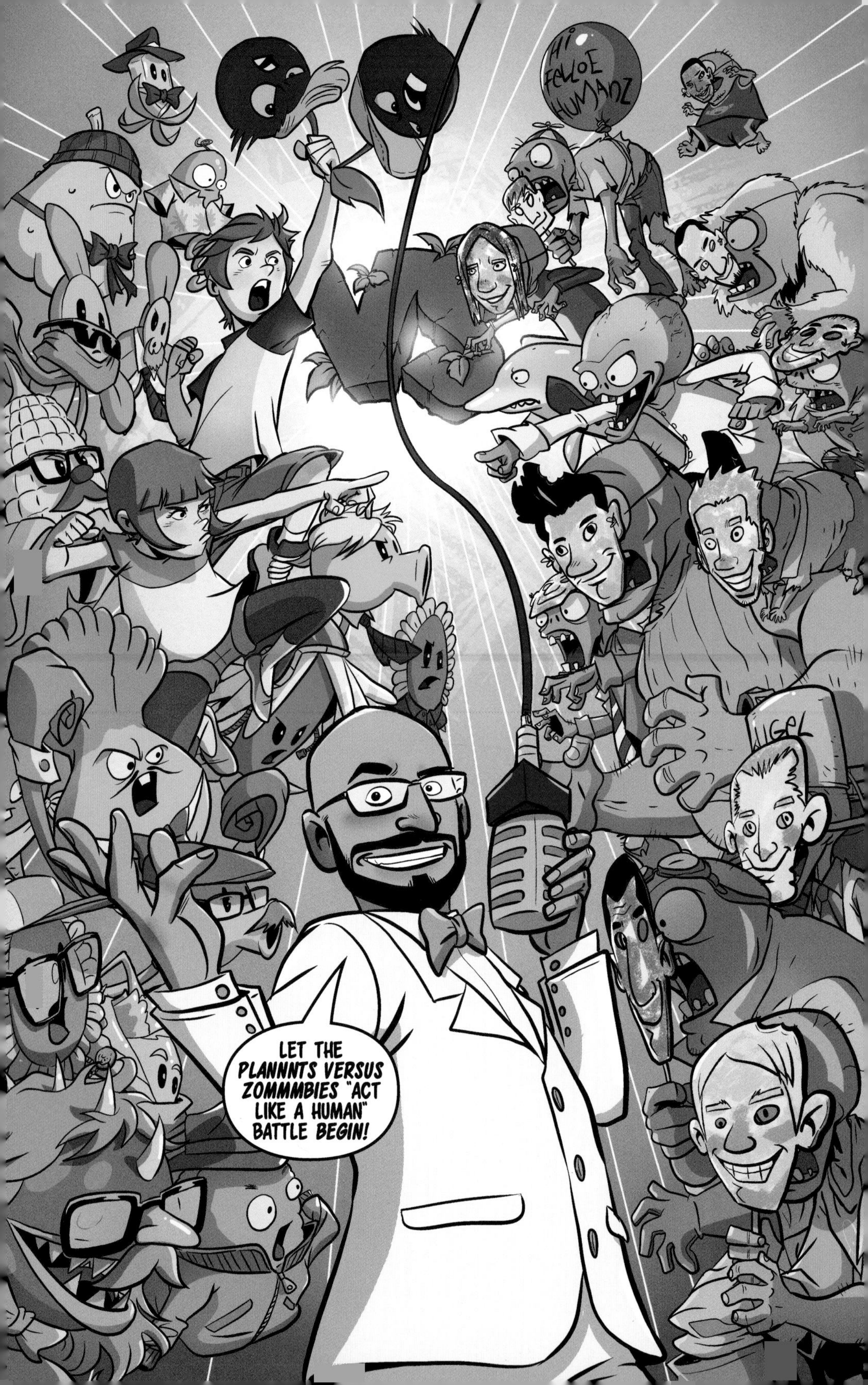
HI FELLOE HUMANZ
LET THE PLANNNTS VERSUS ZOMMMBIES "ACT LIKE A HUMAN" BATTLE BEGIN!

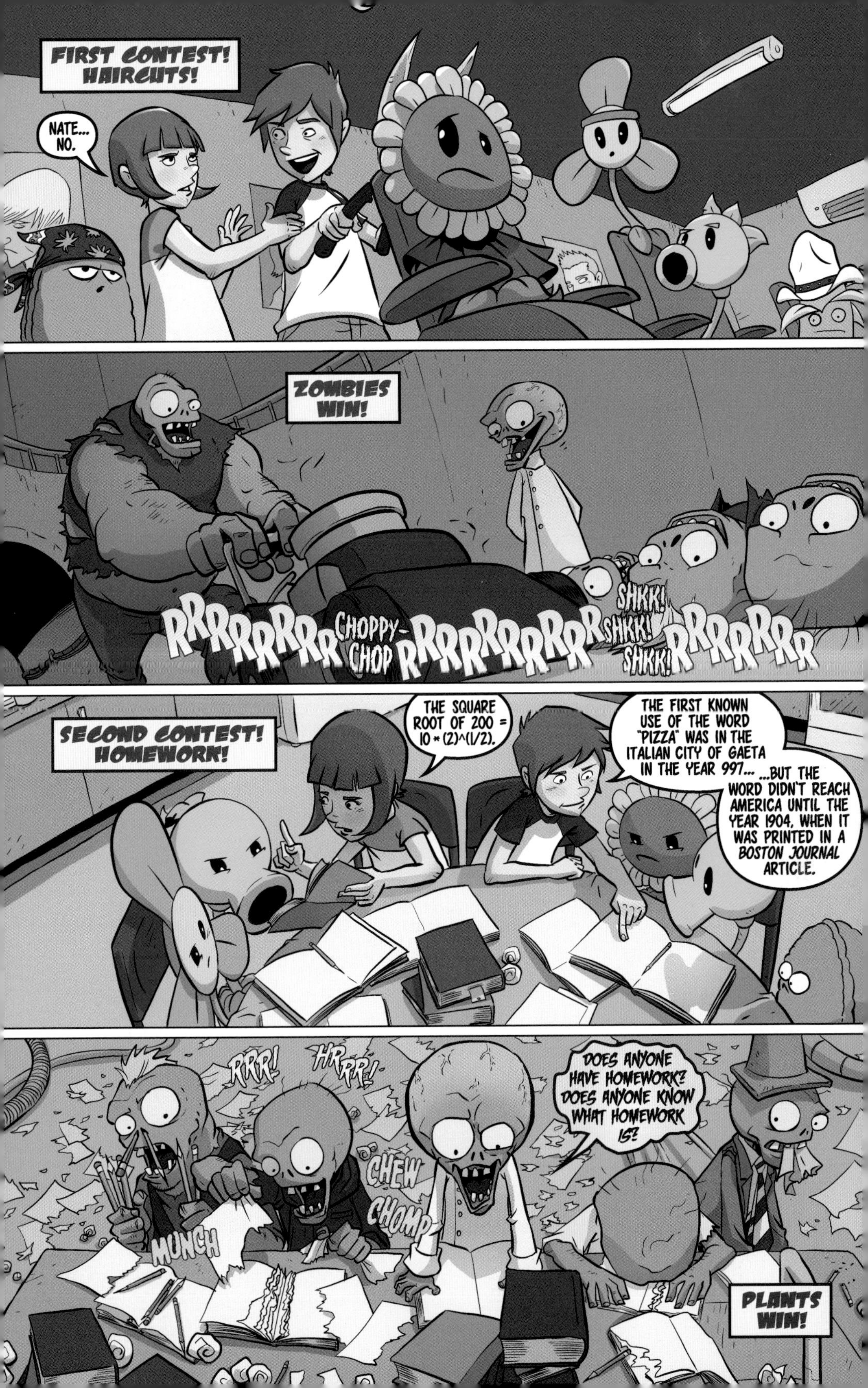
FIRST CONTEST! HAIRCUTS!
NATE... NO.
ZOMBIES WIN!
RRRRRRRRR CHOPPY-CHOP RRRRRRRRRRR SHKK! SHKK! SHKK! RRRRRRRR
SECOND CONTEST! HOMEWORK!
THE SQUARE ROOT OF 200 = 10 * (2)^(1/2).
THE FIRST KNOWN USE OF THE WORD "PIZZA" WAS IN THE ITALIAN CITY OF GAETA IN THE YEAR 997...
...BUT THE WORD DIDN'T REACH AMERICA UNTIL THE YEAR 1904, WHEN IT WAS PRINTED IN A *BOSTON JOURNAL* ARTICLE.
RRR!
HRRR!
DOES ANYONE HAVE HOMEWORK? DOES ANYONE KNOW WHAT HOMEWORK IS?
CHEW
CHOMP
MUNCH
PLANTS WIN!

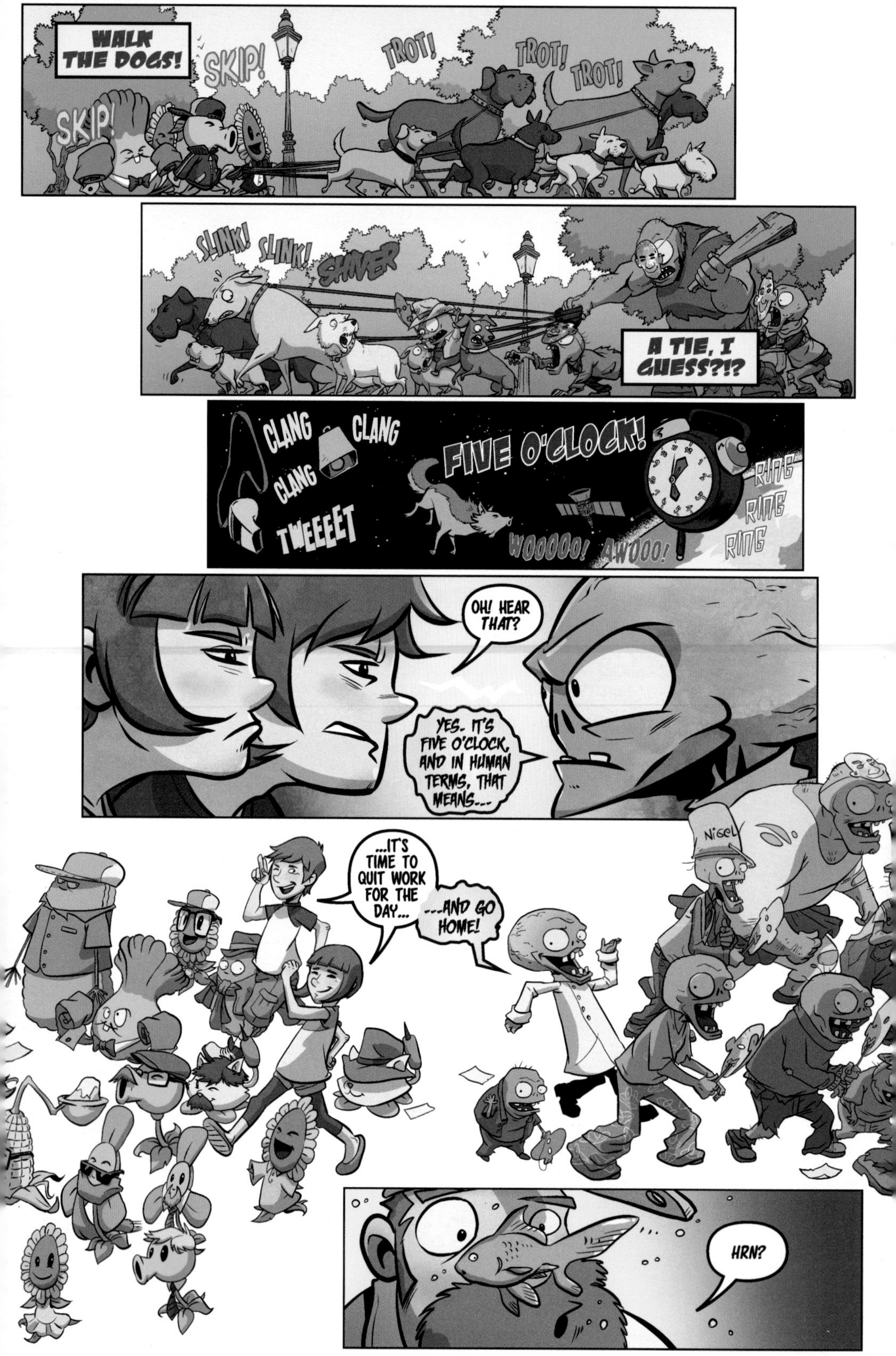
WALK THE DOGS!
SKIP!
SKIP!
TROT!
TROT!
TROT!
SLINK!
SLINK!
SHIVER
A TIE, I GUESS?!?
CLANG
CLANG
CLANG
TWEEEET
FIVE O'CLOCK!
WOOOOO!
AWOOO!
RING
RING
RING
OH! HEAR THAT?
YES. IT'S FIVE O'CLOCK, AND IN HUMAN TERMS, THAT MEANS...
...IT'S TIME TO QUIT WORK FOR THE DAY...
...AND GO HOME!
NIGEL
HRN?

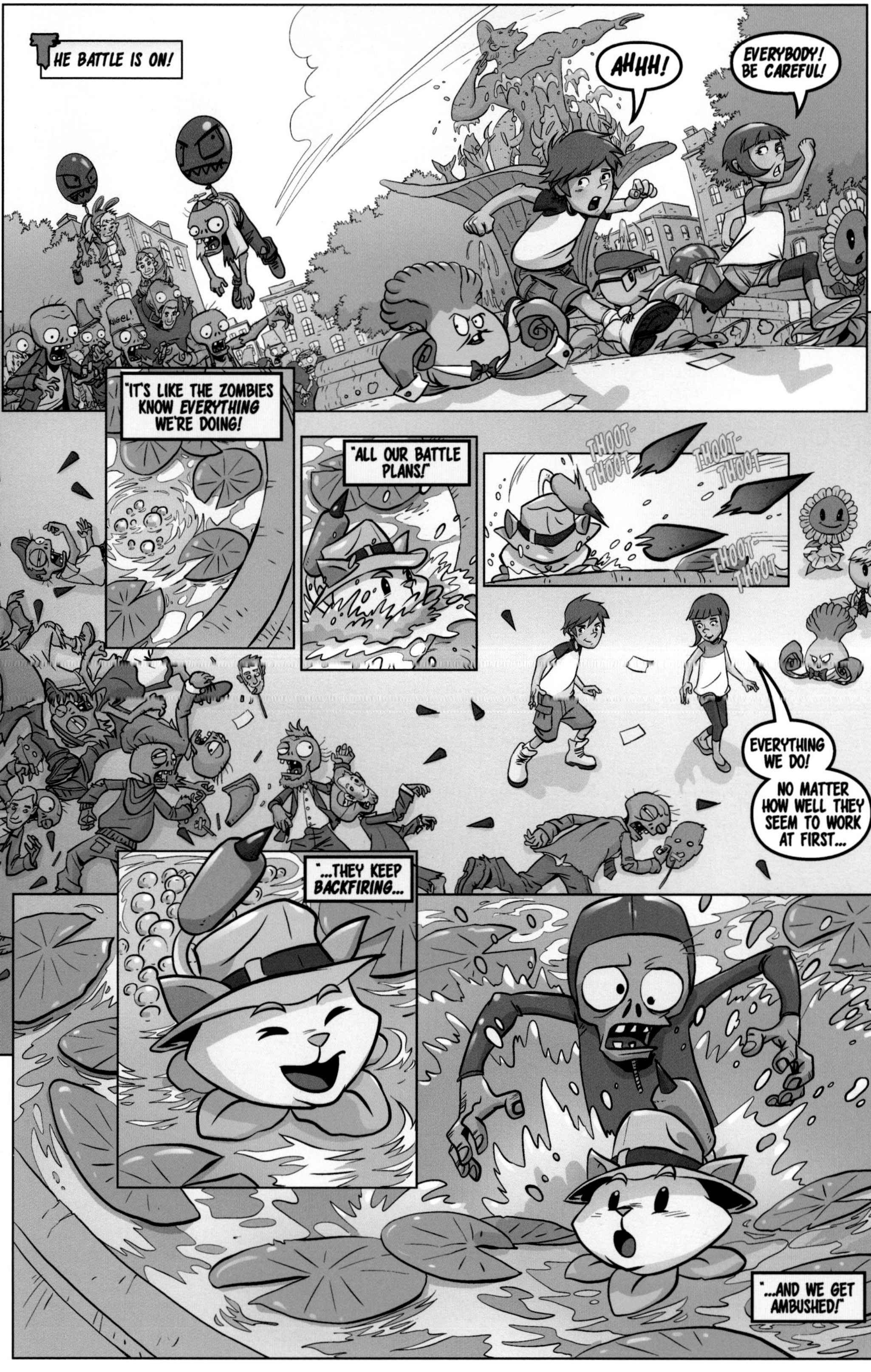
THE BATTLE IS ON!
AHHH!
EVERYBODY! BE CAREFUL!
"IT'S LIKE THE ZOMBIES KNOW EVERYTHING WE'RE DOING!
"ALL OUR BATTLE PLANS!"
THOOT-THOOT
THOOT-THOOT
THOOT-THOOT
EVERYTHING WE DO!
NO MATTER HOW WELL THEY SEEM TO WORK AT FIRST...
"...THEY KEEP BACKFIRING...
"...AND WE GET AMBUSHED!"

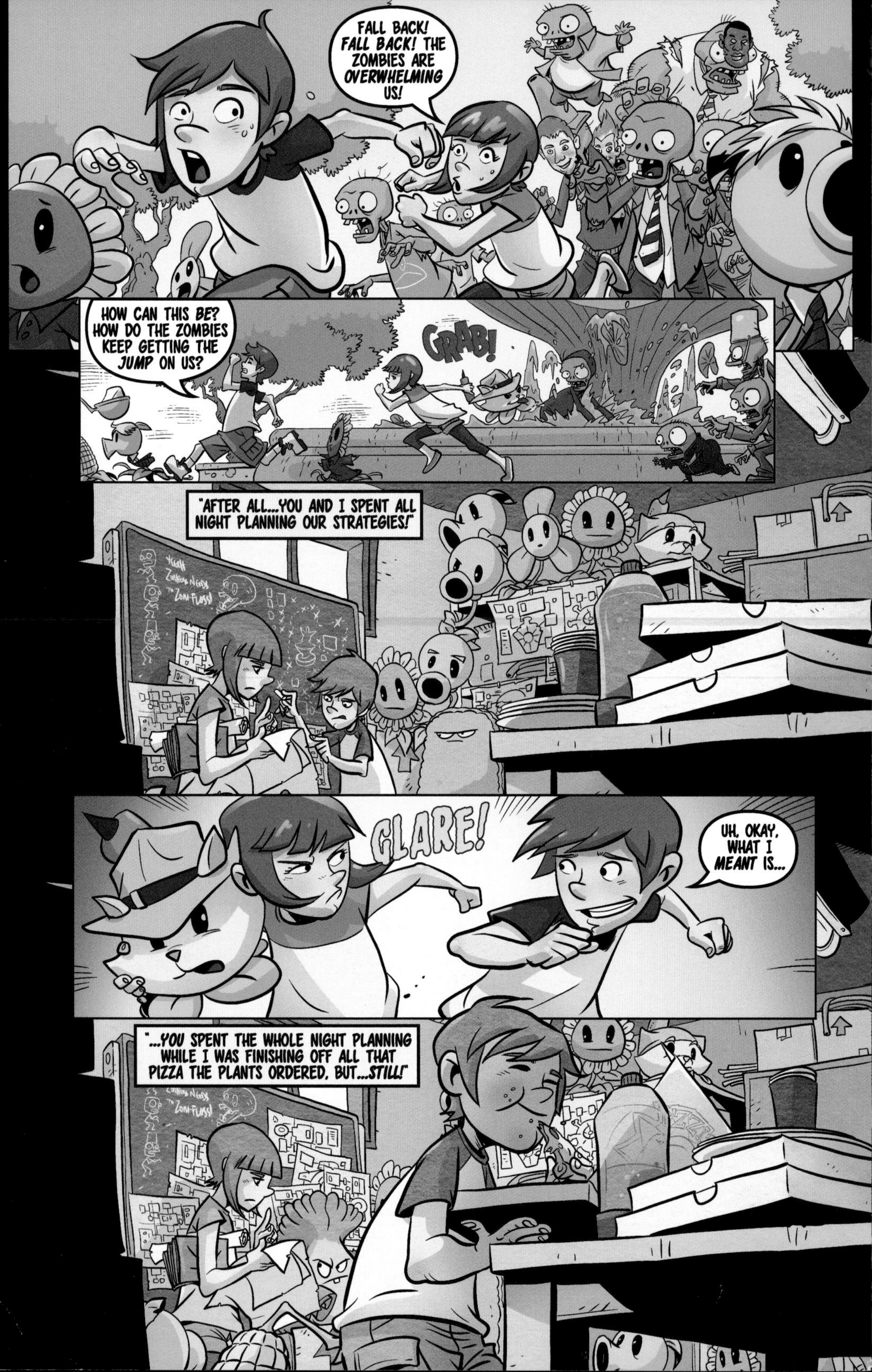
FALL BACK! FALL BACK! THE ZOMBIES ARE OVERWHELMING US!
HOW CAN THIS BE? HOW DO THE ZOMBIES KEEP GETTING THE JUMP ON US?
GRAB!
"AFTER ALL...YOU AND I SPENT ALL NIGHT PLANNING OUR STRATEGIES!"
GLARE!
UH, OKAY, WHAT I MEANT IS...
"...YOU SPENT THE WHOLE NIGHT PLANNING WHILE I WAS FINISHING OFF ALL THAT PIZZA THE PLANTS ORDERED, BUT...STILL!"

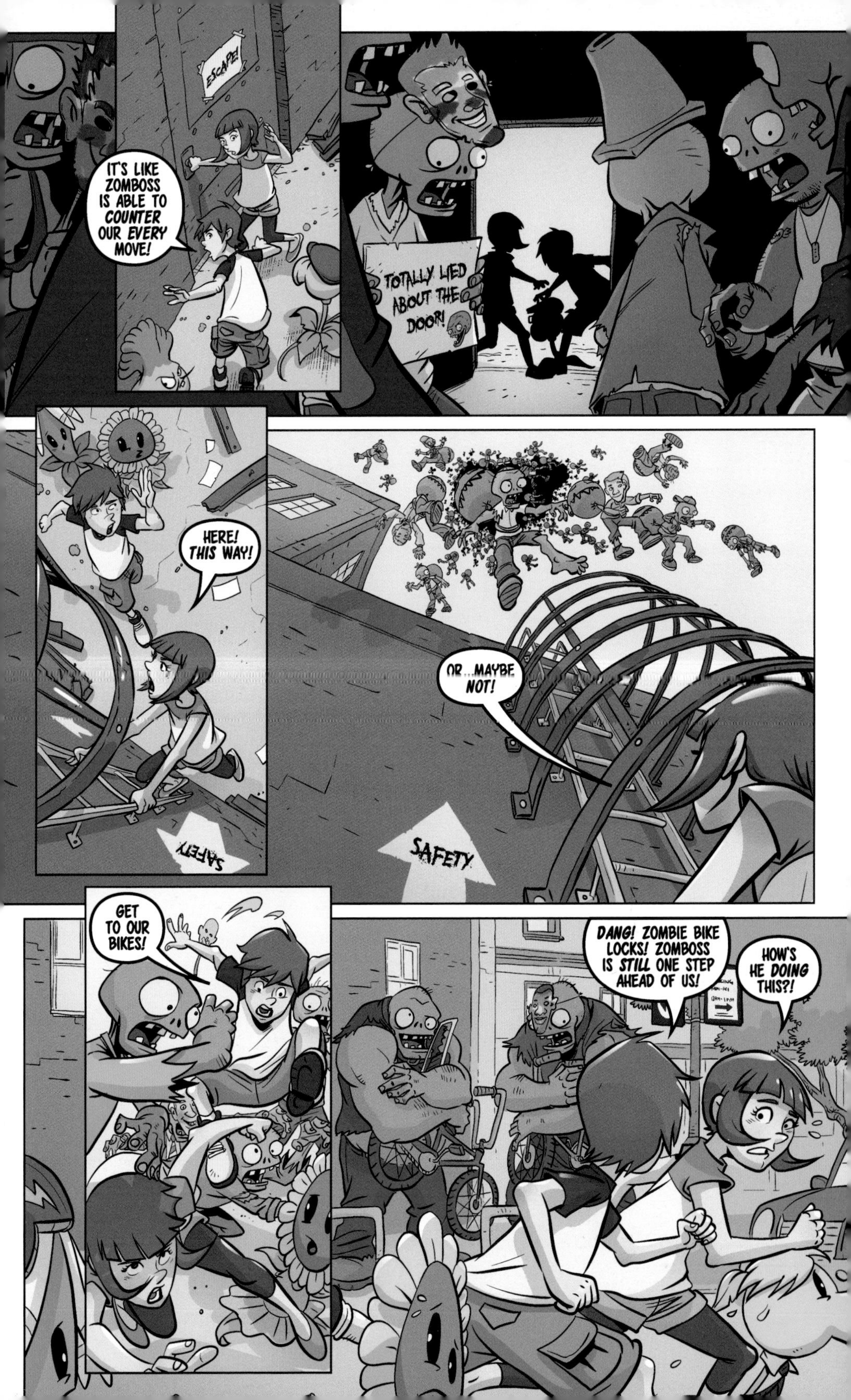
ESCAPE!
IT'S LIKE ZOMBOSS IS ABLE TO COUNTER OUR EVERY MOVE!
TOTALLY LIED ABOUT THE DOOR!
HERE! THIS WAY!
SAFETY
OR...MAYBE NOT!
SAFETY
GET TO OUR BIKES!
DANG! ZOMBIE BIKE LOCKS! ZOMBOSS IS STILL ONE STEP AHEAD OF US!
HOW'S HE DOING THIS?!

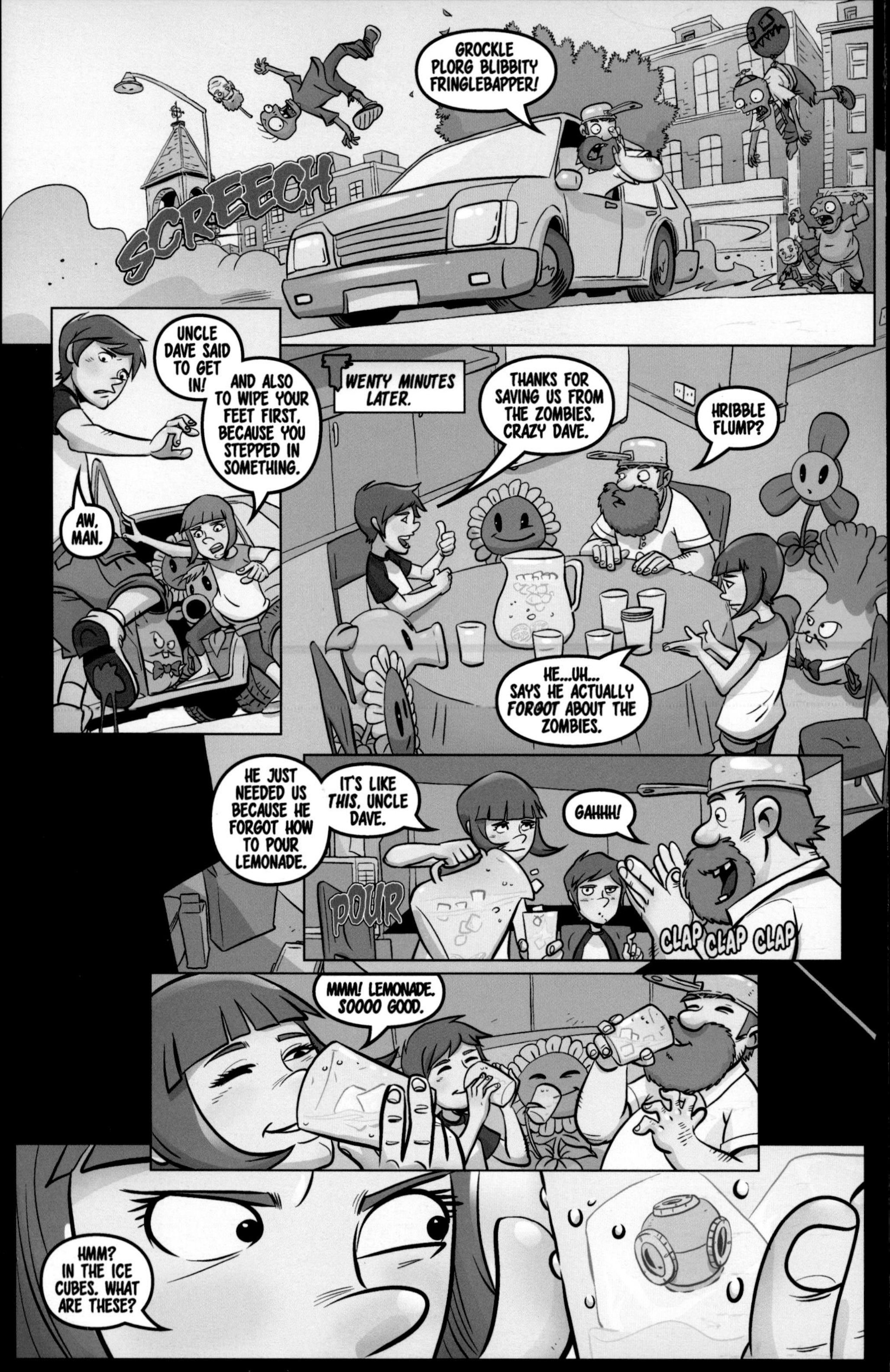
SCREECH
GROCKLE PLORG BLIBBITY FRINGLEBAPPER!
UNCLE DAVE SAID TO GET IN!
AND ALSO TO WIPE YOUR FEET FIRST, BECAUSE YOU STEPPED IN SOMETHING.
AW, MAN.
TWENTY MINUTES LATER.
THANKS FOR SAVING US FROM THE ZOMBIES, CRAZY DAVE.
HRIBBLE FLUMP?
HE...UH... SAYS HE ACTUALLY FORGOT ABOUT THE ZOMBIES.
HE JUST NEEDED US BECAUSE HE FORGOT HOW TO POUR LEMONADE.
IT'S LIKE THIS, UNCLE DAVE.
GAHHH!
POUR
CLAP CLAP CLAP
MMM! LEMONADE. SOOOO GOOD.
HMM? IN THE ICE CUBES. WHAT ARE THESE?

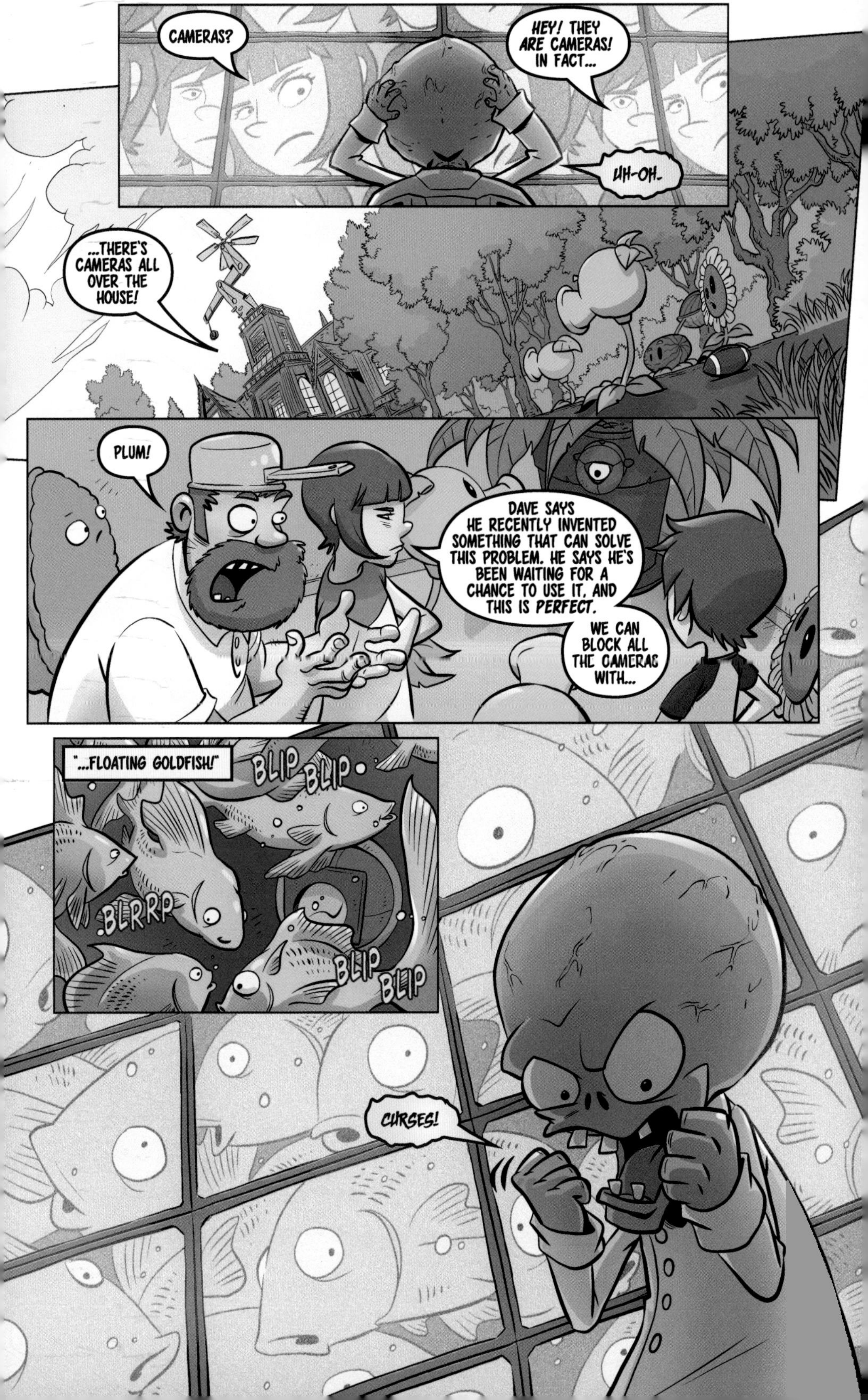
CAMERAS?
HEY! THEY ARE CAMERAS! IN FACT...
UH-OH.
...THERE'S CAMERAS ALL OVER THE HOUSE!
PLUM!
DAVE SAYS HE RECENTLY INVENTED SOMETHING THAT CAN SOLVE THIS PROBLEM. HE SAYS HE'S BEEN WAITING FOR A CHANCE TO USE IT, AND THIS IS PERFECT.
WE CAN BLOCK ALL THE CAMERAS WITH...
"...FLOATING GOLDFISH!"
BLIP BLIP
BLRRP
BLIP BLIP
CURSES!

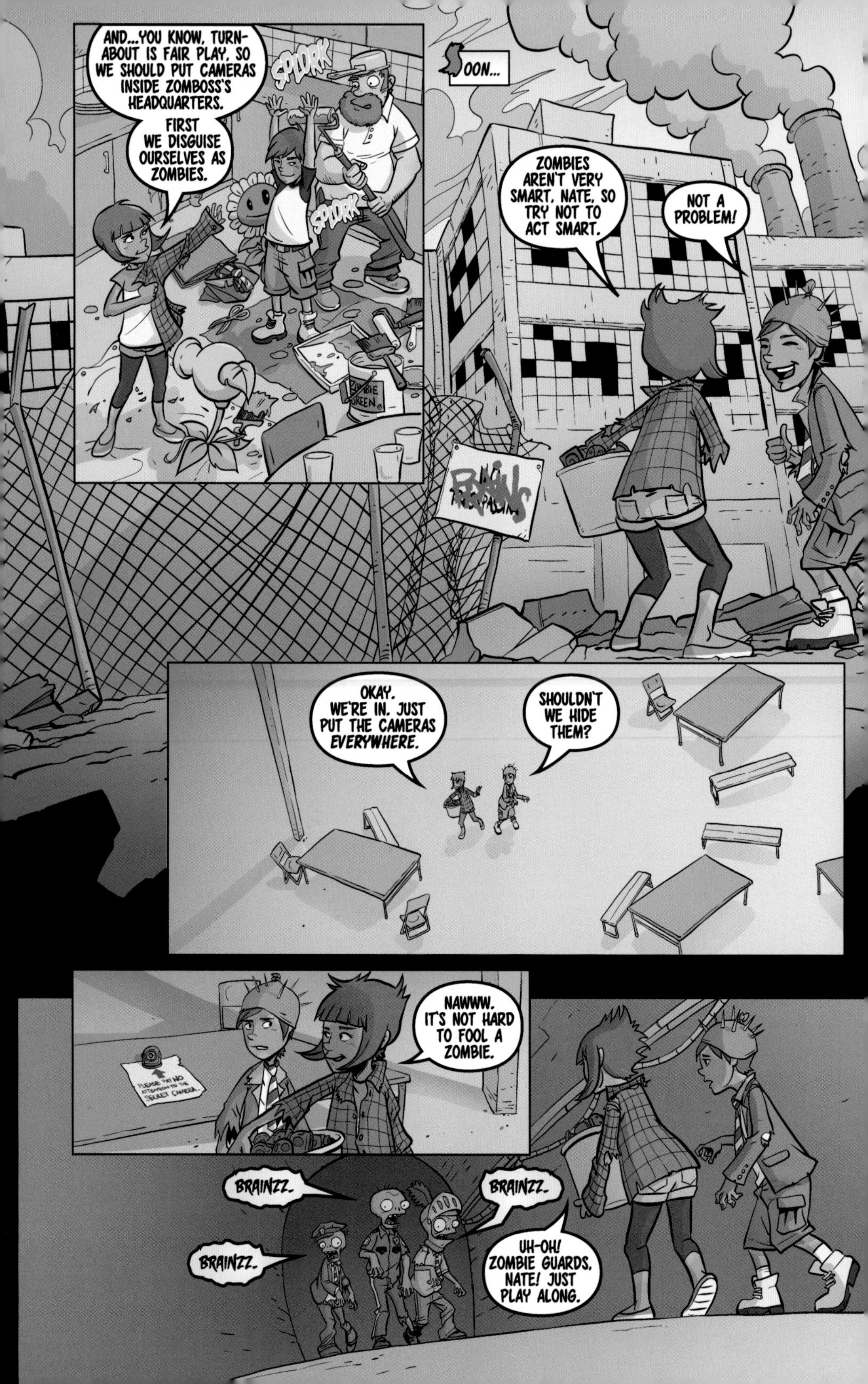
AND...YOU KNOW, TURN-ABOUT IS FAIR PLAY, SO WE SHOULD PUT CAMERAS INSIDE ZOMBOSS'S HEADQUARTERS.
FIRST WE DISGUISE OURSELVES AS ZOMBIES.
SPLORK
SPLORK
ZOMBIE GREEN
SOON...
ZOMBIES AREN'T VERY SMART, NATE, SO TRY NOT TO ACT SMART.
NOT A PROBLEM!
BRAINS
OKAY. WE'RE IN. JUST PUT THE CAMERAS EVERYWHERE.
SHOULDN'T WE HIDE THEM?
PLEASE PAY NO ATTENTION TO THE SECRET CAMERA.
NAWWW. IT'S NOT HARD TO FOOL A ZOMBIE.
BRAINZZ.
BRAINZZ.
BRAINZZ.
UH-OH! ZOMBIE GUARDS, NATE! JUST PLAY ALONG.

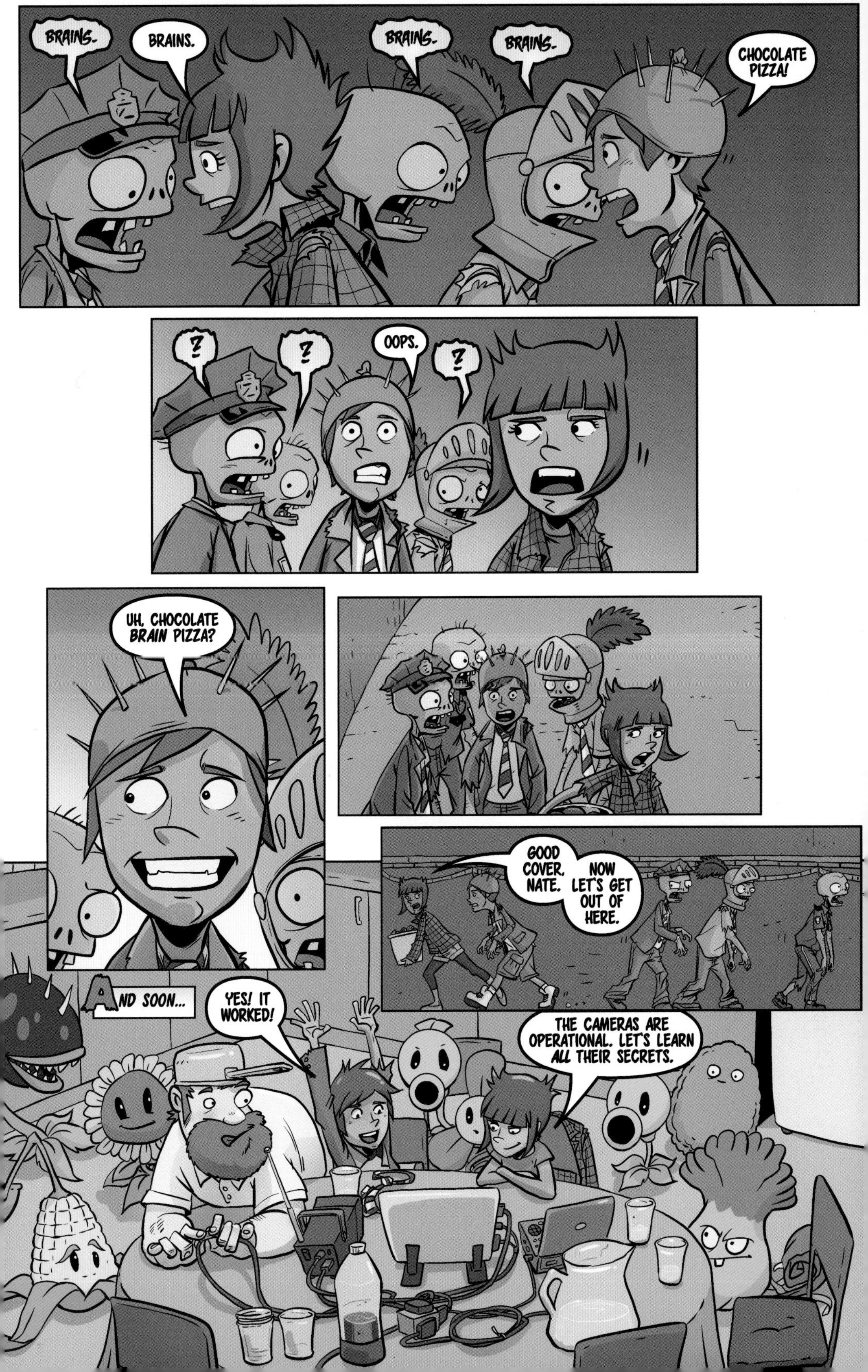
BRAINS.
BRAINS.
BRAINS.
BRAINS.
CHOCOLATE PIZZA!
?
?
OOPS.
?
UH, CHOCOLATE BRAIN PIZZA?
GOOD COVER, NATE.
NOW LET'S GET OUT OF HERE.
AND SOON...
YES! IT WORKED!
THE CAMERAS ARE OPERATIONAL. LET'S LEARN ALL THEIR SECRETS.

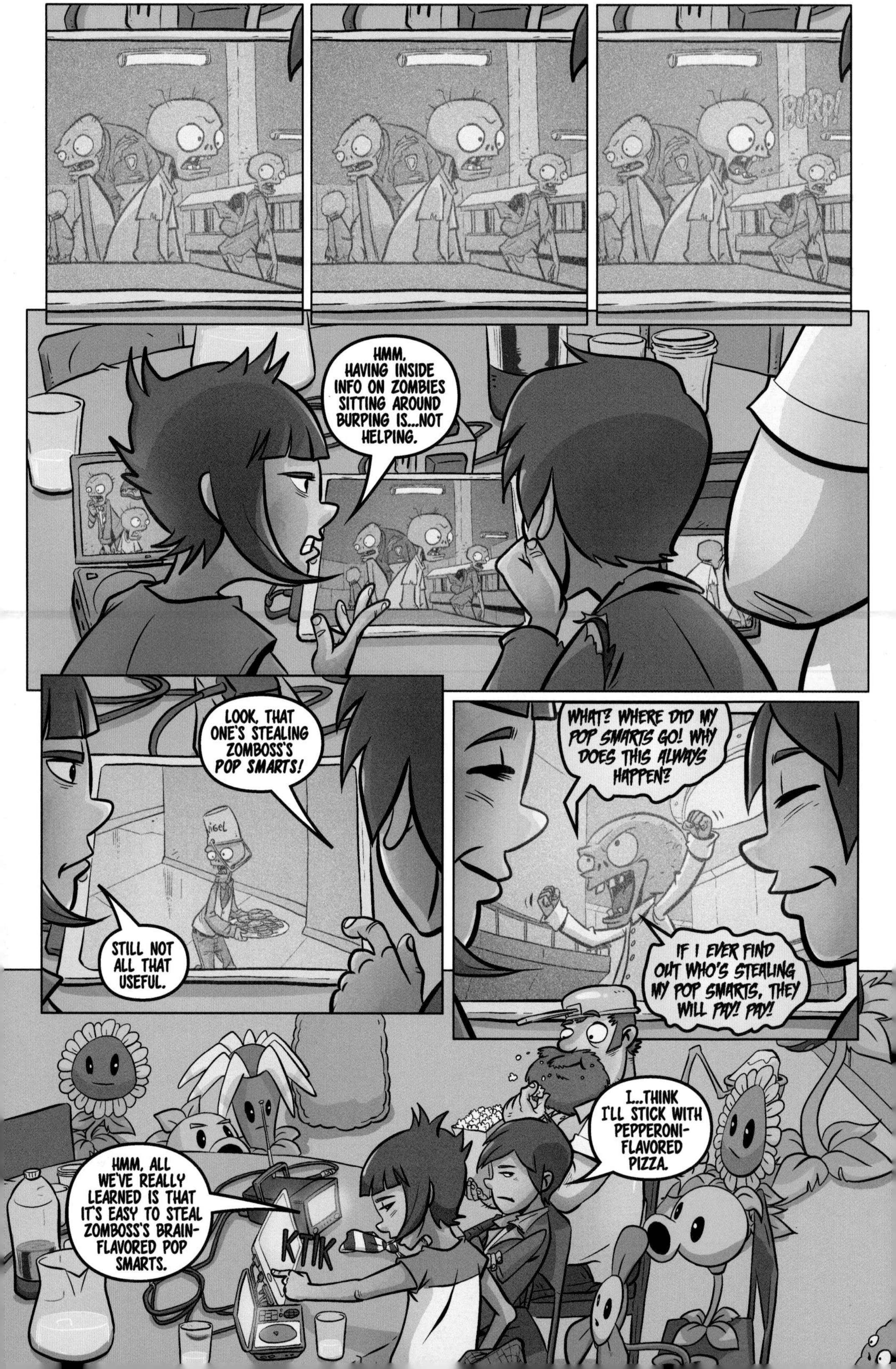

BURP!
HMM, HAVING INSIDE INFO ON ZOMBIES SITTING AROUND BURPING IS...NOT HELPING.
LOOK, THAT ONE'S STEALING ZOMBOSS'S POP SMARTS!
STILL NOT ALL THAT USEFUL.
WHAT? WHERE DID MY POP SMARTS GO! WHY DOES THIS ALWAYS HAPPEN?
IF I EVER FIND OUT WHO'S STEALING MY POP SMARTS, THEY WILL PAY! PAY!
HMM, ALL WE'VE REALLY LEARNED IS THAT IT'S EASY TO STEAL ZOMBOSS'S BRAIN-FLAVORED POP SMARTS.
KTIK
I...THINK I'LL STICK WITH PEPPERONI-FLAVORED PIZZA.

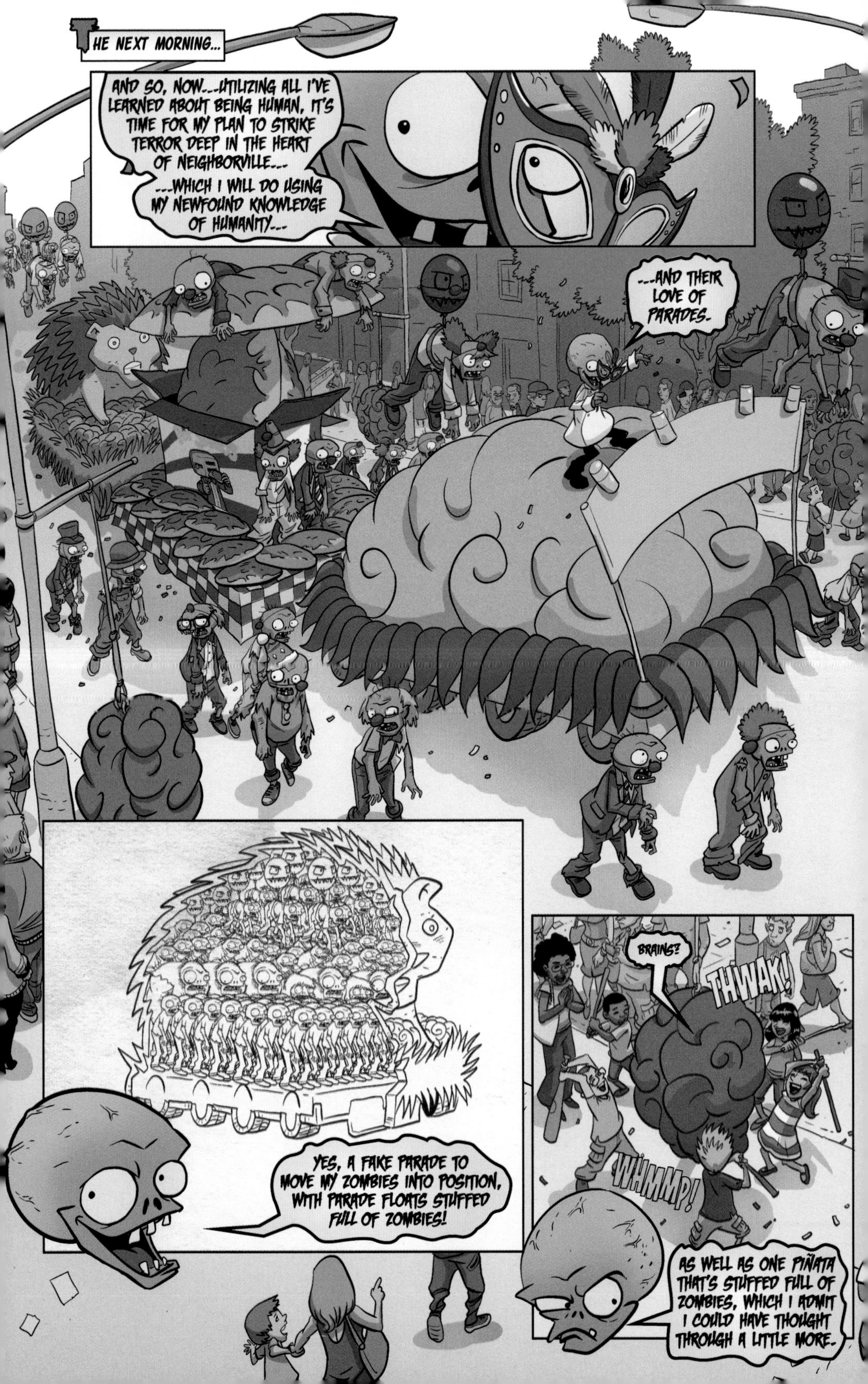
THE NEXT MORNING...
AND SO, NOW...UTILIZING ALL I'VE LEARNED ABOUT BEING HUMAN, IT'S TIME FOR MY PLAN TO STRIKE TERROR DEEP IN THE HEART OF NEIGHBORVILLE...
...WHICH I WILL DO USING MY NEWFOUND KNOWLEDGE OF HUMANITY...
...AND THEIR LOVE OF PARADES.
YES, A FAKE PARADE TO MOVE MY ZOMBIES INTO POSITION, WITH PARADE FLOATS STUFFED FULL OF ZOMBIES!
BRAINS?
THWAK!
WHMMP!
AS WELL AS ONE PIÑATA THAT'S STUFFED FULL OF ZOMBIES, WHICH I ADMIT I COULD HAVE THOUGHT THROUGH A LITTLE MORE.

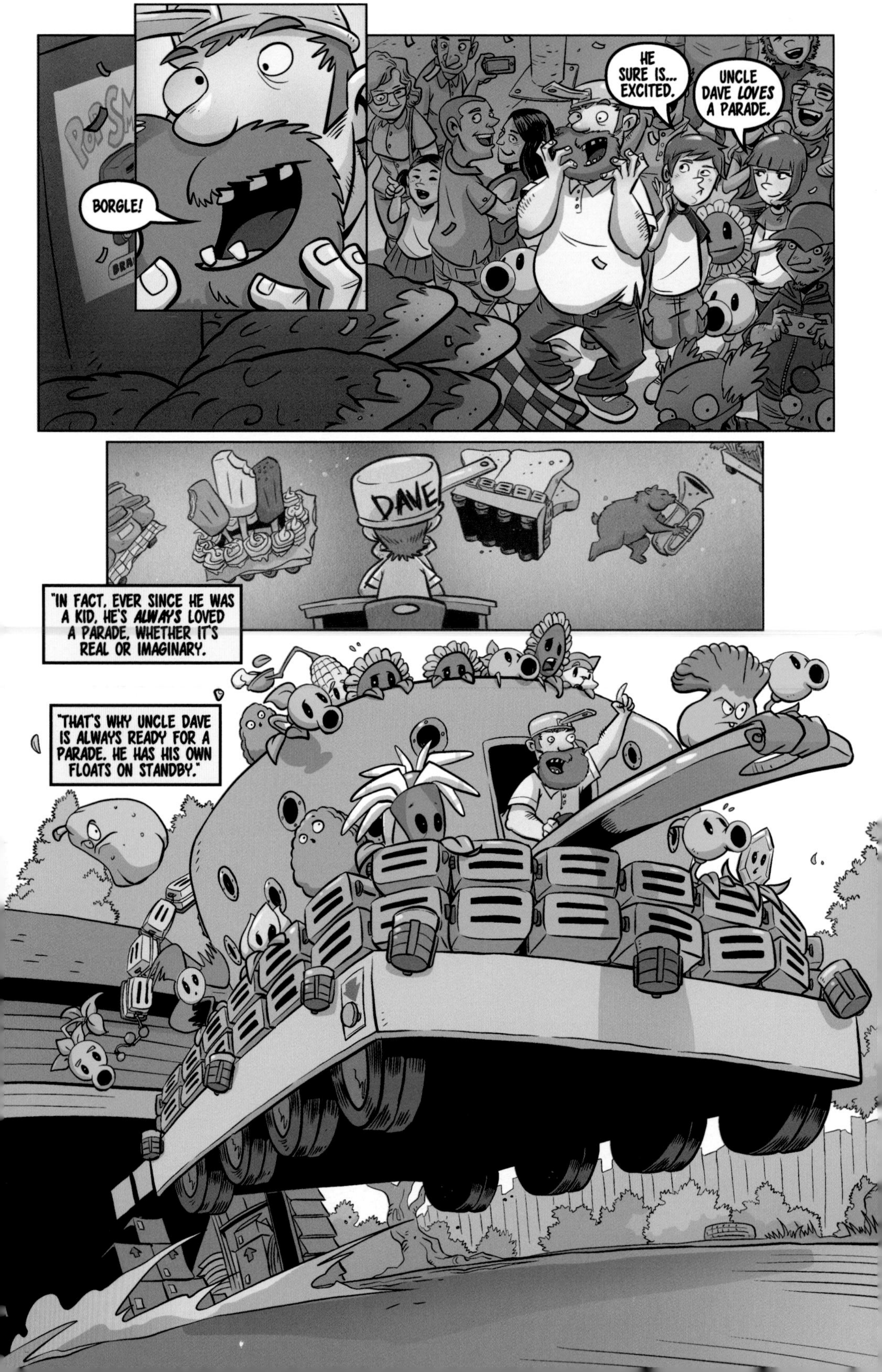
BORGLE!
HE SURE IS... EXCITED.
UNCLE DAVE *LOVES* A PARADE.
DAVE
"IN FACT, EVER SINCE HE WAS A KID, HE'S *ALWAYS* LOVED A PARADE, WHETHER IT'S REAL OR IMAGINARY.
"THAT'S WHY UNCLE DAVE IS ALWAYS READY FOR A PARADE. HE HAS HIS OWN FLOATS ON STANDBY."

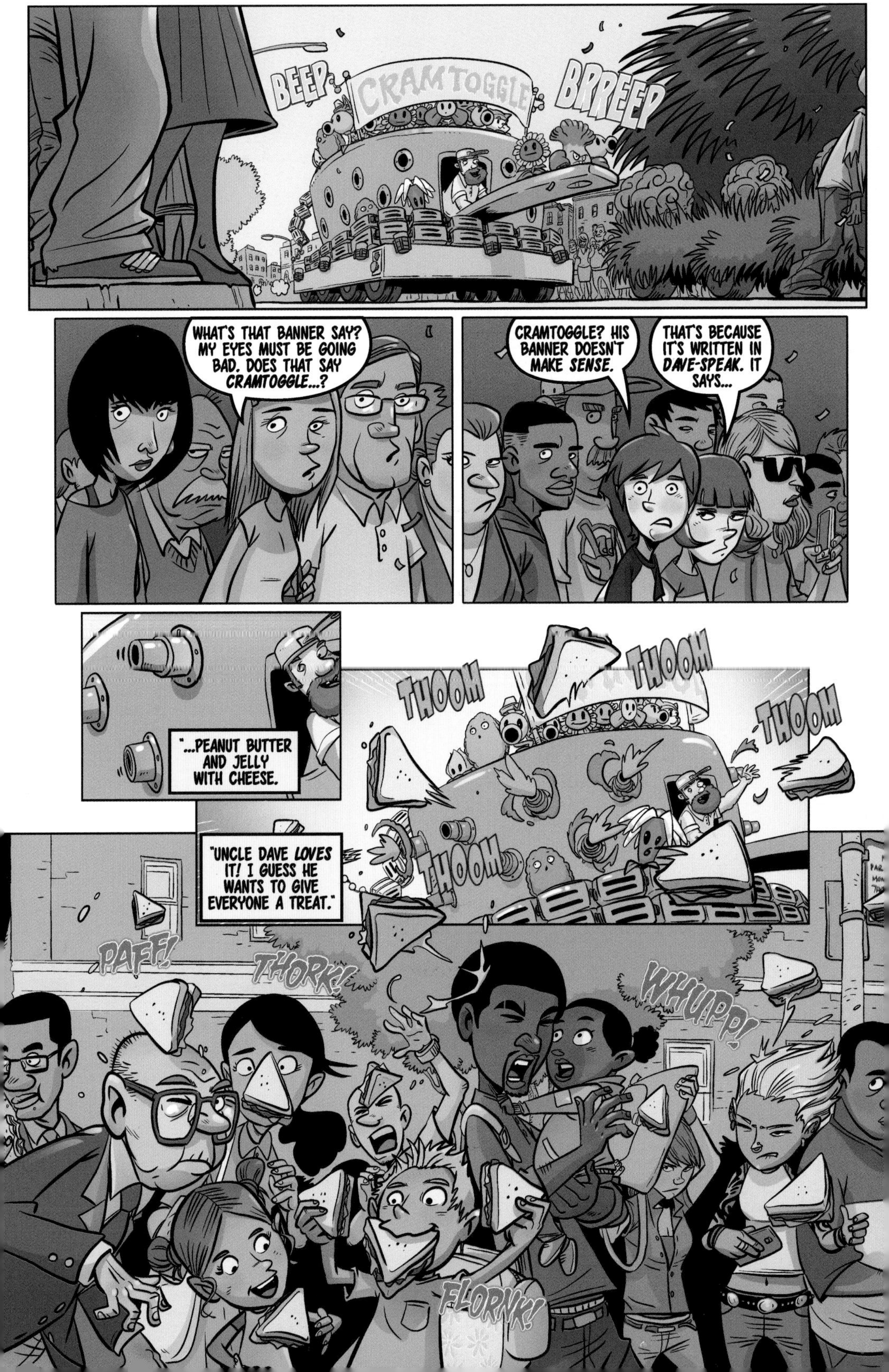
BEEP
CRAMTOGGLE
BRREEP
WHAT'S THAT BANNER SAY? MY EYES MUST BE GOING BAD. DOES THAT SAY CRAMTOGGLE...?
CRAMTOGGLE? HIS BANNER DOESN'T MAKE SENSE.
THAT'S BECAUSE IT'S WRITTEN IN DAVE-SPEAK. IT SAYS...
"...PEANUT BUTTER AND JELLY WITH CHEESE.
THOOM
THOOM
THOOM
"UNCLE DAVE LOVES IT! I GUESS HE WANTS TO GIVE EVERYONE A TREAT."
THOOM
PAFF!
THORK!
WHUPP!
FLORNK!

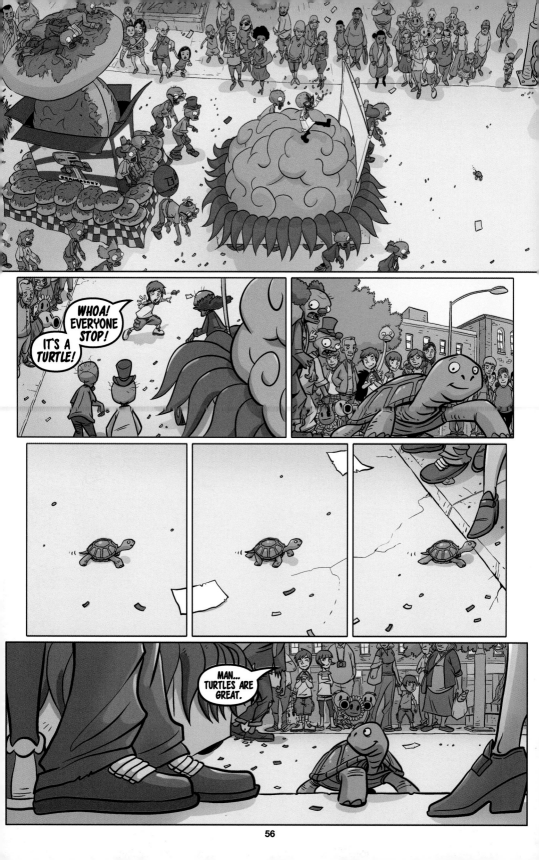

WHOA! EVERYONE STOP!

IT'S A TURTLE!

MAN... TURTLES ARE GREAT.

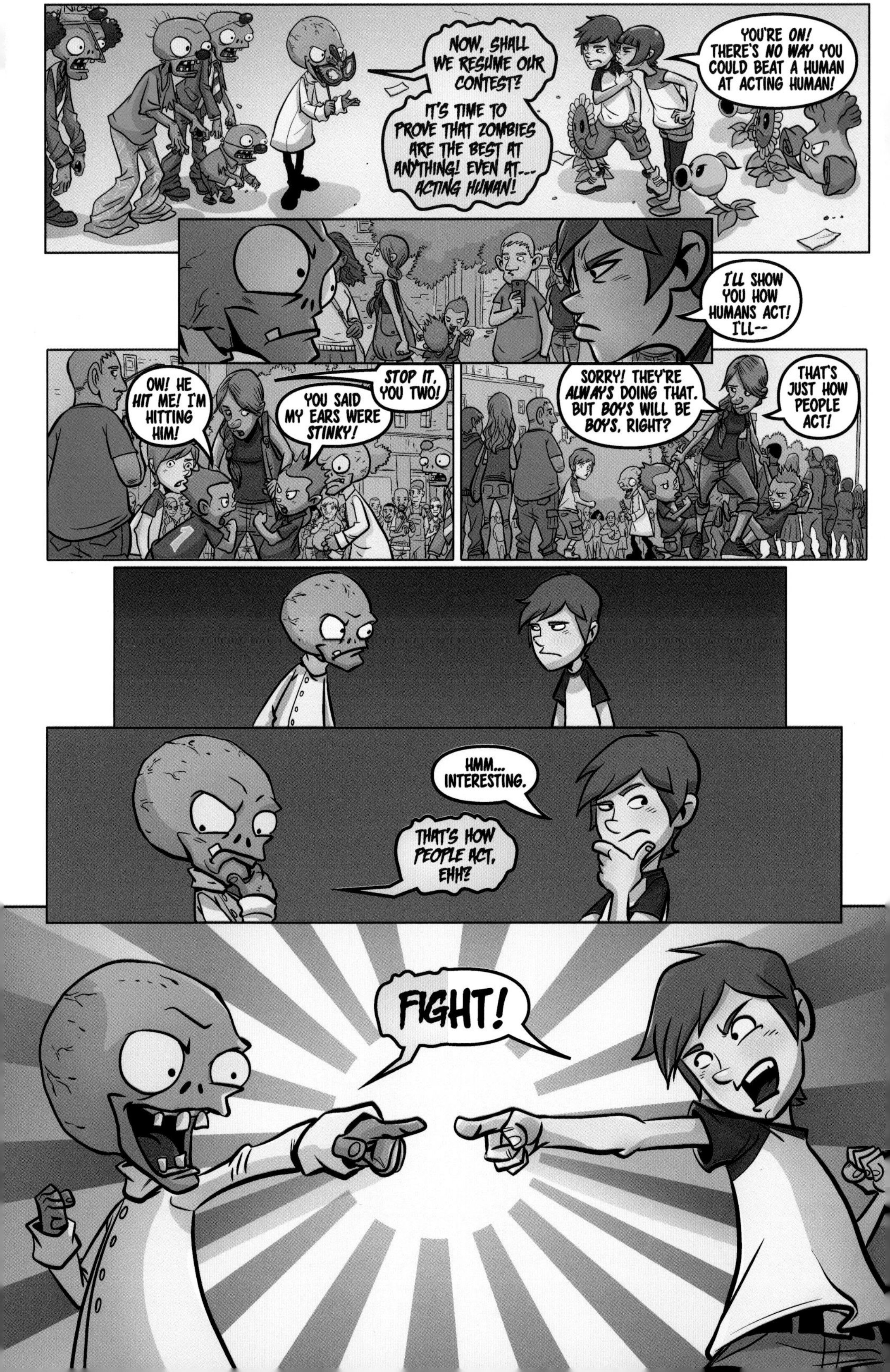
NOW, SHALL WE RESUME OUR CONTEST?
IT'S TIME TO PROVE THAT ZOMBIES ARE THE BEST AT ANYTHING! EVEN AT--- ACTING HUMAN!
YOU'RE ON! THERE'S NO WAY YOU COULD BEAT A HUMAN AT ACTING HUMAN!
I'LL SHOW YOU HOW HUMANS ACT! I'LL--
OW! HE HIT ME! I'M HITTING HIM!
YOU SAID MY EARS WERE STINKY!
STOP IT, YOU TWO!
SORRY! THEY'RE ALWAYS DOING THAT. BUT BOYS WILL BE BOYS, RIGHT?
THAT'S JUST HOW PEOPLE ACT!
HMM... INTERESTING.
THAT'S HOW PEOPLE ACT, EHH?
FIGHT!

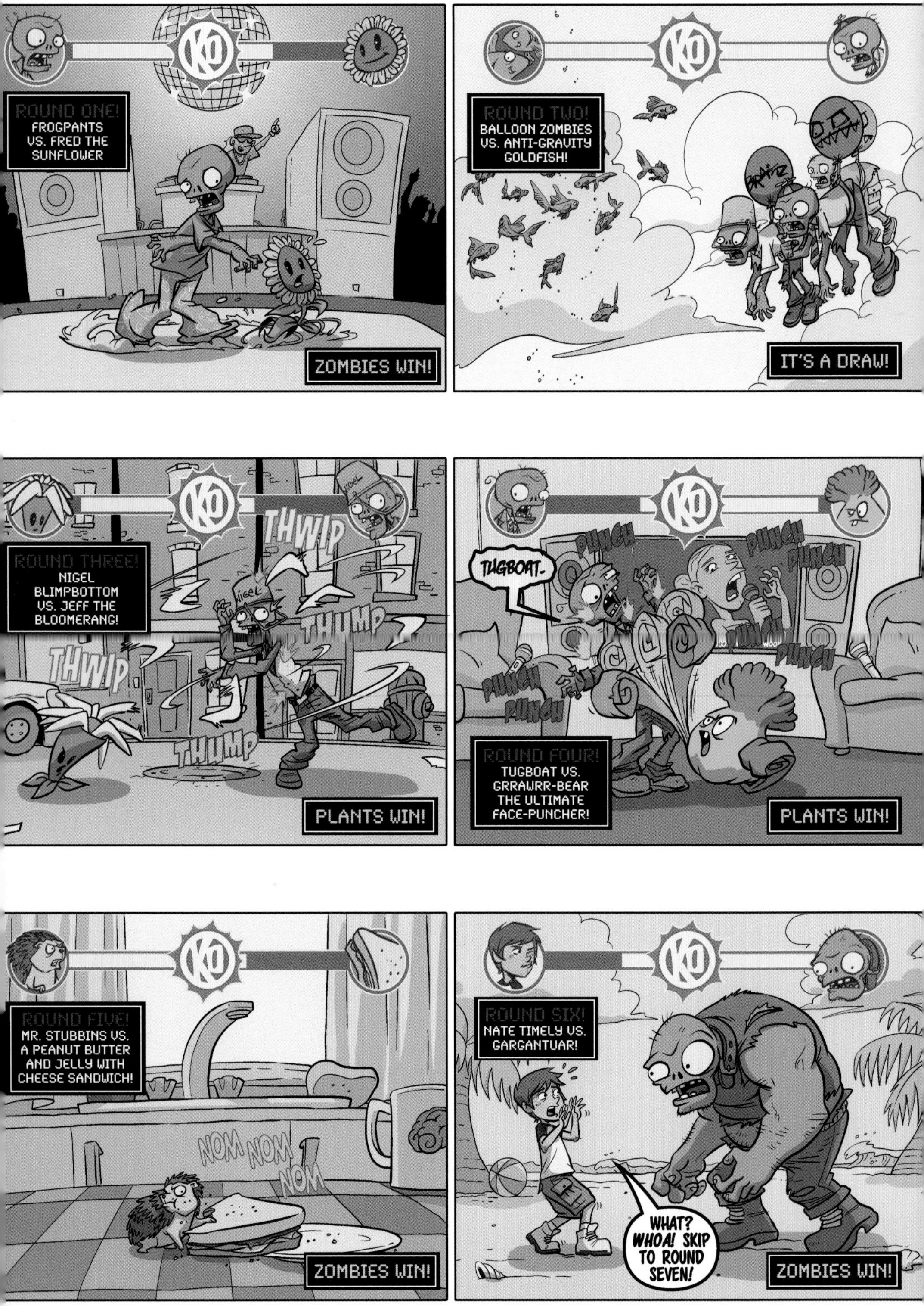
KO
ROUND ONE!
FROGPANTS VS. FRED THE SUNFLOWER
ZOMBIES WIN!
KO
ROUND TWO!
BALLOON ZOMBIES VS. ANTI-GRAVITY GOLDFISH!
IT'S A DRAW!
KO
ROUND THREE!
NIGEL BLIMPBOTTOM VS. JEFF THE BLOOMERANG!
THWIP
THUMP
THWIP
THUMP
PLANTS WIN!
KO
TUGBOAT-
PUNCH
PUNCH
PUNCH
PUNCH
PUNCH
PUNCH
PUNCH
ROUND FOUR!
TUGBOAT VS. GRRAWRR-BEAR THE ULTIMATE FACE-PUNCHER!
PLANTS WIN!
KO
ROUND FIVE!
MR. STUBBINS VS. A PEANUT BUTTER AND JELLY WITH CHEESE SANDWICH!
NOM NOM NOM
ZOMBIES WIN!
KO
ROUND SIX!
NATE TIMELY VS. GARGANTUAR!
WHAT? WHOA! SKIP TO ROUND SEVEN!
ZOMBIES WIN!

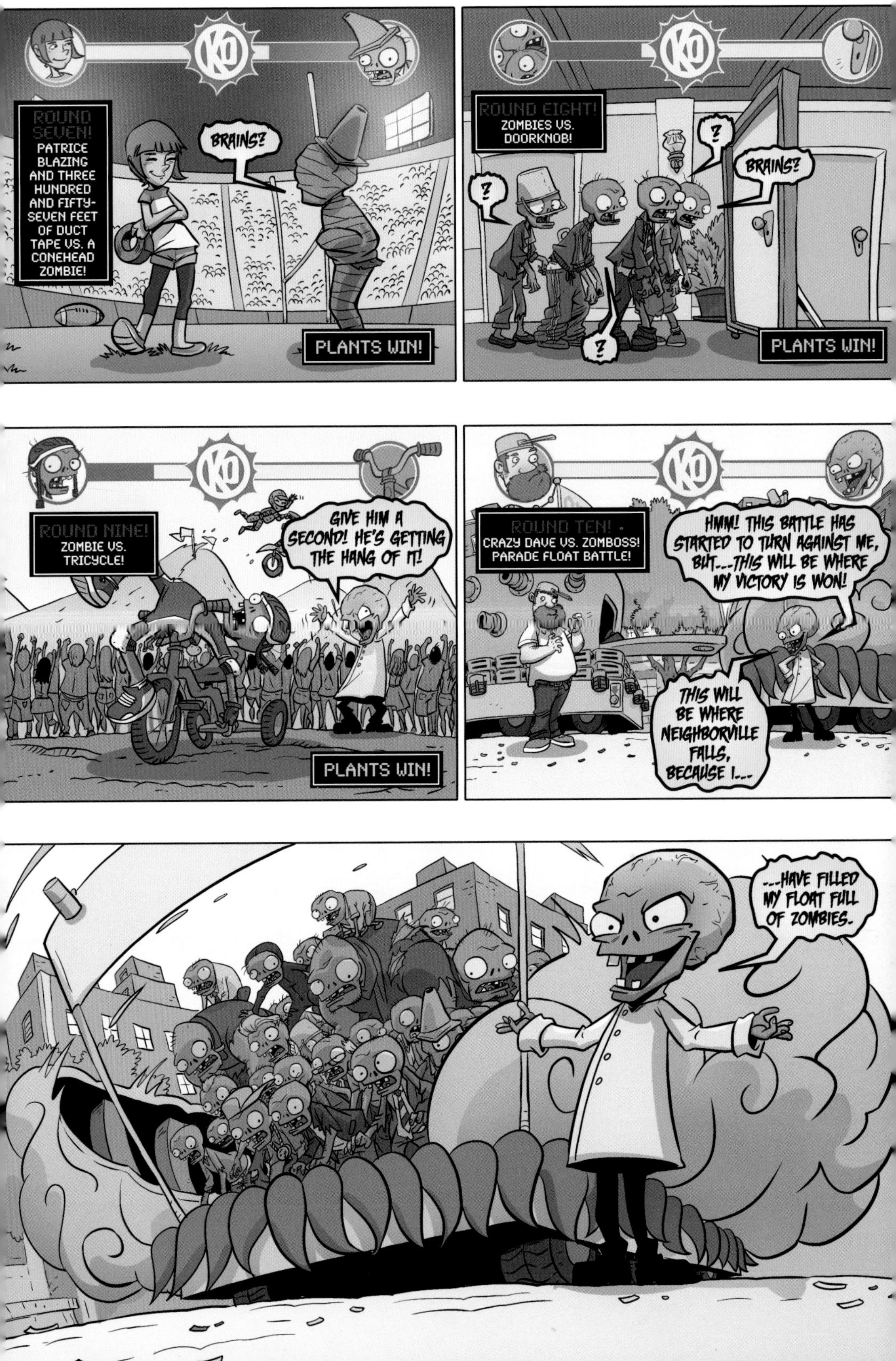
ROUND SEVEN!
PATRICE BLAZING AND THREE HUNDRED AND FIFTY-SEVEN FEET OF DUCT TAPE VS. A CONEHEAD ZOMBIE!
BRAINS?
PLANTS WIN!
ROUND EIGHT!
ZOMBIES VS. DOORKNOB!
?
?
BRAINS?
?
PLANTS WIN!
ROUND NINE!
ZOMBIE VS. TRICYCLE!
GIVE HIM A SECOND! HE'S GETTING THE HANG OF IT!
PLANTS WIN!
ROUND TEN!
CRAZY DAVE VS. ZOMBOSS! PARADE FLOAT BATTLE!
HMM! THIS BATTLE HAS STARTED TO TURN AGAINST ME, BUT... THIS WILL BE WHERE MY VICTORY IS WON!
THIS WILL BE WHERE NEIGHBORVILLE FALLS, BECAUSE I...
...HAVE FILLED MY FLOAT FULL OF ZOMBIES.

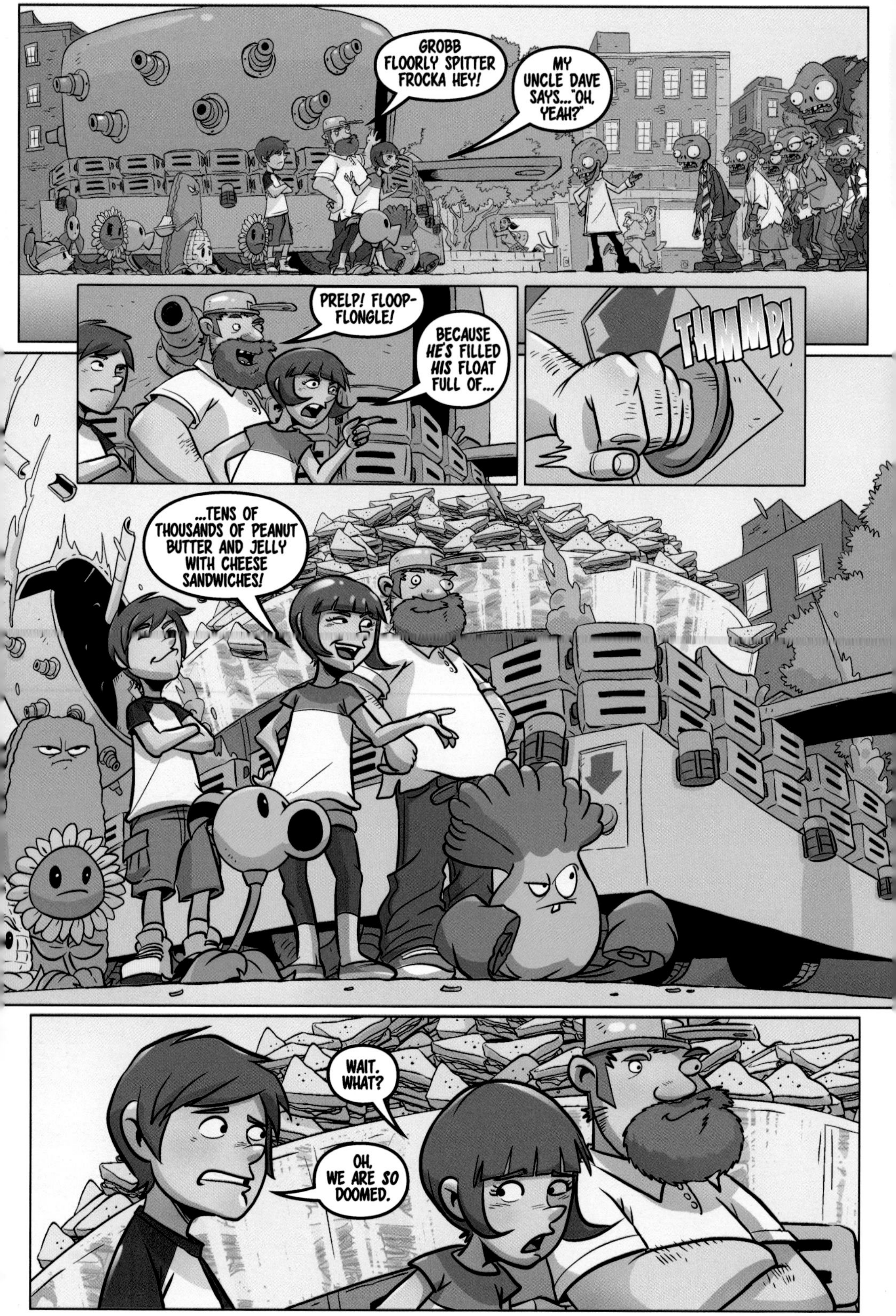
GROBB FLOORLY SPITTER FROCKA HEY!
MY UNCLE DAVE SAYS..."OH, YEAH?"
PRELP! FLOOP-FLONGLE!
BECAUSE HE'S FILLED HIS FLOAT FULL OF...
THMMP!
...TENS OF THOUSANDS OF PEANUT BUTTER AND JELLY WITH CHEESE SANDWICHES!
WAIT. WHAT?
OH, WE ARE SO DOOMED.

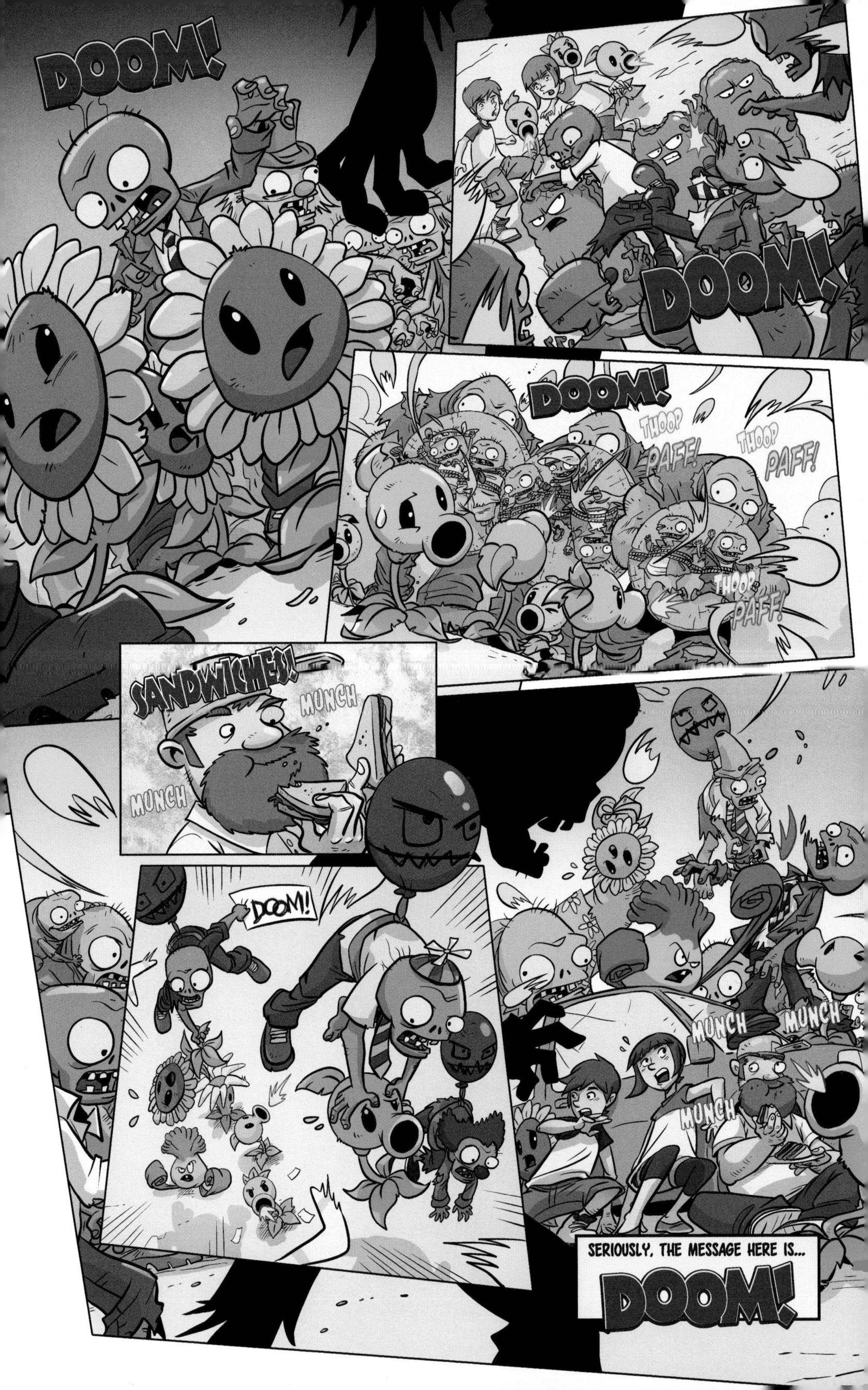
DOOM!
DOOM!
DOOM!
THOOP
PAFF!
THOOP
PAFF!
THOOP
PAFF!
SANDWICHES!
MUNCH
MUNCH
DOOM!
MUNCH
MUNCH
MUNCH
SERIOUSLY, THE MESSAGE HERE IS...
DOOM!

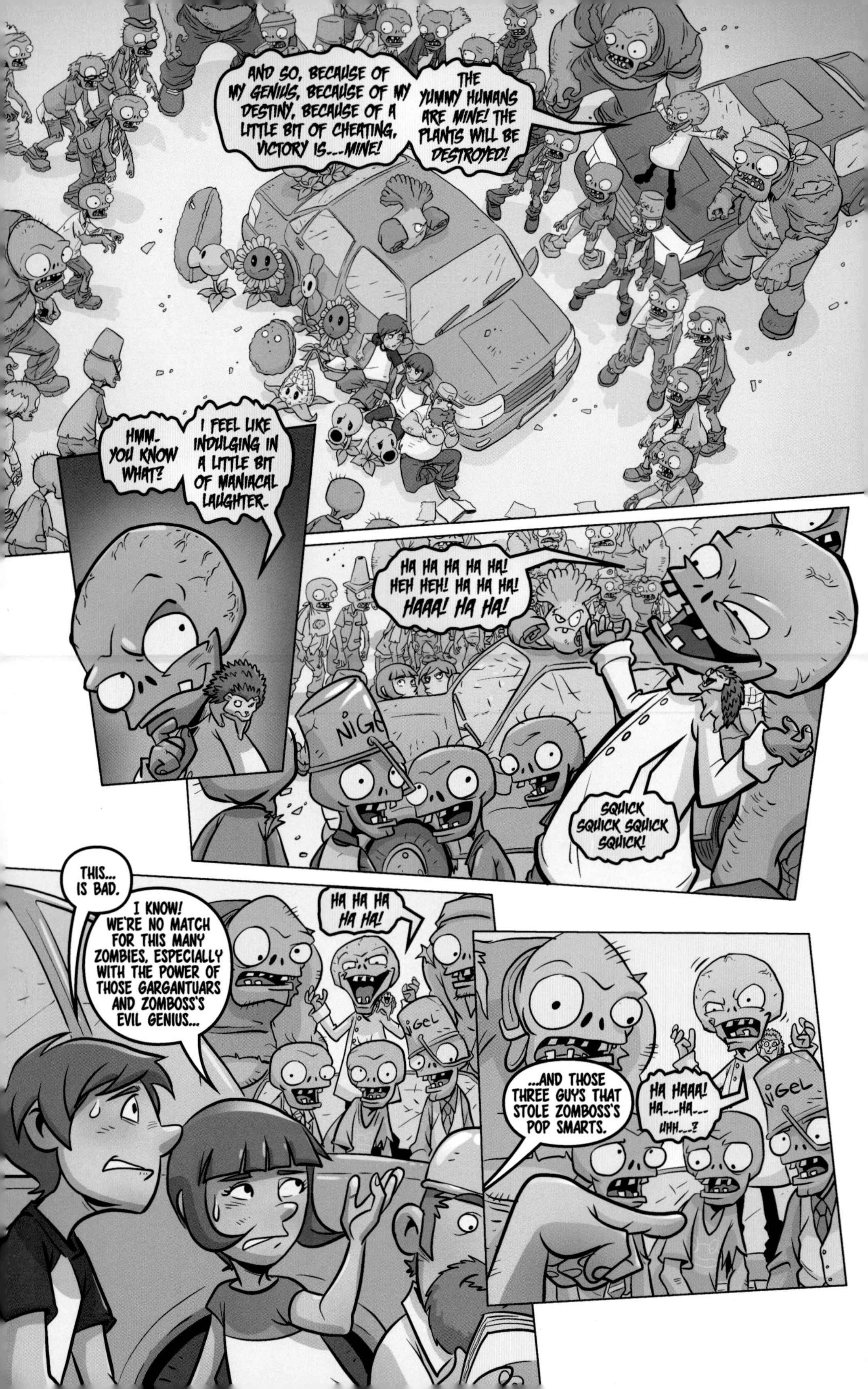
AND SO, BECAUSE OF MY GENIUS, BECAUSE OF MY DESTINY, BECAUSE OF A LITTLE BIT OF CHEATING, VICTORY IS...MINE!
THE YUMMY HUMANS ARE MINE! THE PLANTS WILL BE DESTROYED!
HMM. YOU KNOW WHAT?
I FEEL LIKE INDULGING IN A LITTLE BIT OF MANIACAL LAUGHTER.
HA HA HA HA HA! HEH HEH! HA HA HA! HAAA! HA HA!
NIGEL
SQUICK SQUICK SQUICK SQUICK!
THIS... IS BAD.
I KNOW! WE'RE NO MATCH FOR THIS MANY ZOMBIES, ESPECIALLY WITH THE POWER OF THOSE GARGANTUARS AND ZOMBOSS'S EVIL GENIUS...
HA HA HA HA HA!
...AND THOSE THREE GUYS THAT STOLE ZOMBOSS'S POP SMARTS.
HA HAAA! HA...HA... UHH...?

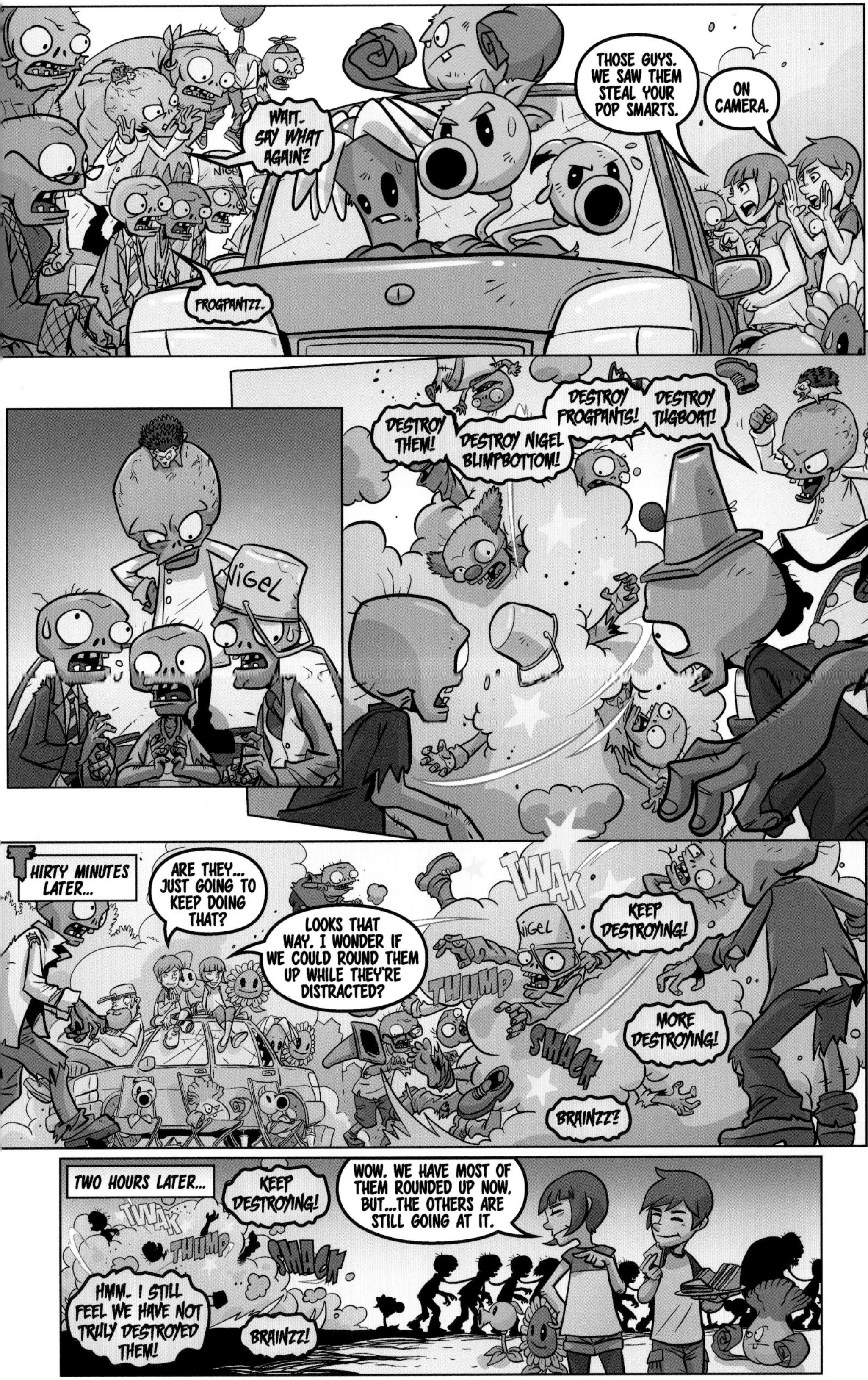
THOSE GUYS. WE SAW THEM STEAL YOUR POP SMARTS.
ON CAMERA.
WAIT. SAY WHAT AGAIN?
FROGPANTZZ.
DESTROY THEM!
DESTROY NIGEL BLIMPBOTTOM!
DESTROY FROGPANTS!
DESTROY TUGBOAT!
NIGEL
THIRTY MINUTES LATER...
ARE THEY... JUST GOING TO KEEP DOING THAT?
LOOKS THAT WAY. I WONDER IF WE COULD ROUND THEM UP WHILE THEY'RE DISTRACTED?
TWAK
KEEP DESTROYING!
THUMP
SMACK
MORE DESTROYING!
BRAINZZ?
TWO HOURS LATER...
KEEP DESTROYING!
WOW. WE HAVE MOST OF THEM ROUNDED UP NOW, BUT...THE OTHERS ARE STILL GOING AT IT.
TWAK
THUMP
SMACK
HMM. I STILL FEEL WE HAVE NOT TRULY DESTROYED THEM!
BRAINZZ!

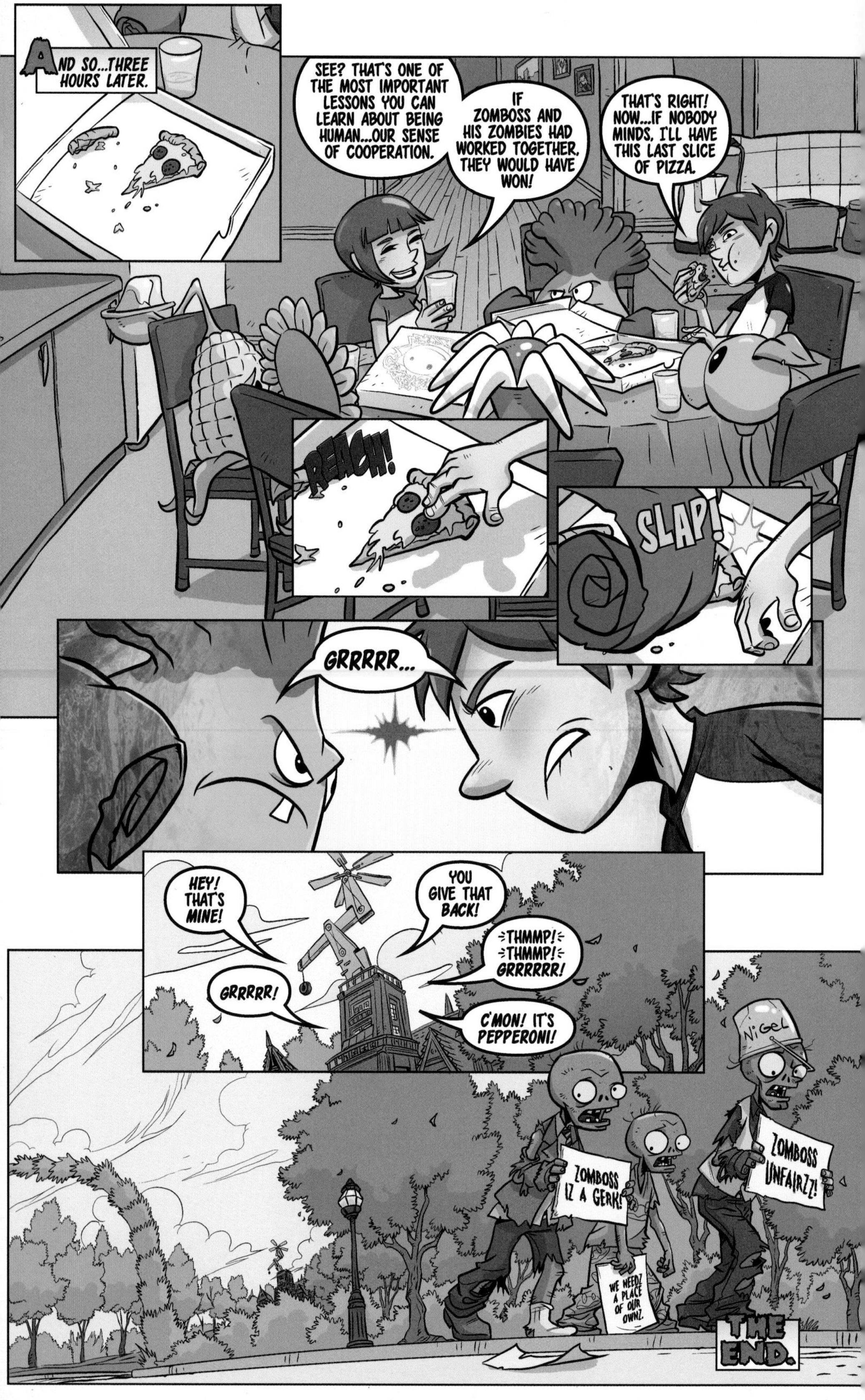
AND SO...THREE HOURS LATER.
SEE? THAT'S ONE OF THE MOST IMPORTANT LESSONS YOU CAN LEARN ABOUT BEING HUMAN...OUR SENSE OF COOPERATION.
IF ZOMBOSS AND HIS ZOMBIES HAD WORKED TOGETHER, THEY WOULD HAVE WON!
THAT'S RIGHT! NOW...IF NOBODY MINDS, I'LL HAVE THIS LAST SLICE OF PIZZA.
REACH!
SLAP!
GRRRRR...
HEY! THAT'S MINE!
YOU GIVE THAT BACK!
GRRRRR!
THMMP! THMMP! GRRRRRR!
C'MON! IT'S PEPPERONI!
NiGeL
ZOMBOSS IZ A GERK!
ZOMBOSS UNFAIRZZ!
WE NEEDZ A PLACE OF OUR OWNZ.
THE END.

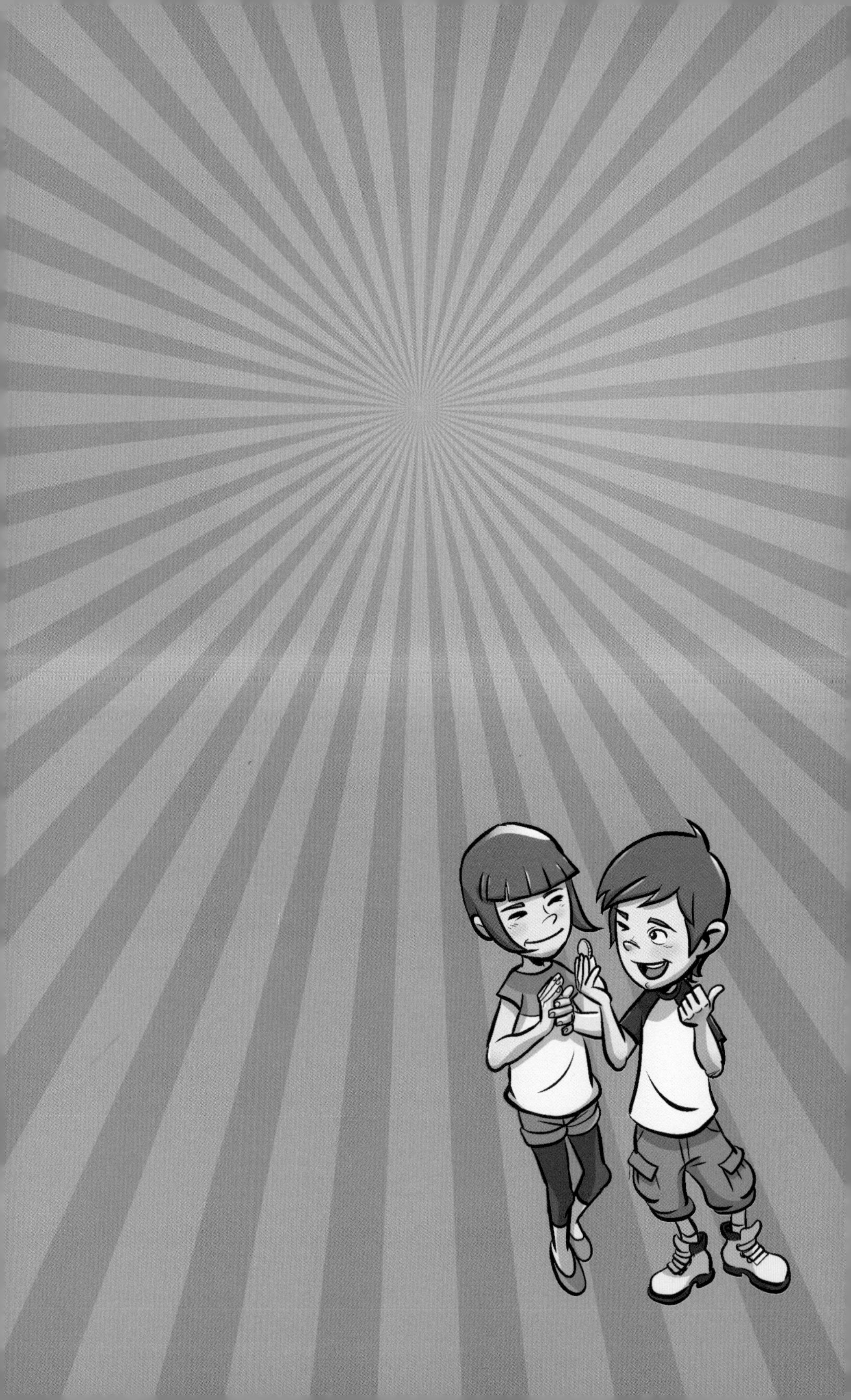

BONUS STORIES

CHESTBEARD'S REVENGE!

Written by PAUL TOBIN
Art by KARIM FRIHA
Letters by STEVE DUTRO

A DAY IN THE LIFE(ISH) OF A ZOMBIE!

Written by PAUL TOBIN
Art by NNEKA MYERS
Letters by STEVE DUTRO

THE ZOMBIE THAT WAS AFRAID OF THE DARK

Written by PAUL TOBIN
Art by NNEKA MYERS
Letters by STEVE DUTRO

KNOW YOUR ZOMBIE HOLIDAYS!

Written by PAUL TOBIN
Art by BRIAN CHURILLA
Letters by STEVE DUTRO

THE DEVELOPMENT OF THE BALLOON ZOMBIE

Written by PAUL TOBIN
Art by BRIAN CHURILLA
Letters by STEVE DUTRO

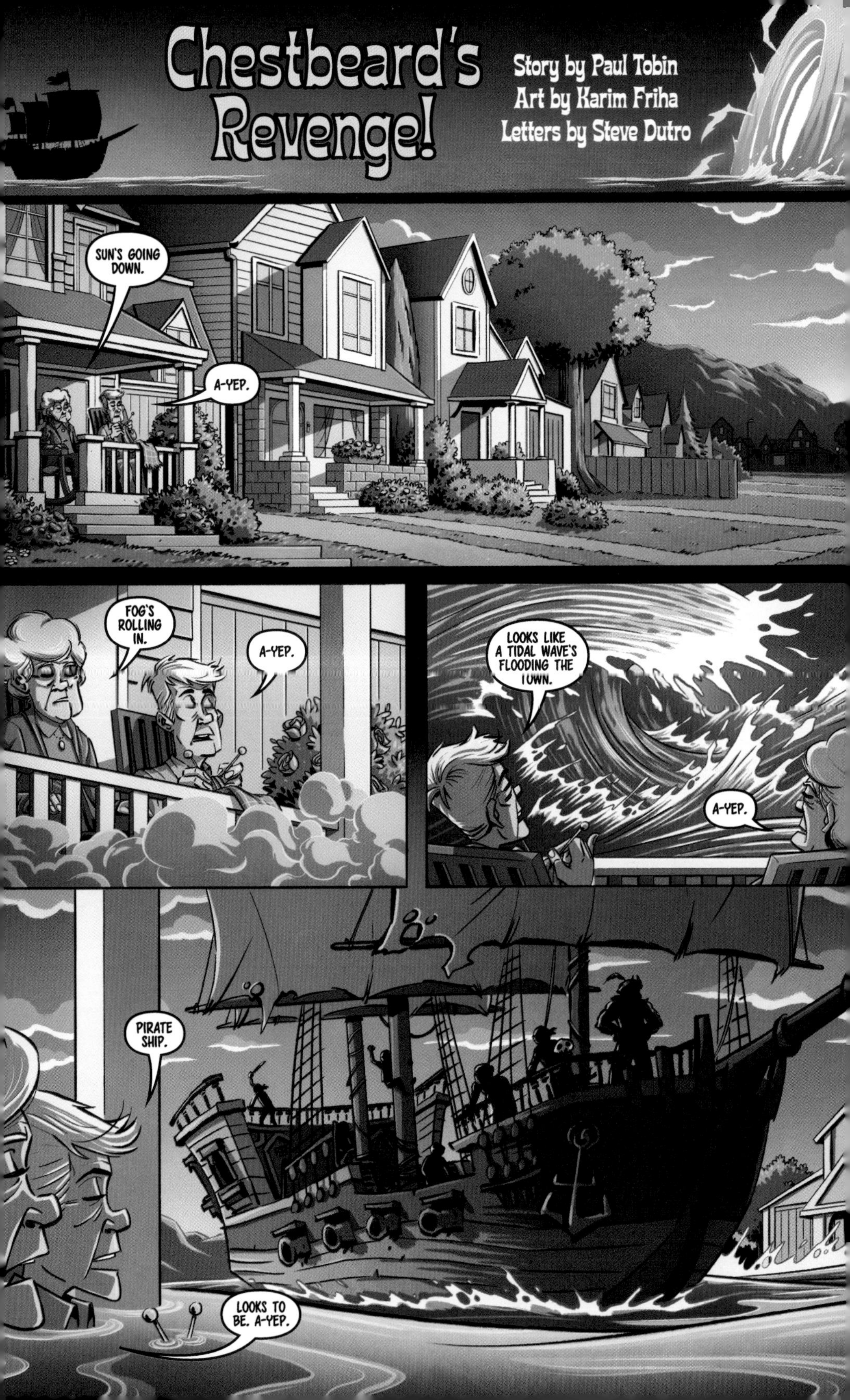
Chestbeard's Revenge!
Story by Paul Tobin
Art by Karim Friha
Letters by Steve Dutro
SUN'S GOING DOWN.
A-YEP.
FOG'S ROLLING IN.
A-YEP.
LOOKS LIKE A TIDAL WAVE'S FLOODING THE TOWN.
A-YEP.
PIRATE SHIP.
LOOKS TO BE. A-YEP.

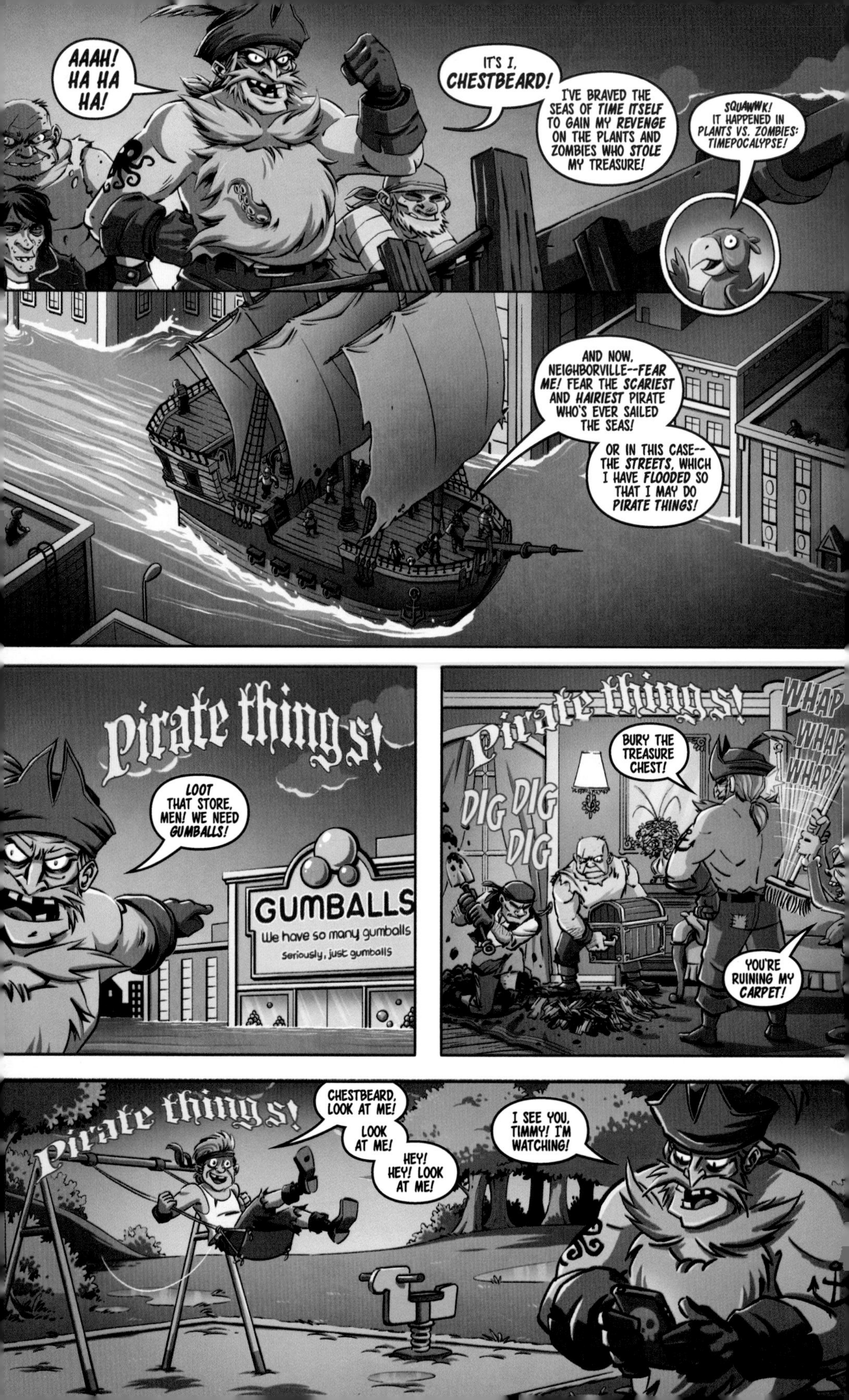

AAAH! HA HA HA!
IT'S I, CHESTBEARD!
I'VE BRAVED THE SEAS OF TIME ITSELF TO GAIN MY REVENGE ON THE PLANTS AND ZOMBIES WHO STOLE MY TREASURE!
SQUAWWK! IT HAPPENED IN PLANTS VS. ZOMBIES: TIMEPOCALYPSE!
AND NOW, NEIGHBORVILLE--FEAR ME! FEAR THE SCARIEST AND HAIRIEST PIRATE WHO'S EVER SAILED THE SEAS!
OR IN THIS CASE--THE STREETS, WHICH I HAVE FLOODED SO THAT I MAY DO PIRATE THINGS!
pirate things!
LOOT THAT STORE, MEN! WE NEED GUMBALLS!
GUMBALLS
We have so many gumballs
Seriously, just gumballs
pirate things!
WHAP
WHAP
WHAP
BURY THE TREASURE CHEST!
DIG DIG DIG
YOU'RE RUINING MY CARPET!
pirate things!
CHESTBEARD, LOOK AT ME!
LOOK AT ME!
HEY! HEY! LOOK AT ME!
I SEE YOU, TIMMY! I'M WATCHING!

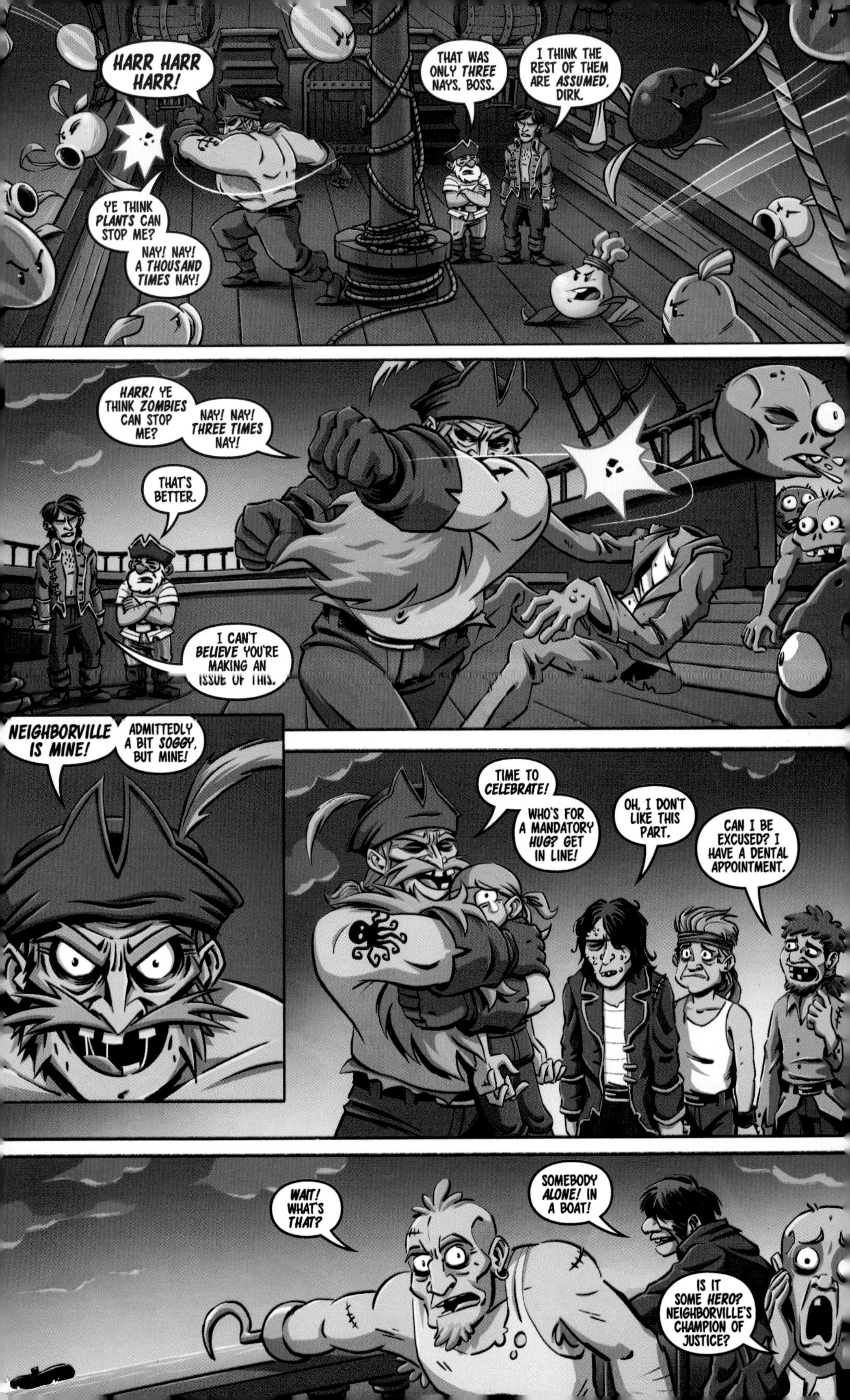
HARR HARR HARR!
YE THINK PLANTS CAN STOP ME?
NAY! NAY! A THOUSAND TIMES NAY!
THAT WAS ONLY THREE NAYS, BOSS.
I THINK THE REST OF THEM ARE ASSUMED, DIRK.
HARR! YE THINK ZOMBIES CAN STOP ME?
NAY! NAY! THREE TIMES NAY!
THAT'S BETTER.
I CAN'T BELIEVE YOU'RE MAKING AN ISSUE OF THIS.
NEIGHBORVILLE IS MINE!
ADMITTEDLY A BIT SOGGY, BUT MINE!
TIME TO CELEBRATE!
WHO'S FOR A MANDATORY HUG? GET IN LINE!
OH, I DON'T LIKE THIS PART.
CAN I BE EXCUSED? I HAVE A DENTAL APPOINTMENT.
WAIT! WHAT'S THAT?
SOMEBODY ALONE! IN A BOAT!
IS IT SOME HERO? NEIGHBORVILLE'S CHAMPION OF JUSTICE?

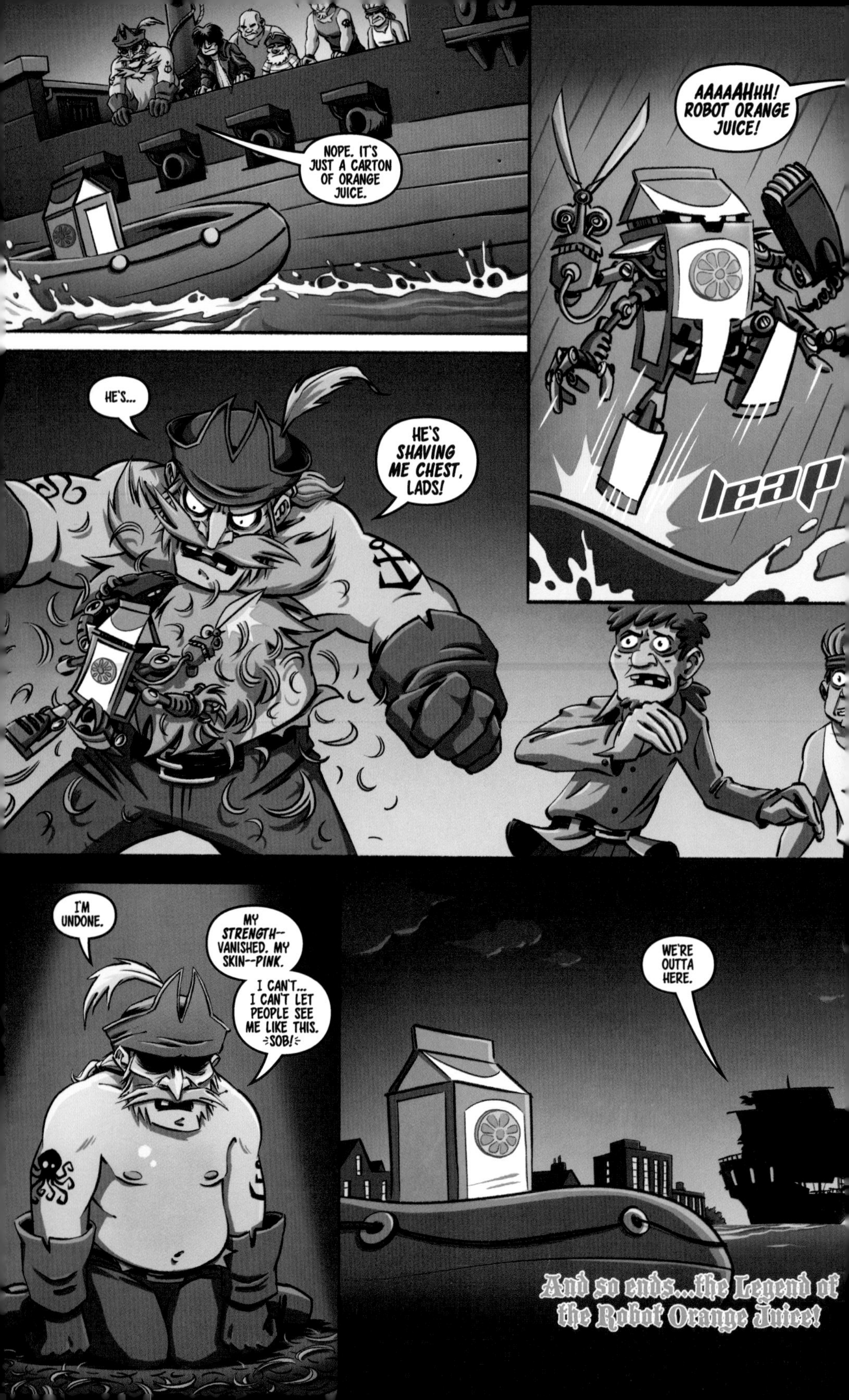
NOPE. IT'S JUST A CARTON OF ORANGE JUICE.
AAAAAHHH! ROBOT ORANGE JUICE!
LEAP
HE'S...
HE'S SHAVING ME CHEST, LADS!
I'M UNDONE.
MY STRENGTH--VANISHED. MY SKIN--PINK.
I CAN'T... I CAN'T LET PEOPLE SEE ME LIKE THIS. SOB!
WE'RE OUTTA HERE.
And so ends...the Legend of the Robot Orange Juice!

Story by **Paul Tobin** • Art by **Nneka Myers** • Letters by **Steve Dutro**

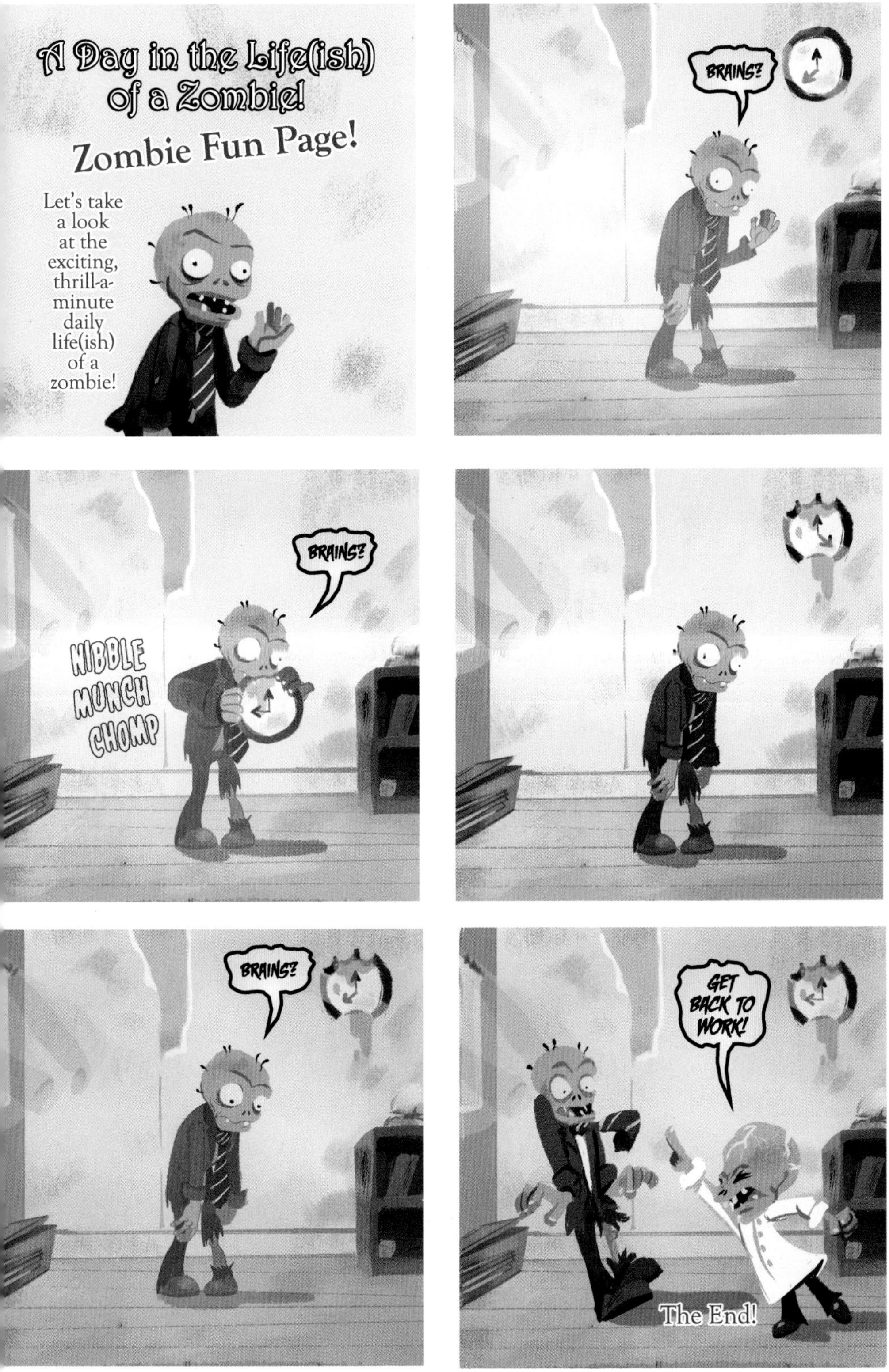

A Day in the Life(ish) of a Zombie!
Zombie Fun Page!
Let's take a look at the exciting, thrill-a-minute daily life(ish) of a zombie!
BRAINS?
BRAINS?
NIBBLE MUNCH CHOMP
BRAINS?
GET BACK TO WORK!
The End!

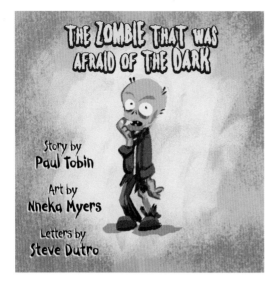

THE ZOMBIE THAT WAS AFRAID OF THE DARK

Story by
Paul Tobin

Art by
Nneka Myers

Letters by
Steve Dutro

EEP!

Once there was a zombie who was afraid of the dark.

He refused to step one foot into the night, because who knew what scary things might be lurking in the darkness?

BRAAAINZZ?

His friends tried to coax him outside with flashlights.

BRAINZ?

They tried to coax him out with candles.

And with one hundred and seventy-two lightning bugs on leashes.

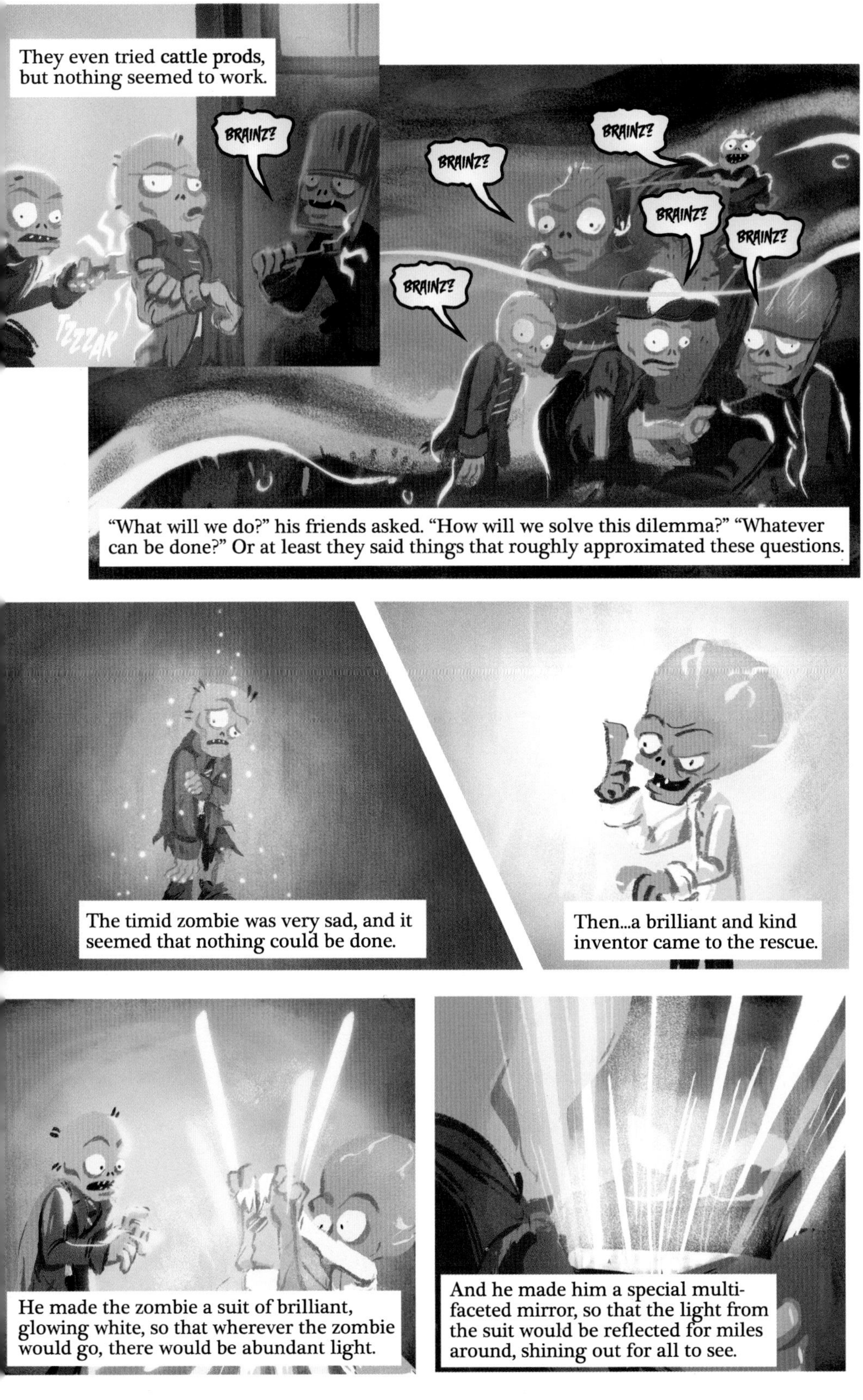
They even tried cattle prods, but nothing seemed to work.
BRAINZ?
TZZZAK
BRAINZ?
BRAINZ?
BRAINZ?
BRAINZ?
BRAINZ?
"What will we do?" his friends asked. "How will we solve this dilemma?" "Whatever can be done?" Or at least they said things that roughly approximated these questions.
The timid zombie was very sad, and it seemed that nothing could be done.
Then...a brilliant and kind inventor came to the rescue.
He made the zombie a suit of brilliant, glowing white, so that wherever the zombie would go, there would be abundant light.
And he made him a special multi-faceted mirror, so that the light from the suit would be reflected for miles around, shining out for all to see.

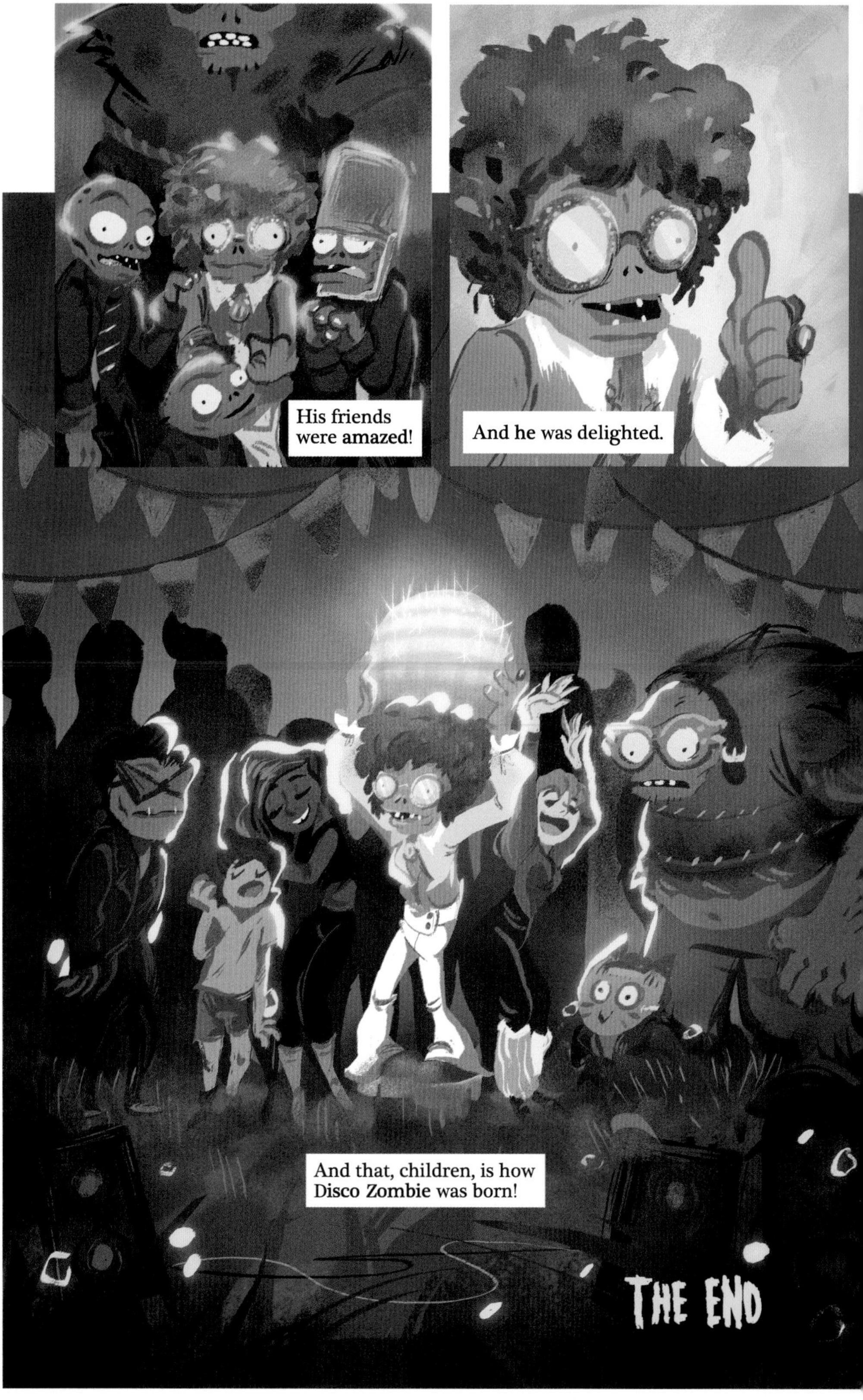
His friends were amazed!
And he was delighted.
And that, children, is how Disco Zombie was born!
THE END

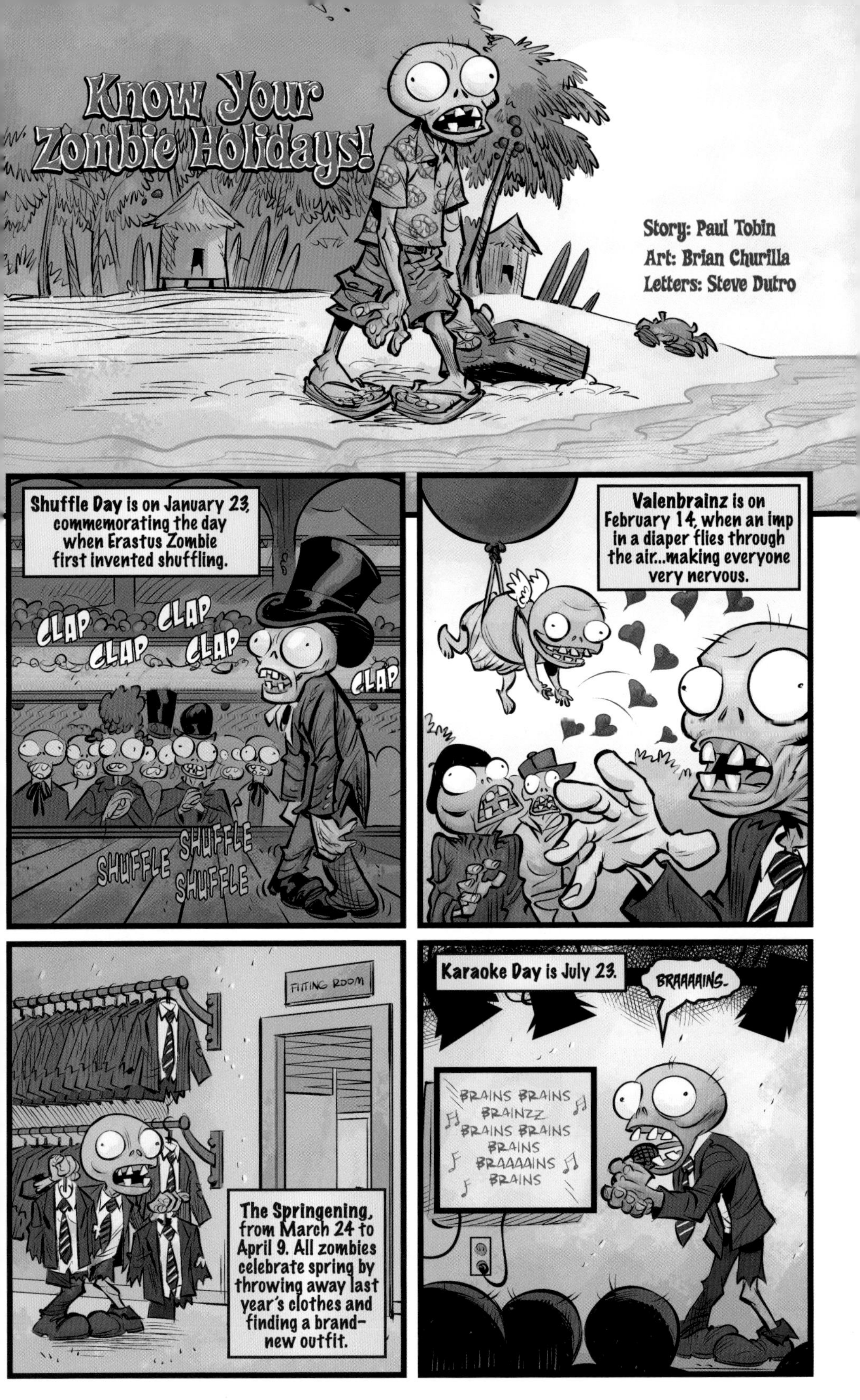
Know Your Zombie Holidays!
Story: Paul Tobin
Art: Brian Churilla
Letters: Steve Dutro
Shuffle Day is on January 23, commemorating the day when Erastus Zombie first invented shuffling.
CLAP
CLAP
CLAP
CLAP
CLAP
SHUFFLE
SHUFFLE
SHUFFLE
Valenbrainz is on February 14, when an imp in a diaper flies through the air...making everyone very nervous.
FITTING ROOM
The Springening, from March 24 to April 9. All zombies celebrate spring by throwing away last year's clothes and finding a brand-new outfit.
Karaoke Day is July 23.
BRAAAAINS.
BRAINS BRAINS
BRAINZZ
BRAINS BRAINS
BRAINS
BRAAAAINS
BRAINS

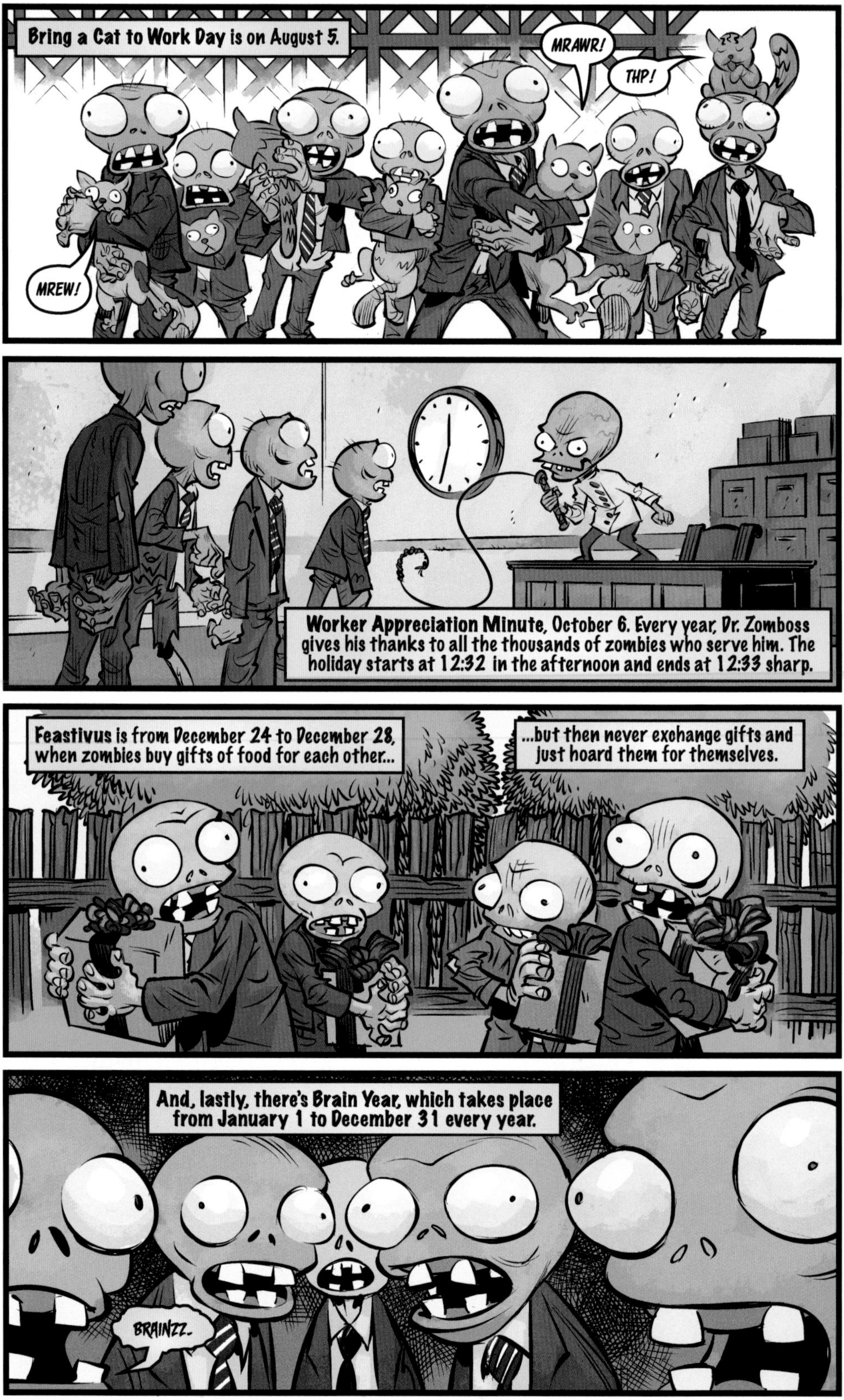
Bring a Cat to Work Day is on August 5.
MRAWR!
THP!
MREW!
Worker Appreciation Minute, October 6. Every year, Dr. Zomboss gives his thanks to all the thousands of zombies who serve him. The holiday starts at 12:32 in the afternoon and ends at 12:33 sharp.
Feastivus is from December 24 to December 28, when zombies buy gifts of food for each other...
...but then never exchange gifts and just hoard them for themselves.
And, lastly, there's Brain Year, which takes place from January 1 to December 31 every year.
BRAINZZ.

The end.

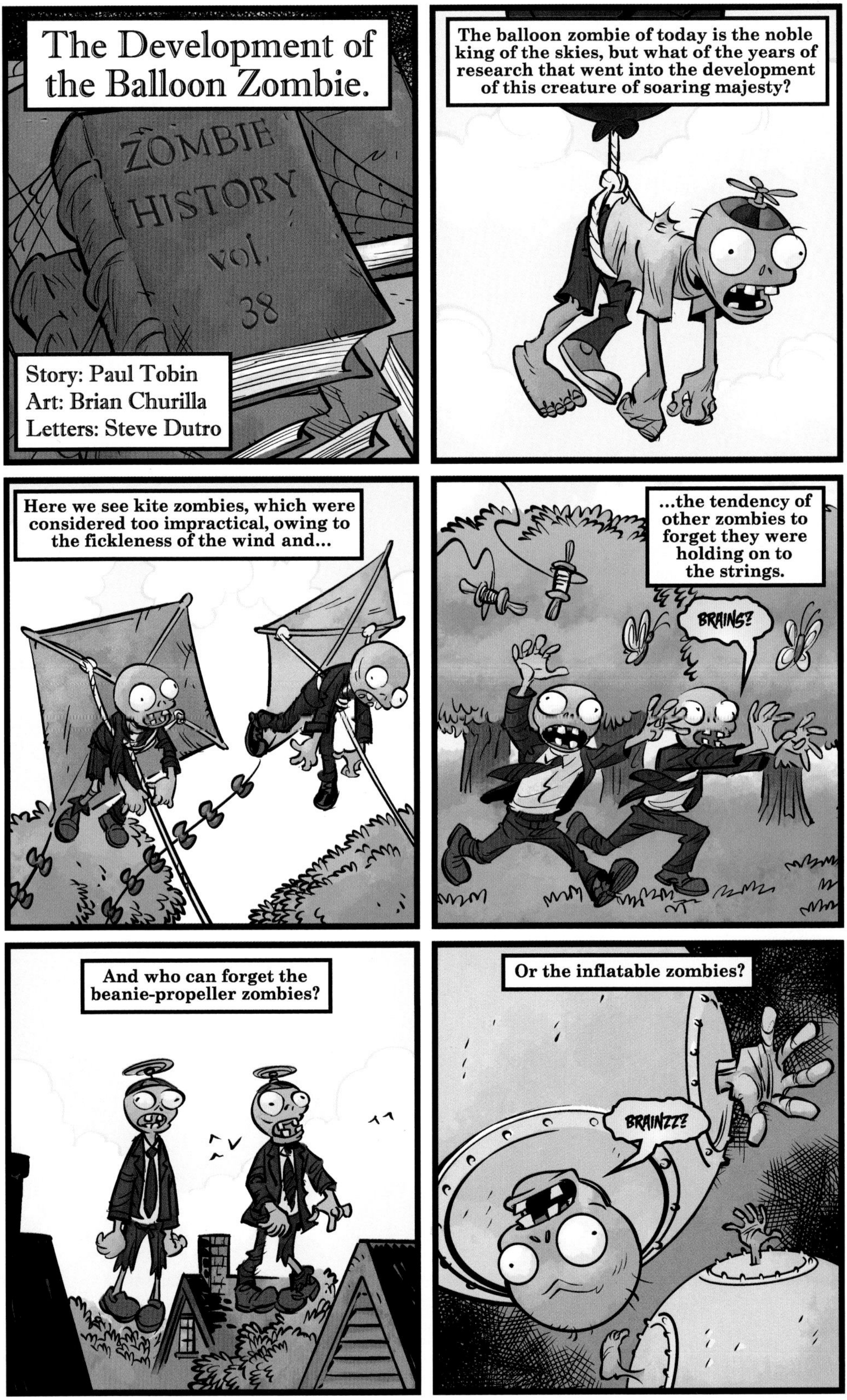
The Development of the Balloon Zombie.
ZOMBIE HISTORY vol. 38
Story: Paul Tobin
Art: Brian Churilla
Letters: Steve Dutro
The balloon zombie of today is the noble king of the skies, but what of the years of research that went into the development of this creature of soaring majesty?
Here we see kite zombies, which were considered too impractical, owing to the fickleness of the wind and...
...the tendency of other zombies to forget they were holding on to the strings.
BRAINS?
And who can forget the beanie-propeller zombies?
Or the inflatable zombies?
BRAINZZ?

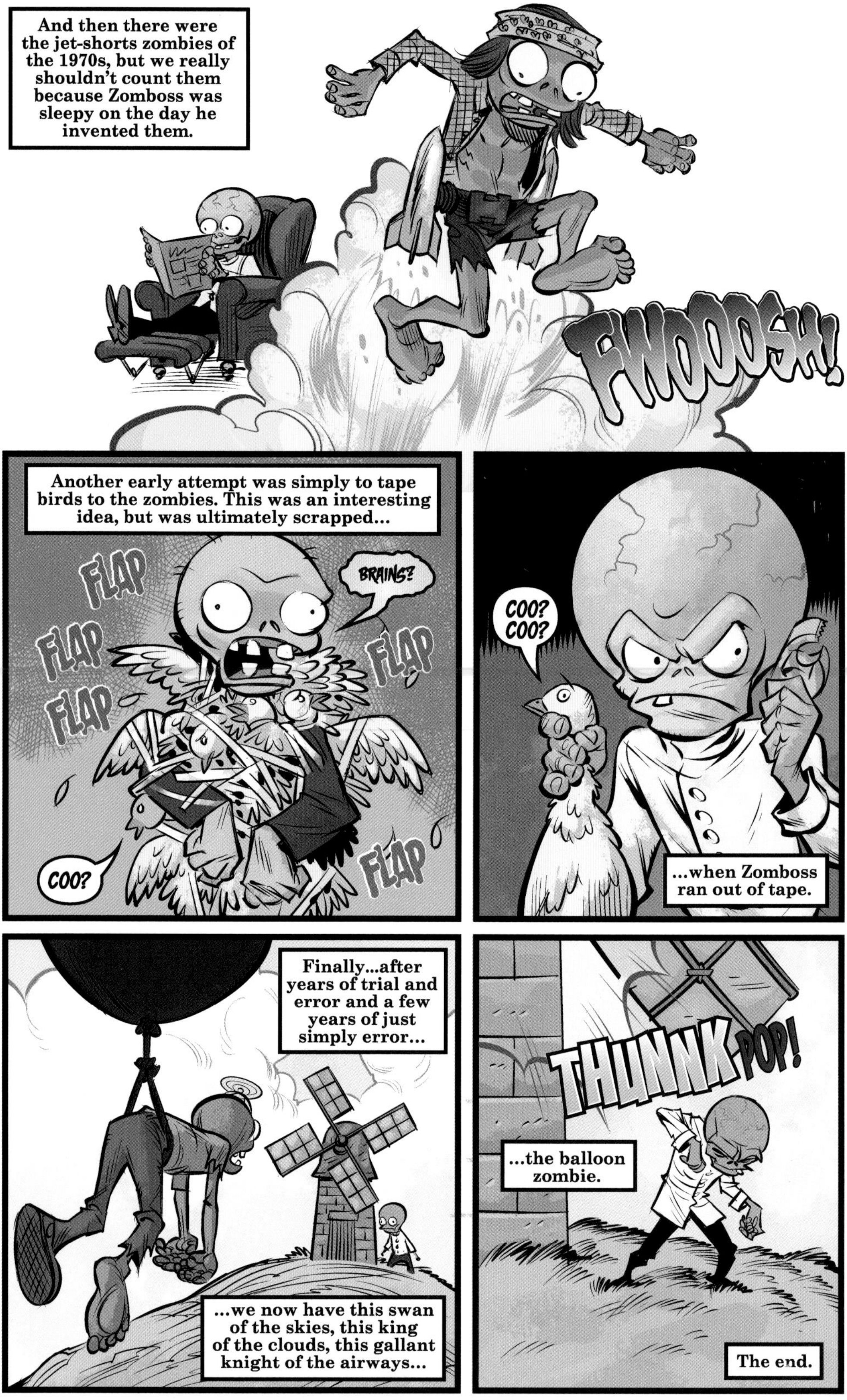
And then there were the jet-shorts zombies of the 1970s, but we really shouldn't count them because Zomboss was sleepy on the day he invented them.
FWOOOSH!
Another early attempt was simply to tape birds to the zombies. This was an interesting idea, but was ultimately scrapped...
FLAP
BRAINS?
FLAP
FLAP
FLAP
FLAP
COO?
COO? COO?
...when Zomboss ran out of tape.
Finally...after years of trial and error and a few years of just simply error...
...we now have this swan of the skies, this king of the clouds, this gallant knight of the airways...
THUNNK
POP!
...the balloon zombie.
The end.

LANTS VS. ZOMBIES #4
ver inks by ANDIE TONG

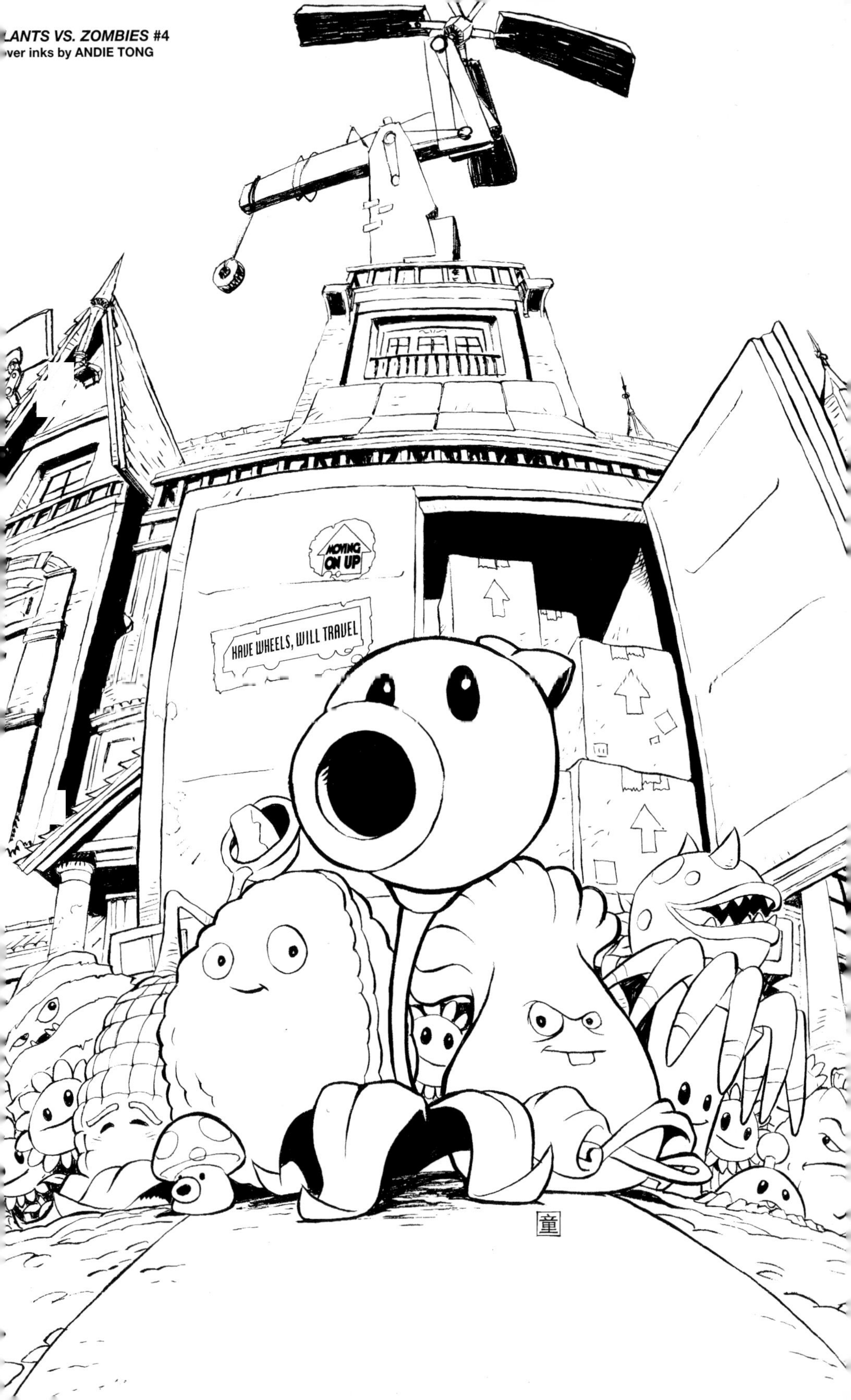
MOVING ON UP
HAVE WHEELS, WILL TRAVEL
童

PLANTS VS. ZOMBIES #5
cover inks by ANDIE TONG

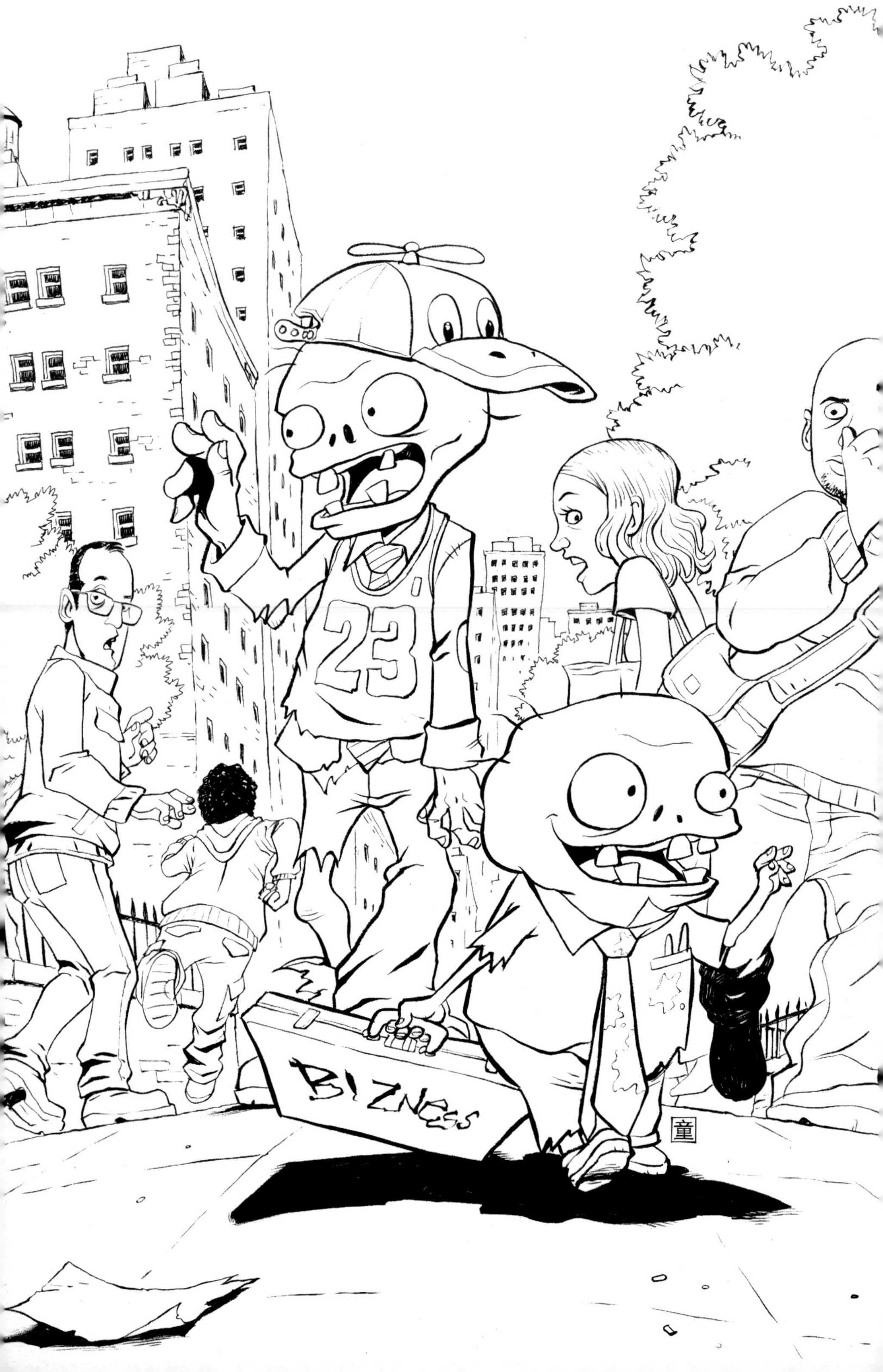
23
BIZNESS
童

PLANTS VS. ZOMBIES #5
cover by ANDIE TONG

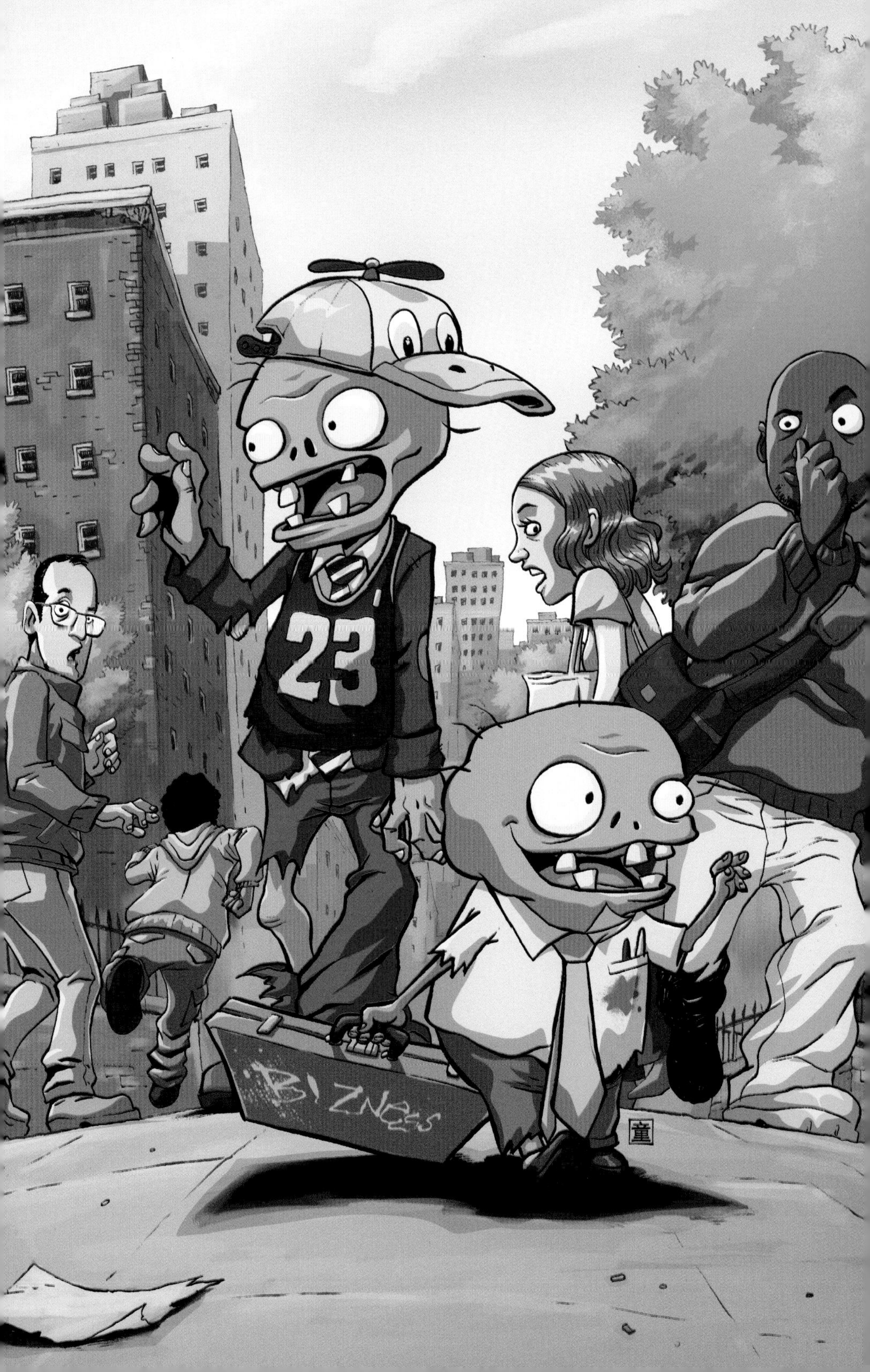
23

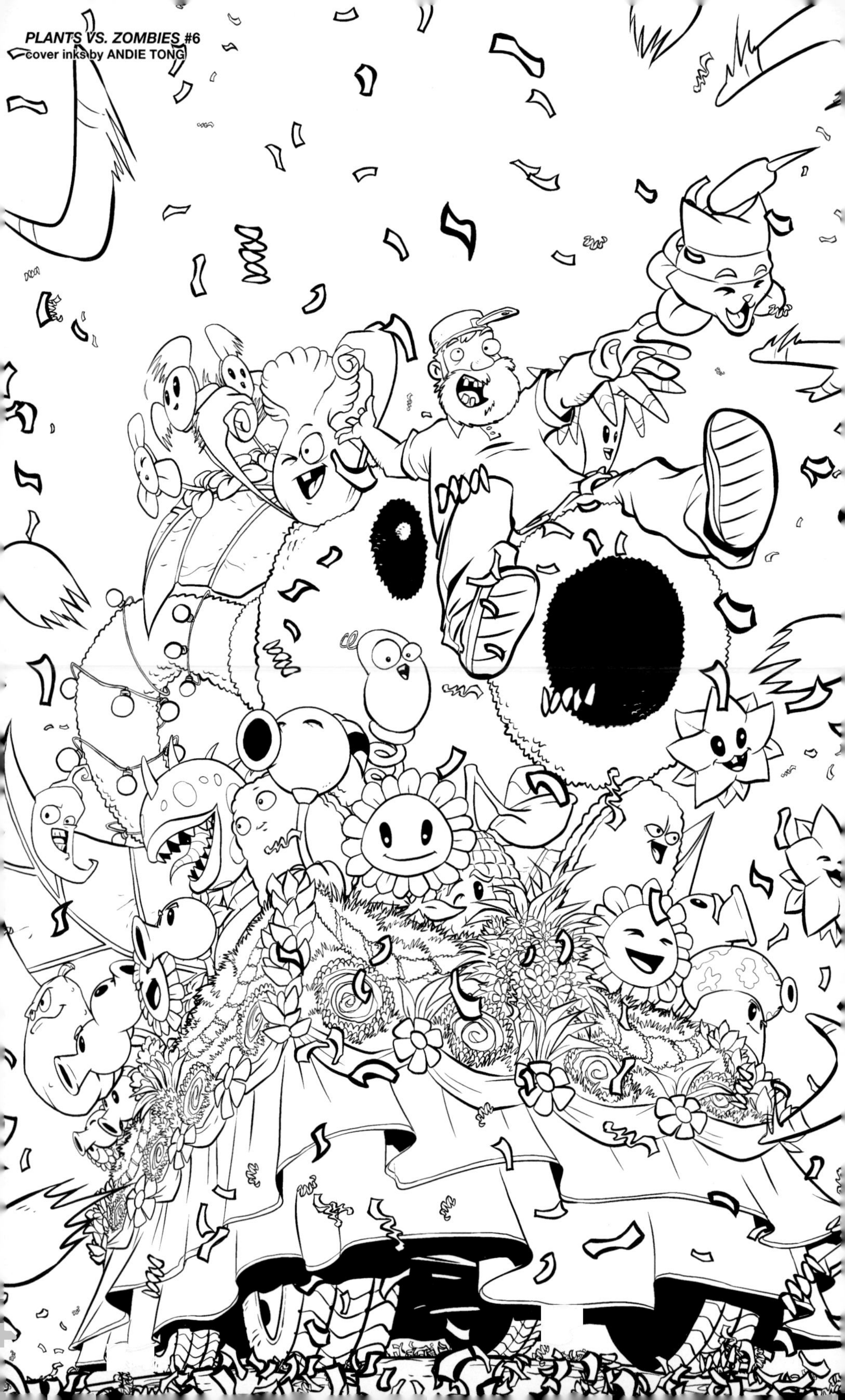

PLANTS VS. ZOMBIES #6
cover inks by ANDIE TONG

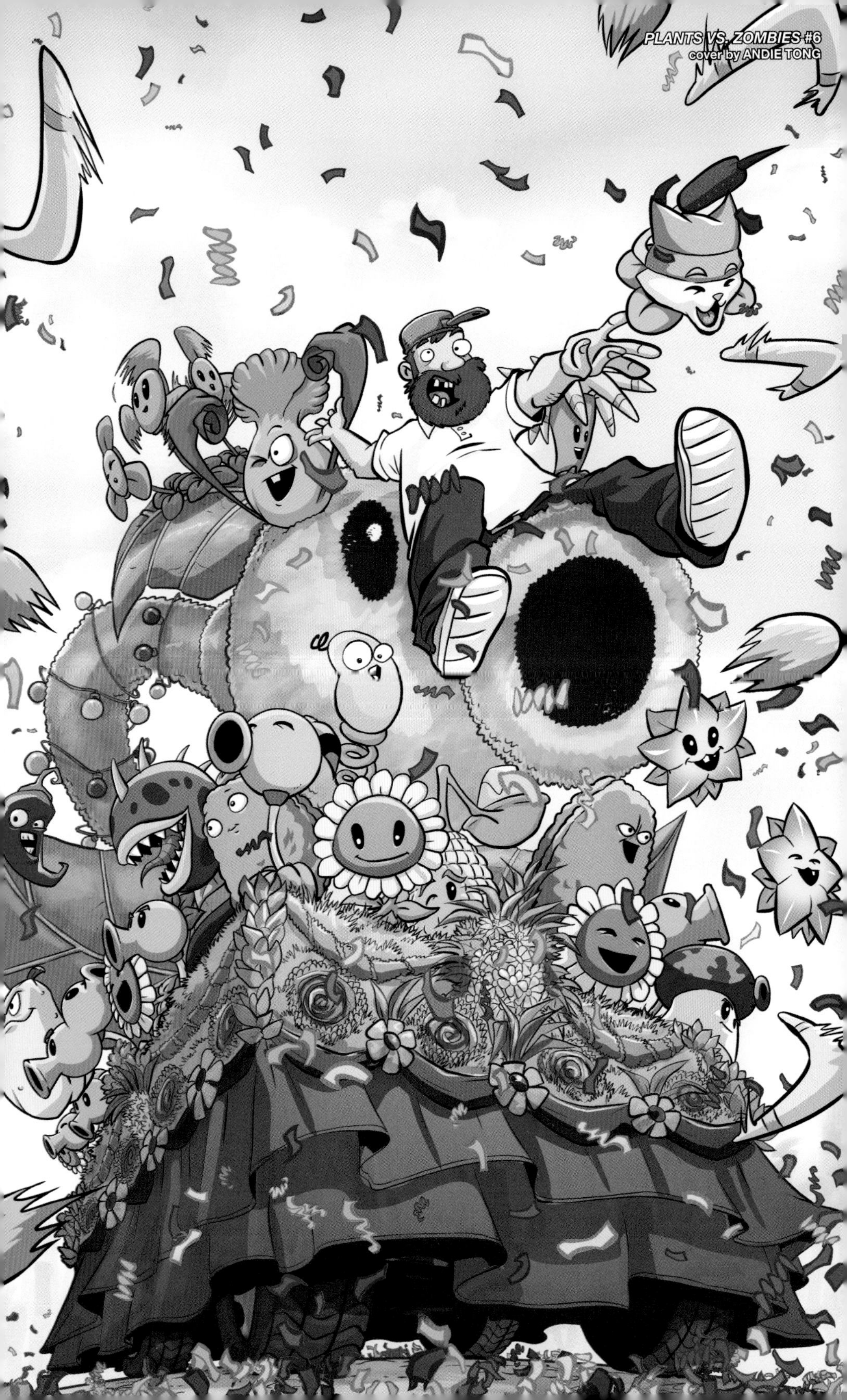

PLANTS VS. ZOMBIES #6
cover by ANDIE TONG

CREATOR BIOS

Paul Tobin

Andie Tong

PAUL TOBIN is a critically acclaimed freckled person who has a detailed plan for any actual zombie invasion, based on creating a vast perfume and cologne empire—both of which would be vitally important in a zombie-infested world. Paul was once informed he "walks funny, like, seriously," but has recovered from this childhood trauma to write hundreds of comics for Marvel, DC, Dark Horse, and many others, including such creator-owned titles as *Colder* and *Bandette*, as well as *Prepare to Die!*—his debut novel. His *Genius Factor* series of novels about a fifth-grade genius and his war against the Red Death Tea Society begins in March of 2016 from Bloomsbury Publishing. Despite his many writing accomplishments, Paul's greatest claim to fame is his ability to win water levels in *Plants vs. Zombies* without using any water plants.

ANDIE TONG started off as a multimedia designer in 1997 and migrated to doing comics full time in 2006. Since then he has worked on titles such as *Tron: Betrayal*, *Spectacular Spider-Man*, *The Batman Strikes!*, *Smallville*, *The Wheel of Time*, *Tales of the TMNT*, *Masters of the Universe*, and *Starship Troopers*, working for companies such as Disney, Marvel, DC Comics, Panini, Dark Horse, and Dynamite Entertainment, and has made commercial illustrations for numerous advertising agencies including Nike, Universal, CBS, Mattel, and Hasbro. When he gets the chance, Andie does concept design for various companies and also juggles illustration duties on a range of children's picture storybooks for HarperCollins. Malaysian born, Andie migrated to Australia at a young age and then moved to London in 2005. In 2012, he journeyed back to Asia and currently resides in Singapore with his wife and two children.

Matthew J. Rainwater

Steve Dutro

Residing in the cool, damp forests of Portland, Oregon, **MATTHEW J. RAINWATER** is a freelance illustrator whose work has been featured in advertising, web design, and independent video games. On top of this, he also self-publishes several comic books, including *Trailer Park Warlock*, *Garage Raja*, and *The Feeling Is Multiplied*—all of which can be found at MattJRainwater.com. His favorite zombie-bashing strategy utilizes a line of Bonk Choys with a Wall-nut front guard and Threepeater covering fire.

STEVE DUTRO is a comic book letterer from northern California who can also drive a tractor. He graduated from the Kubert School and has been in the comics industry for decades, working for Dark Horse (*The Fifth Beatle*, *The Evil Dead*, *Eden*), Viz, Marvel, and DC. Steve's last encounter with zombies was playing zombie paintball in a walnut orchard on Halloween. He tried to play the *Plants vs. Zombies* video game once but experienced a full-on panic attack and resolved to stick with calmer games . . . like *Gears of War*.

PLANTS VS. ZOMBIES: LAWNMAGEDDON
Crazy Dave—the babbling-yet-brilliant inventor and top-notch neighborhood defender—helps his niece Patrice and young adventurer Nate Timely fend off a zombie invasion that threatens to overrun the peaceful town of Neighborville in *Plants vs. Zombies: Lawnmageddon!* Their only hope is a brave army of chomping, squashing, and pea-shooting plants! A wacky adventure for zombie zappers young and old!
ISBN 978-1-61655-192-6 | $9.99

THE ART OF PLANTS VS. ZOMBIES
Part zombie memoir, part celebration of zombie triumphs, and part anti-plant screed, *The Art of Plants vs. Zombies* is a treasure trove of never-before-seen concept art, character sketches, and surprises from PopCap's popular *Plants vs. Zombies* games!
ISBN 978-1-61655-331-9 | $9.99

PLANTS VS. ZOMBIES: TIMEPOCALYPSE
Crazy Dave helps Patrice and Nate Timely fend off Zomboss's latest attack in *Plants vs. Zombies: Timepocalypse!* This new standalone tale will tickle your funny bones and thrill your brains through any timeline!
ISBN 978-1-61655-621-1 | $9.99

PLANTS VS. ZOMBIES: BULLY FOR YOU
Patrice and Nate have followed Crazy Dave throughout time—but are they ready to investigate a strange college campus to keep the streets safe from zombies?
ISBN 978-1-61655-889-5 | $9.99

PLANTS VS. ZOMBIES: GARDEN WARFARE
Based on the hit video game, this comic tells the story leading up to the events in *Plants vs. Zombies: Garden Warfare 2!*
ISBN 978-1-61655-946-5 | $9.99

PLANTS VS. ZOMBIES: GROWN SWEET HOME
Armed with newfound knowledge of humanity, Dr. Zomboss launches a strike at the heart of Neighborville . . . and also sparks a series of all-star plant-versus-zombie brawls!
ISBN 978-1-61655-971-7 | $9.99

MORE DARK HORSE ALL-AGES TITLES

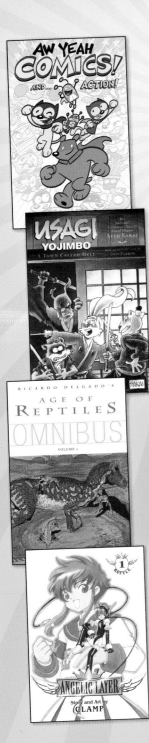

AW YEAH
COMICS!
AND... ACTION!

AW YEAH COMICS! AND . . . ACTION!

Cornelius and Alowicious are just your average comic book store employees, but when trouble strikes, they are . . . Action Cat and Adventure Bug! Join their epic all-ages adventures as they face off—with the help of Adorable Cat and Shelly Bug—against their archnemesis, Evil Cat, and his fiendish friends!

ISBN 978-1-61655-558-0 | $12.99

USAGI
YOJIMBO
A TOWN CALLED HELL
STAN SAKAI
SAKAI

USAGI YOJIMBO

In his latest adventure, the rabbit *ronin* Usagi finds himself caught between competing gang lords fighting for control of a town called Hell, confronting a *nukekubi*—a flying cannibal head—and crossing paths with the demon Jei!

Volume 25: Fox Hunt
ISBN 978-1-59582-726-5 | $16.99

***Volume 26: Traitors of the Earth* | $16.99**
ISBN 978-1-59582-910-8

***Volume 27: A Town Called Hell* | $16.99**
ISBN 978-1-59582-970-2

RICARDO DELGADO'S
AGE OF
REPTILES
OMNIBUS
VOLUME 1

AGE OF REPTILES OMNIBUS

When Ricardo Delgado first set his sights on creating comics, he crafted an epic tale about the most unlikely cast of characters: dinosaurs. Since that first Eisner-winning foray into the world of sequential art he has returned to his critically acclaimed *Age of Reptiles* again and again, each time crafting a captivating saga about his saurian subjects.

ISBN 978-1-59582-683-1 | $24.99

1
BATTLE
ANGELIC LAYER
Story and Art by
CLAMP

ANGELIC LAYER BOOK 1

Junior-high student Misaki Suzuhara just arrived in Tokyo to live with her TV-star aunt and attend the prestigious Eriol Academy. But what excites Misaki most is Angelic Layer—an arena game where you control a miniature robot fighter with your mind! Can Misaki's enthusiasm and skill take her to the top of the arena?

ISBN 978-1-61655-021-9 | $19.99

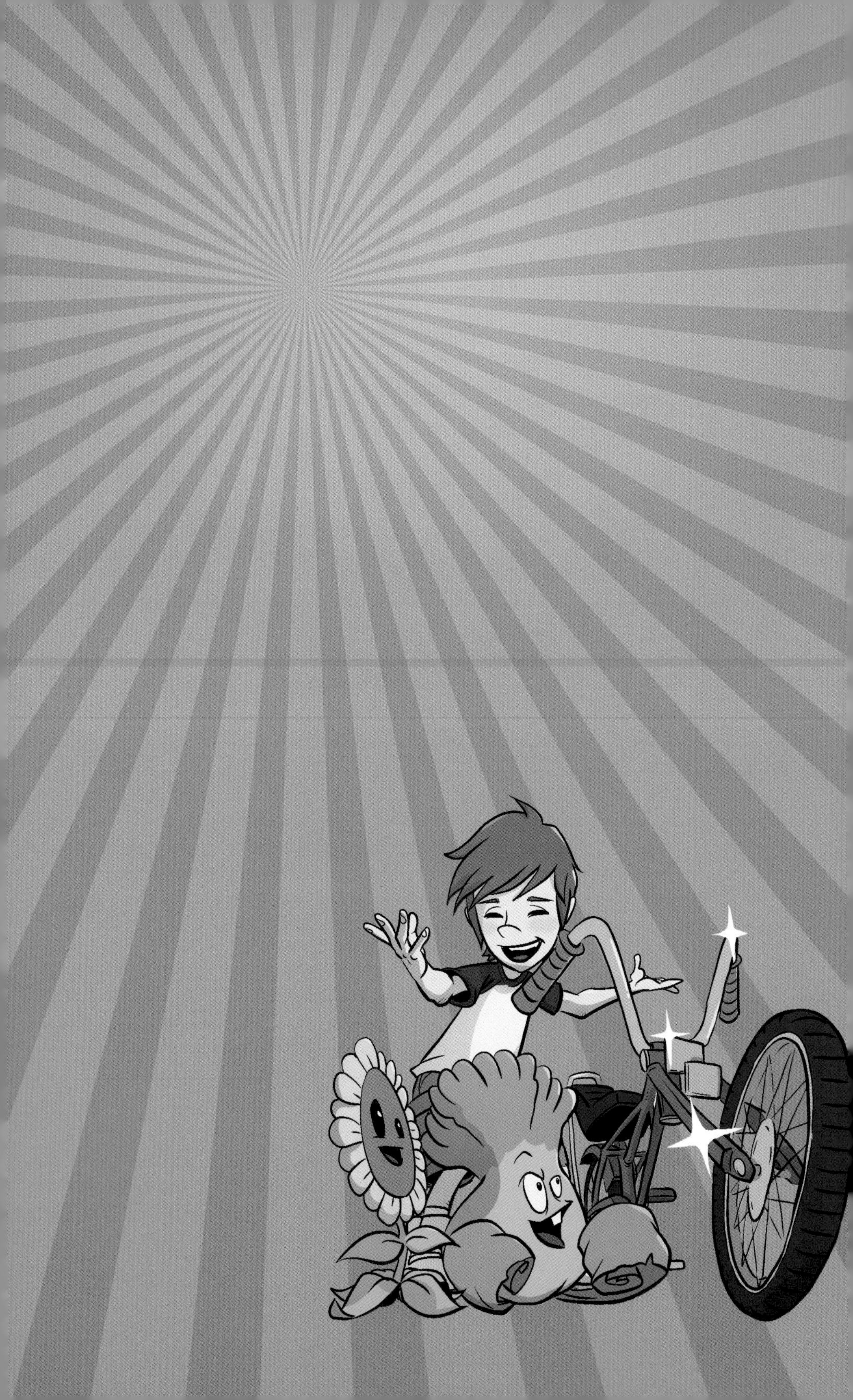

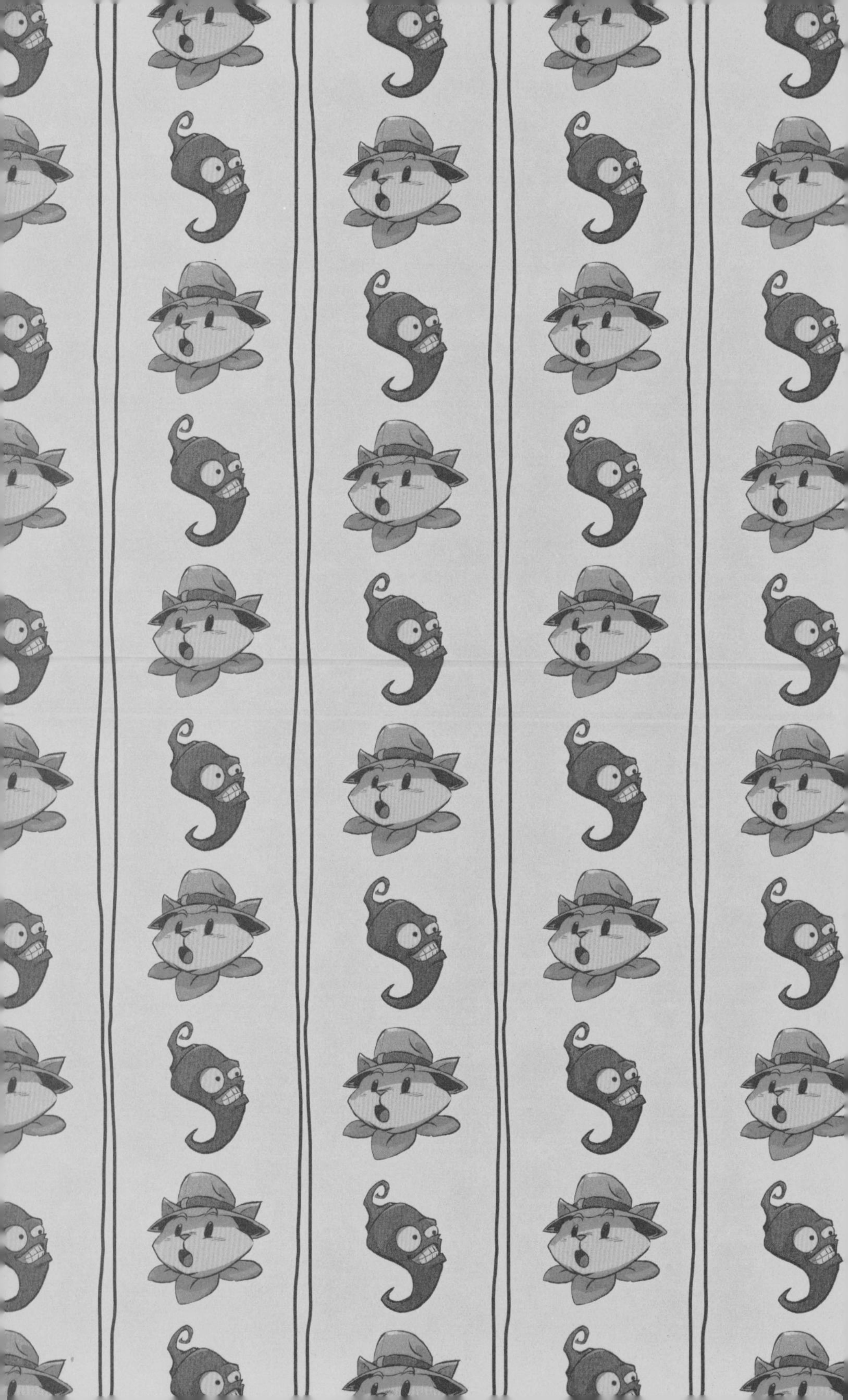